Hank had known she'd be back.

Still, it was with a note of mocking humor that he said to her, "I didn't think I'd see you this morning."

"That's because you don't know me," she cheerily responded. "He's beautiful," she said of the proud-looking horse.

Hank smiled. "We've won a few trophies together, haven't we, boy?"

"Tell me about the mustangs," Kit prodded. "What are they like?"

"They used to be used as cow ponies, but they've been replaced by animals of better quality. Every once in a while I break one to use for range work."

"I'll bet you're very good at it, too," she remarked.

"And how would you know that?" he asked.

"I simply judged how good you are from the number of bronc-riding trophies you've won. Why'd you leave the rodeo circuit?"

"I don't need the crowds anymore, and I sure as hell don't need the trophies. You know something, lady? You ask too many questions."

Dear Reader,

When two people fall in love, the world is suddenly new and exciting, and it's that same excitement we bring to you in Silhouette Intimate Moments. These are stories with scope, with grandeur. The characters lead the lives we all dream of, and everything they do reflects the wonder of being in love.

This month, Silhouette Intimate Moments has two exciting projects to present to you. First, read *Sea Gate*, by Maura Seger, if you're looking for a romance with a difference. Romantic fantasy has always been a part of these books, but in *Sea Gate*, we go one step farther to fantasy of a different kind. Just for a moment, suppose that the legend of Atlantis had a basis in reality, and that the inhabitants of that watery world had survived into the present day. What if a woman from their world met a man from ours and discovered that love is always the same, no matter where you live?

Bestselling author Heather Graham Pozzessere has a treat in store for you too. She's written an exciting short story called "Shadows on the Nile," and the first chapter is included in all the Silhouette Books titles for this month. But the remaining five chapters will be published only in Silhouette Intimate Moments, and we hope you'll join us next month and every month through March to follow the rocky course of love in the shadow of the Pyramids.

And, as always, we will continue to bring you the best romantic fiction available today, written by authors whose way with words is guaranteed to touch your heart.

Leslie J. Wainger
Senior Editor
Silhouette Books

Nancy Morse

Run Wild, Run Free

Silhouette Intimate Moments

Published by Silhouette Books New York

America's Publisher of Contemporary Romance

SILHOUETTE BOOKS
300 East 42nd St., New York, N.Y. 10017

ISBN: 0-373-07210-4

First Silhouette Books printing October 1987

America's Publisher of Contemporary Romance

Printed in the U.S.A.

Books by Nancy Morse

Silhouette Intimate Moments

Sacred Places #181
Run Wild, Run Free #210

NANCY MORSE

is an avid reader of everything from novels to cereal boxes. Her love of reading has inspired her to write and keep writing, and she is the author of several historical and contemporary romances. Her passion for books is also responsible for her deep interest in Native American history and culture. She is the proud possessor of many Indian artifacts and considers her collection not just a hobby but her link with the past.

When she is not working or writing, she enjoys traveling. Although she is a native of New York, she and her husband have toured Europe and northern Africa. Other favorite activities include the theater, working up a sweat at aerobics class and being with friends.

Chapter 1

I said *no*, dammit! Can't you ever just let anything be?" demanded a deep, angry male voice.

Standing behind the open window, Kit Sloan couldn't see the two men who approached the house, but their tone of voice made it obvious they were in the midst of an argument.

"But the purse is up to a hundred thousand this year, Hank." Kit thought this voice sounded equally perturbed, but thinner, older. "When are you gonna get it through your thick head that the Chaparral needs money? Last winter nearly ruined us. If this one's as bad, we ain't gonna make it. All right, so we lost some of our best mares. We need to replace that stock, and we need the money to do it. Horse-breeding ain't worth a damn if you ain't got the horses to breed. I keep telling you that, but all you want to do is chase that damned fool horse over half the state of Wyoming. I'm telling you, Hank, you gotta come to your senses and quit chasing him. Ain't seven years long enough?''

In a voice so tightly controlled that it bordered on dangerous, Hank Reardon replied, ''So, you want me to quit chasing the stallion and take up the rodeo circuit again. Is that right, Pete?''

Feeling awkward at listening in on a private argument, Kit moved away from the window and tried to concentrate her attention on the room. The study at the Chaparral was obviously a man's room. Dark walnut shelves lined the walls, stocked with leather-bound volumes of Dickens and Twain that were interspersed with journals on animal husbandry and every possible aspect of horse-breeding. An ancient-looking rolltop desk filled a space against one wall. Two brass-studded brown leather chairs sat before a stone and mortar fireplace, flanking a sofa upholstered in soft, plush velour of burnt umber. A large Navajo rug of vibrant red, black and buff was spread across the hardwood floor. The overhanging boughs of the trees outside the window made the room cool and dark and a faint aroma of linseed oil and leather hung in the air.

Kit wandered from the shelves to a glass case that housed an assortment of blue ribbons, trophies and plaques. There were awards for National Bronc Busting Champion six years in a row, Best All-Round Winner at Cheyenne, fastest time in calf-roping at Calgary, and scores of other awards from dozens of competitions across the United States and Canada. Kit was impressed. This Hank Reardon had obviously roped and bucked his way to the top of the rodeo circuit—no small feat, considering the bumps and bruises and broken bones he surely had suffered along the way. Not to mention the prize money he must have won. She remembered reading somewhere that rodeo riders earned good money. From the mounds of research she'd done in preparation for this assignment, Kit had also learned that Hank Reardon had quit the rodeo circuit seven years before, although no mention was ever made of what had caused his abrupt disappearance from the circuit after an impressive fifteen-year run. Having never met the man, Kit could only surmise that he'd gotten too old to compete. With the image of a rusty old rodeo veteran fixed in her mind, Kit was lured back to the open window by the sound of the voices from outside.

"Tell me something, Pete," Hank Reardon demanded. "Is there anything else you think I should do?"

"Yeah. I think you ought to bury the dead."

Kit heard a warning grate in Hank Reardon's tone when he said, "We go back a long way, Pete. If anyone but you had said that to me, I'd have decked him."

Sullenly the other man replied, "Yeah, I know. But I also know you've got too much hate rumbling around inside of you because of that horse. I say put that energy to good use and sign up for some of the events. Nothing hard. Just the easy-money stuff."

From behind the window, Kit nodded knowingly. It was just as she'd thought—Hank Reardon *was* getting on in age. No wonder he'd stopped competing. That might also account for the ranch's run-down appearance, which Kit had noticed as she'd driven in earlier.

"After we get rid of the people who come to adopt the mustangs, we can load Dakota into the trailer and head for Cheyenne," the man called Pete suggested. "We could be there in time to register. What do you say, Hank, huh?"

There was a pause. Then, in a voice that suddenly sounded tired, Hank Reardon said, "I don't know, Pete. I can't promise anything. This is the time of year when he comes back, and I've got to be here. I'm going to get him this year, Pete. I know it. I'm going to get him."

"But Hank—"

A horse's frenzied whinny from the corral stopped Pete in midplea. Hank's tone turned harsh as he muttered a string of epithets. "You tell Quint that if he doesn't stop treating the horses like that, he can collect his wages and get the hell out of here. I won't put up with any of the hands mistreating the horses."

"Aw, you know Quint, Hank. He thinks he's top rider and likes to show off. That's all."

"Yeah? Well, he can show off somewhere else. I don't like his style or his methods."

"Quint'll probably score big points at Cheyenne this year," Pete noted, then added slyly, "seeing as how there's no one better to compete against him."

Hank let the pointed remark pass without a reply, and the two men parted company. From the window Kit saw one of them emerge into view. He moved his lanky frame in the direction of the barn. That, she surmised, was Pete.

While she waited for Hank Reardon, Kit thought of the research she'd done and made mental notes of questions she wanted to ask him about the annual wild horse roundup and adoption that she'd come to Wyoming to photograph.

The program had been started ten years before by the Bureau of Land Management as an incentive to Americans who wanted to adopt wild horses. Homes were being sought for the animals because they were trampling western rangelands in pursuit of food and because they faced starvation as a result of overpopulation.

Kit's editor at *Human Interest Magazine*, where she was a staff photographer, thought the roundup and adoption would make a good photo essay. Once she'd arrived in Wyoming, her natural curiosity had taken over. Who were these people who came from all over the country to adopt wild horses? Who were the men who rounded up the mustangs? And where did Hank Reardon, owner of the Chaparral ranch, aging rodeo rider, fit into the picture?

Just then the door to the study swung open. An imperceptible breeze rushed into the room, picking up a strand of Kit's auburn hair and blowing it into her eyes as she turned from the window.

The darkness of the tree-shaded room and the light just beyond the doorway created a silhouette that seemed to fill the entire space. Kit blinked as the tall figure stepped into the room, passing from light to shadow in long strides. He walked to a table, where he removed his gloves and slapped them down, saying without even looking up, "You're early. We haven't even gone out to round up the horses yet. If you come back in a few days, we should have something for you."

Hank's movements ground to a halt as an unexpectedly feminine voice replied, "I haven't come to adopt a horse, Mr. Reardon."

The sound of that voice—smooth, beguiling, somewhat tentative, but mostly confident—spun Hank Reardon's head in her direction toward the window. A ray of sunlight slanted through the branches of the tree outside, illuminating her hair and teasing it with red sparkles while playing softly against the contours of her face. Her unexpected beauty rendered him speechless, an unsettling feeling for him. He moved forward in order to shake the sensation. "If you're not here to adopt a wild horse, then what are you here for? My housekeeper sent word that you wanted to see me."

In those first few moments, Kit scrambled to collect her thoughts. He was handsome in a way she couldn't define. Beneath the wide brim of his Stetson she saw a strong, unflinching jaw, a full, finely shaped mouth, tatters of dark curly hair. Two things struck her simultaneously: for one,

Hank Reardon was not an old cowboy. On the contrary, he exuded raw vitality, and she could see that he was not yet forty. The other was his eyes, as blue as the sky on this fine June day. Kit felt momentarily trapped by those thick-lashed eyes. Beyond their unexpected and startling beauty was something she almost wished she hadn't seen. A suffering in their depths, she thought, an anguish that beckoned for her to fly across the room and offer him comfort, although for what she didn't know. But Kit stayed rooted to her spot, not daring to give in to such a foolish impulse, for in his eyes was also a simmering fury that she did not understand but felt acutely. As he swept his gaze over her, Kit became increasingly uncomfortable. A chill crept along her spine, displacing any urge she might have had to comfort him.

When he had drunk his fill with those blue eyes, he turned and began to walk away. Kit noticed the play of muscles beneath his shirt, which spanned his broad back, and the fluidity of his gait, muscles working in harmony to create a symmetry of motion that held Kit's gaze. Something quick and dangerous emanated from him, heating up the surrounding air.

Kit nervously cleared her throat, then volunteered, "My name is Kit Sloan." When that produced no visible sign of recognition, she prompted, "You know, from *Human Interest Magazine*. I'm here to take pictures of the adoption. I'm sure they told you I was coming."

He gave her a brief but thorough look. "So, you're the photographer they sent."

She nodded.

"That's funny. I thought—" He wasn't really sure what he'd thought.

"Then you *were* expecting me?"

Hank walked to the sofa and tossed his hat onto it. "Yeah. Sure."

His reaction baffled her. "Yeah. Sure."? That was it? "You'll pardon my asking," she said, "but if you were expecting me, why do I get the distinct impression that you're surprised to see me?"

Hank mentally replayed the phone call from the people at the magazine asking if he would consent to a photographer coming out to shoot the event. He'd been tempted to turn them down. Who needed some nosy photographer butting into things? Pete had persuaded him to do it, reasoning that the publicity might be good for the Chaparral's flagging horse-breeding business. Hank wasn't sure he cared, but Pete had been so insistent that he'd given in. It had been easier to say yes than explain all the reasons for saying no. If he'd thought for a minute, though, that they'd send a woman, and one as beautiful as this one, he would have stuck to his guns in the first place. And besides, he'd assumed the photographer would be there one day, maybe two at the most, just to take pictures of the people who came to adopt the horses. So there was an edge of impatience to his tone when he told her, "Well, like I said, you're early."

"That's all right," Kit replied. "I like to get a jump on things, anyway. Sort of peruse the area before I actually get down to work. It gives me a better feel for what I'm going to photograph."

Hank responded with a disgruntled mutter. When he looked at her again, his eyes flashed with annoyance from his suntanned face. "Look, when I agreed to this thing, I had no idea they'd send a woman—and one who probably doesn't even know which end of a horse points forward."

Kit came forward in a fluid motion that gave no hint of the anger building rapidly inside her. She kept her voice low and calm and said, "If I weren't qualified to do this job, I wouldn't be here. I assure you, Mr. Reardon, I know my way around horses. As a matter of fact, I can attest to looking at one end of a horse at this very moment, and let's just say it's not the end that points forward."

A flash of fury, a swift retort, even a dangerous glint from those icy blue eyes—Kit would have expected anything from him other than the laughter that rippled from his throat. It startled her, not only by its sudden interruption of the tension in the room but by its ring of genuine humor. "I guess I had that coming," he admitted. "Okay, so I'll assume you know your way around horses. But we've got a hundred mustangs to round up in the next few days, and the range is no place for a woman."

"That's a sexist remark if I've ever heard one," she said sourly.

He replied, "It wasn't meant to be." He hadn't meant it the way it sounded. The fact was, he'd seen women who could ride better than some men he knew. He assessed her thoughtfully, scanning her face with his eyes, then moving them slowly over the rest of her. It was just that he wasn't sure how the other men would react to her presence. Emotions ran high on a roundup. It wasn't just the horses and nature they competed with out there; it was with one another. There was definitely something about this woman that was hard to ignore, and the last thing he needed was to give the men something else to compete for.

If he was trying to disconcert her, he was doing a good job of it, she mused. Unable to take any more of his scrutiny, Kit lifted her hands into the air, wiggled her fingers at him and said sardonically, "I take pictures with these, Mr. Reardon."

"You're going to need more than those," he responded. "Whoever rides with me does his—or *her*—share of the work."

It wasn't so much the unnecessary emphasis on gender as his assumption that she'd be riding with them that made Kit pause on the verge of a retort. This was something she hadn't anticipated, but it could be just the thing to give her photo essay the impact it needed. The idea of a roundup in action intrigued her. Still, she wasn't entirely certain she liked the idea of spending the next few days in the company of this dark and brooding man, whose manners left something to be desired.

"When do we ride out?" she asked.

"Day after tomorrow. But you might want to change your mind. This isn't a cushy outfit I run here. If you're looking for a carpeted tent with a wood stove, a cot and a hot shower, I'd suggest you try one of the local outfitters that take tourists into the mountains to view the scenery."

"I'm not here to view the scenery."

"We don't provide wool socks, biodegradable soap, sleeping bags or insect repellent," he said almost triumphantly.

"Fine."

"We don't serve pork chops, mashed potatoes and gravy for dinner, either."

"I guess that rules out apple pie for dessert, then," she said flippantly.

There was something admirable about the way she stood her ground that pleased Hank in spite of himself. An involuntary smile made its way across his lips, softening those relentless features and stunning Kit with its impact before it retreated behind another hard look.

Refusing to be intimidated by his expression or by his eyes, which sent ripples of uncertainty through her, Kit tried a bolder approach. "I'd like to ask you a few questions, if you don't mind."

"Questions?" He seized upon the word as if she'd uttered an obscenity. "What kind of questions?"

Her hand went up to her throat, and it was apparent by the flutter in her voice that she'd meant no harm. "Just some background stuff, that's all." So much for the bold approach, Kit thought with a gulp.

Hank looked into her baffled green eyes and regretted his harshness. When had he become so suspicious of everyone's motives? he asked himself. If he had stopped and considered it, he would have known the precise moment when he stopped trusting, but Hank chose not to think about it. No good ever came from thinking. All it did was prolong a pain he'd begun to believe would never leave him.

"I've got a mare about to foal over at the barn," he said. "If you promise not to get in the way, yeah, sure, it would be all right. Come on." He grabbed his dusty Stetson, slapped it back on his head and strode from the room.

Kit trailed Hank out into the fading sunshine to a weather-beaten barn. A horse's throaty whinnies from within signaled that something was wrong in the last stall.

As they approached, Kit could see that the mare was down, her eyes rolling, head tossing. A man she recognized as Pete was kneeling at her side, stroking her neck and speaking soothing words to her.

"What's wrong?" asked Hank as he hurried in.

"I was afraid of this," said Pete. "The foal hasn't turned."

"Did you call Doc Ryan?"

"He'll be here as soon as he can, but—" He didn't have to say it; it was written all over his face.

"Damn." Hank spoke softly, for he didn't want to startle the mare. "It might strangle on the cord."

"What do you want to do, Hank?" Pete asked in a voice tight with urgency.

Hank was already pushing up the sleeves of his shirt. "Maybe I can turn it. Pete, keep her attention. This is her first, and she's bound to be nervous." He dropped to his knees in the hay and positioned himself to receive the foal, working his hands deep within the mare. Sweat trickled from his brow into his eyes, catching in a tangle of dark lashes to blur his vision. He hunched a shoulder in a vain attempt to wipe it away, swearing softly under his breath.

At the first sign of his discomfort, Kit came forward. She untied the bandanna that was knotted around his neck. Brushing smoothly and swiftly, she dabbed at the perspiration that rolled down his brow and the sides of his face. She received only a faint nod of the head from him for her effort.

Tense seconds ticked by. Finally Hank said, "I think I've got it." Then, "No, dammit, the foal's too slippery. I can't grab it." He placed the palm of one hand against the mare's frothy coat, and with the other he reached far inside, searching for the foal's head. A muffled curse signaled his failure to turn the foal.

Pete shot an anxious glance back at Hank. "We gotta do something!"

"I know, dammit, I know."

From off to the side, Kit suggested, "Try a rope."

The two men looked at her in unison, Pete's expression questioning, Hank's faintly mocking. "I've seen it done that way before," she explained in answer to their looks. But when that failed to convince them, she added with a smattering of disgust at their skepticism, "I used to help my dad deliver foals on the farm, okay?"

Hank and Pete exchanged a brief look before Hank withdrew his hands and hurried to get a rope. When he raced back with one, Kit said, "Put a loop in it, then see if you can get it around the foal's forelegs."

"Easy, girl," Pete crooned to the mare. "It won't be long now."

Hank worked against time to locate the foal's forelegs, feeling around in the wet darkness. Somehow, he found them and managed to secure the loop. He grasped the end, braced himself and began to pull. But there was no movement in the rope. "Okay, lady, if you know so much about horses, come grab hold of this rope while I maneuver this rascal around."

Without hesitation, Kit wound the rope around her hands, waited until Hank gave the word, then slowly pulled. She was concentrating so hard that she didn't see Hank leave his place and come up behind her. When his hands closed around her waist, she gasped and almost dropped the rope before collecting herself.

"We'll pull together," he said. "At the next contraction."

His hands burned into her flesh, searing through the fabric of her shirt. His arm around her rib cage felt like a cinch of steel. Her breasts rested against his arm as she and Hank pulled together. Her heart began to thump wildly. But when the mare's next contraction came, she had little thought for her own feelings. She was, for the time being, only dimly aware of Hank's arm, which held her pinned close to him, and of the hard male body pressed against her back. She was wrapped up in the splendor of birth as the tiny foal appeared legs first into the world.

Kit let the rope slip from her grasp, and for those first few seconds all she could do was try to regain her breath as she watched the wet little animal in the hay. As Kit began to breathe more evenly, she realized that Hank's arm was no longer around her. Those places on her that had come in contact with him burned as though scorched by flame, and only now did his nearness have its fullest impact on her.

Kit, Hank and Pete stood back as the mare got to her feet, cleaned her foal and gently nudged him to stand. Only after the horse was up on its wobbly legs did Hank get around to performing the introductions. Pete smiled at Kit and said, "Thanks for your help, Missy. We couldn't have done it without you."

Kit smiled back. "She'll give you a lot of good foals. She's got heart."

"Yeah," he agreed. "Like you."

Kit blushed at the compliment. Hank, who noticed it, turned to the older man and asked, "You got everything under control here now, Pete?"

"Sure, Hank. You two go on."

Dusk was descending over the peaks when Hank and Kit emerged from the barn. He walked her to her car and held the door open for her as she got in. "You were right," he said. "You do know your way around horses."

Kit started the engine. "I was raised on a farm in up-state New York," she explained.

He watched her a few moments longer with an unreadable look on his face, then said finally, "We ride out day after tomorrow at sunrise." The fading light played across his face, casting his handsome features into partial shadow before he turned away and headed back to the house.

The setting sun's last rays shot fiery beams between the darkening battlements of the Tetons. Wispy pink clouds snagged atop knife-edged crags, and the distant sound of thunder rumbled from behind the peaks as Kit drove back to the motel in Jackson. It was dark by the time she got there and pulled into the gravel parking lot, which was lit by a neon sign proclaiming "Silver Spur Motel" in sputtering letters. She could hear the throb of country and western music coming from the lounge as she made her way to her room, where she collapsed on the bed, fully clothed. She lay atop the chenille bedspread, staring up at the white plaster ceiling. As she followed with her eyes a tiny crack that snaked off to a far corner of the room, she thought of how draining an experience her first meeting with Hank Reardon had been. In spite of all Kit's attempts to remain detached from her subject, it had taken just one look from those eyes and she'd been reeled in like a helpless minnow.

After a while Kit rose wearily, stripped off her clothes, washed her face, pulled on a T-shirt and climbed back into bed. She was too tired to notice much except the ache in her bones. She slept deeply, but far from soundly, for into her dreams came the harsh intrusion of a pair of steely blue eyes and the dismal realization that they had affected her more than she cared to admit.

The moon climbed higher into the sky as Kit slept, and one by one the lights of Jackson went out.

Chapter 2

A stream of sunlight through the venetian blinds fell across Kit's eyes. She stirred, rustling her hair, which was spread in a dark mass across the white pillowcase. Yawning, she sat up, swung her bare legs around and got out of bed. On her way to the bathroom, she switched on the radio. The soft strains of a Willie Nelson ballad floated into the steam-filled bathroom as she showered.

Kit emerged from the bathroom wrapped in the white motel towel and sat on the bed to blow-dry her hair. As the heat evaporated the moisture, the tresses turned lighter until they shone with characteristic red and gold sparkles. When her hair was practically dry, she turned the dryer off to let the summer air finish the job.

Humming along to the music, Kit dressed in a pair of white cotton shorts, T-shirt, white socks and sneakers. The pouch of cosmetics that she carried with her but seldom used remained untouched on the dresser as Kit slung her camera bag over her shoulder and set out to explore.

Jackson's downtown streets still had their wooden sidewalks covered by canopies projecting from false facades, reminiscent of the Old West. But Kit quickly noticed that the stylish cowboy hats worn by the people around her shaded the soft city faces of tourists. They flocked to Jackson each year both for the rodeo that was held five nights a week and to the lively melodrama theaters around town.

The mighty Tetons were obscured by a massive butte in whose shadow Kit had driven for over an hour on her way to the Chaparral the previous day. Nevertheless, everywhere she looked she was struck by the nostalgic air of the town. Most of the restaurants, shops and motels had authentic-looking decor. She stopped in some shops to browse as she strolled down the street. Now and then she paused to pull her camera from its bag and get off a few shots, rendering her impressions of Jackson, Wyoming, if not for posterity, then for her own personal scrapbook. When the rumblings of her stomach reminded Kit she hadn't eaten breakfast, she left the trappings of the Old West to the tourists and opted for an ordinary-looking coffee shop.

Inside, she sat on a stool at the counter and waited fifteen minutes before she was even noticed by the waitress. Kit smiled wryly to herself. The moment she'd set foot outside New York City, the pace had slackened considerably. It would take some getting used to, she mused.

It had been like that, only in reverse, when she'd arrived in New York City eight years earlier, fresh out of college. Neither her degree nor her upbringing in Beaver Falls, population six thousand if you didn't count the livestock, had prepared her for the pace of Manhattan. Over the years, of course, she'd adapted to it, yet here it was, culture shock all over again, and she couldn't help but roll her eyes at her long wait for breakfast. Her stomach was grumbling mightily by the time her breakfast—eggs over easy with home fries and piping-hot rolls—was set before her.

Kit sat there happily munching on a crisp strip of bacon and sipping coffee when her attention was drawn to a nearby booth where three men were hunched over their plates. One was an elderly man with white hair and a lined face. The second was a stone-faced man of middle age who looked straight down as he ate. The third was a youngster, no more than sixteen, whose cowboy hat was tilted back on his head at a rakish angle. The profiles of all three were identical. That three generations of the same family sat together intrigued Kit, but what intrigued her more was their conversation.

"Aw, come on, Nate," said the oldest man. "You know the BLM's required to place the healthy animals it captures in private hands. That or destroy 'em."

Without raising his eyes, the man called Nate replied, "If you ask me, that's the only way to get rid of them. Varmints! That's all those mustangs are. And I ain't the only one who thinks so. Ride on out to the Chaparral and ask Reardon what he thinks of those wild horses." He snorted derisively, adding, "Half of Reardon's herd's out there, thanks to that old piebald."

The boy popped a French fry into his mouth and said, "Man, they sure don't get along, do they? Mr. Reardon and that old piebald, I mean."

The boy received a sharp glance from his father. "Don't go talking about things you know nothing about. Whatever's between Reardon and that horse is none of our business."

The boy shrugged. "Wonder why he does it, that's all."

"Does what?"

"Keeps those wild mustangs on his place. I mean, if he hates the mustangs so much, why does he bother rounding them up and keeping them there so's they can be adopted? You'd think he wouldn't want any part of them."

Kit saw the boy's father and grandfather exchange a look that said there were still some things the boy did not understand. The father swallowed the last of the black coffee in his cup, slapped his hat back on his head, swiped the check up off the table and left the booth, muttering, "I guess he's got his reasons."

Kit watched as the three filed out of the coffee shop, then piled into a battered pickup truck parked by the curb and disappeared down the street.

"Excuse me, miss," said Kit, turning back to the waitress.

"Sure, hon, what can I get you? More coffee?"

"Yes, thanks."

As the waitress poured the piping-hot brew into Kit's cup, Kit asked, "Tell me, do you know Hank Reardon?"

The woman glanced up. "He comes in once in a while. Why?"

Kit shrugged. "I met him yesterday. He seemed a little standoffish, if you know what I mean."

"Oh, I know what you mean, all right, but I don't know the man personally. It's just as well I don't. Those good-looking types are nothing but trouble."

Kit laughed and asked the woman if she was married.

"Married?" she exclaimed, her face assuming a horrified expression. "Hell no. Leastways not anymore. Take my word for it, honey; if you take their money, then you gotta take their baloney, too." She chuckled wryly. "So, you met Hank Reardon, huh? You gonna adopt one of those wild horses?"

"No. I'm going to take some photographs of the adoption for *Human Interest Magazine*."

With a shrug, the waitress said, "Never heard of it. It's funny, though, that anyone would want to go out to the Chaparral to take pictures of wild horses."

"Funny? Why's that?" Kit asked.

"It just doesn't seem like the kind of thing Reardon would want. Men," she huffed disparagingly. "Who can figure 'em out?"

Kit swung her legs around and slid off the stool. "Say, would you mind if I took your picture?"

The woman raised disbelieving eyebrows. "You want to take *my* picture?"

"Sure. Maybe I'll use it."

The waitress looked flabbergasted. Her hands went up to the sides of her head to smooth her hair. "Should I go put some lipstick on?"

"No, don't," said Kit. "You're fine just the way you are. Just go ahead and do what you usually do."

The woman looked very unsure of herself as she moved off to go about her work. Kit noticed that now and then she snuck a peek over her shoulder at the camera.

"Don't think of the camera," said Kit as she lined up her subject in the viewfinder. She liked what she saw: touches of age, the fine lines of weary skin. But there was also a grit and endurance about the woman that intrigued Kit. She knew just how to catch and meld those qualities into something that transcended the elegance and beauty the woman lacked. It wasn't beauty that Kit was after. With a few simple techniques, she could have made the woman look beautiful. But Kit wanted to show the world that this was a strong woman, one whose wit and intelligence prevailed despite the small corner she'd relegated herself to, out here in this oasis of Western nostalgia in the vast Teton wilderness.

Kit finished up her meal and asked for the check.

"Sure, hon," said the waitress. "So, what do you think? Get anything you think you might use?"

"Could be. I'll need you to sign this just in case." Kit took a release form from her bag and slid it across the counter. The waitress pulled the pen from behind her ear and signed.

Kit left the coffee shop and set out to explore. Before long, she was laden with packages holding an assortment of souvenirs for friends back home—picturesque postcards of the Old West, campy T-shirts. For her loft, she'd found an Indian basket woven of aromatic sweet grass. As Kit made her way back to the motel, she was unaware of the way the sunlight bounced off her hair, setting the dark tresses on fire and bringing out the rich russet tones. But the man who watched her from beneath the brim of his Stetson was only too aware of it.

Hank Reardon had been steering his pickup down the street, one arm braced on the open window, features relaxed beneath the shadow of his hat, when, at the sight of Kit striding along just up ahead, his muscles tensed and his fingers tightened around the steering wheel.

She was taller than he remembered from the day before. Five seven, he estimated, and most of it leg. Long, slender, bronzed legs, just as he imagined the rest of her must be. It wasn't easy to ignore the way her hair brushed her shoulders like a shaggy mane, or the graceful swing of her hips, but it was impossible to ignore those legs. He followed her at a respectful distance, eyes glued to the tall, easy-moving figure. Lazy sex—that's what she exuded, he thought. He didn't know what else to call it. Hank pressed his foot to the accelerator and urged the pickup to move beyond her. He used her preoccupation with window-shopping to drive past her and park further up the street. He climbed down from the cab. Leaning against the fender, he lit a cigarette and smoked in thoughtful silence as he watched her stroll closer.

Something made Kit turn away from the store window and look over her shoulder. When she saw him, she tensed. Willing her muscles to relax, she approached. She gave him an easy smile and held out her hand. "Mr. Reardon, good morning."

He took her hand and held it. Her grip was stronger than he'd expected. He liked that; strength was something he admired in a woman. Her eyes interested him as well, the way she looked at him forthrightly, with a candid eagerness. He noticed the absence of makeup. Good, he thought. The last thing he needed out on the range was a woman who fussed before a mirror every morning. He knew this one wouldn't. He noticed that she was assessing him in a like manner. He liked that, too; it showed curiosity. It seemed to him as if she were seeking a way to frame his face for the camera, an angle at which to photograph him.

"What are you doing in town?" she asked.

He ceased his perusal of her face. His hand felt strangely empty when she removed hers. He flicked his cigarette butt to the ground. "I came to pick up some feed." Gesturing to the bags, he said, "Can I give you a hand with those?"

"Sure," she said, handing him one of the bags. "Thanks. I was just toting this stuff back to the motel." Kit laughed. A ring of self-mockery in her tone, she confessed, "I'm a sucker for souvenirs. You wouldn't believe the things I let myself get talked into buying."

Hank fell into step beside her as they continued down the sidewalk. He noticed again the scent of her, the same fragrance of fresh-cut flowers that had invaded his senses the previous afternoon as he'd stood close behind her in the barn. It wasn't a sophisticated, haughty scent, but something more basic; the elemental mixture of her natural aroma and traces of a summer garden created a potion that muddled his senses.

Kit felt inside her an unexplained nervousness in his presence. In an attempt to banish it, she opted for small talk. "Doesn't the owner of the Chaparral have more important things to do than ride into town for feed? Don't you have people to do those things for you?" She looked up in time to see a glimmer of contempt race across his face. Had she said the wrong thing? she wondered.

"Yes," he said. "I do. The fact is, I told one of my hands to do it over a week ago, but he didn't." It was only this morning that he'd discovered that his instructions to Dan Quint had gone unheeded, Hank thought. It wasn't the first time Quint had neglected to do something Hank had asked him to do. Half to himself, he said, "I guess I'm going to have to talk to Quint about it."

Kit recalled that Quint's name had come up in the conversation she'd overheard between Hank and Pete. Now, as then, she detected a keen note of hostility in Hank's voice. "Is he new on the job?" she asked.

Hank shook his head. "Me and Quint go back about ten years."

"You're friends, then," she ventured as they reached the hotel.

"Hell, no! I didn't like that guy from the first day he hired on."

"Why do you keep him around?"

He shrugged. "Quint does his job better than most."

"When he does it, you mean."

His voice deepened when he said, "Yeah."

They entered the motel room, and Kit gestured toward the bed, saying, "You can put that bag over there."

Hank did so, then stepped back, hands in his jeans pockets, and looked around, thinking, if he'd seen one motel room, he'd seen them all. In his years on the rodeo circuit it seemed at times that he *had* seen them all. This one, however, was not like all the others, for in the corners of the dresser mirror and hanging about the room were glossy black and white photographs.

"Sorry about the mess," said Kit.

"How'd you manage this?" He gestured around at the prints hung like wash.

She nodded toward the bathroom. "In there."

"With what?"

"I bring my own equipment with me on a shoot," she explained. "I prefer, of course, to work in my own darkroom, but as you can see, I've learned to improvise."

"When did you accomplish all this?" he asked.

"I got up late last night. Couldn't sleep." She let it go at that, remembering that the truth was that she'd awakened in the middle of the night in a sweat, her T-shirt clinging to her body. Knowing it would be useless to lie there in the darkness staring at the shadows, she'd risen and hastily assembled the trays of chemical solutions and the water bath, fitted an appropriate bulb into the overhead fixture and developed the film she'd exposed the previous day, on her drive out to the Chaparral.

"I love darkroom work," she said. "Even under the worst of conditions," she added with a laugh, aiming a sardonic look at the bathroom. "It relaxes me."

What she didn't say was that she'd needed relaxing after the disturbing dream she'd been having. What would he think if he knew? She could just picture the way his blue eyes would flash with typical male pride.

It didn't appear that Hank had gotten much sleep either, Kit thought as she noted the day-old stubble that spiked his chin and the weariness etched in fine lines around his eyes. The hours Kit had spent in the darkroom had accounted for her lack of sleep last night, but what, she wondered, accounted for his?

Hank studied the shots she'd taken of the Tetons, nodding with appreciation. She'd captured them just the way he saw them, teeming with majesty, bursting with beauty. It was where he felt most at home. Sometimes in the dead of night, he'd throw a saddle on Dakota and they'd gallop off into the mountains. Or maybe he'd be out riding the range and the impulse to go up to the higher altitudes would overtake him. He'd give Dakota his head, and they'd climb to places where the air was thin and the sky so close it seemed he could almost touch it with his hand. And there he'd stay until it was time to come back—a day, maybe two, or however long it took for the pain to recede.

He needed the mountains; he derived his own strength from theirs. He needed their sheer beauty to remind him that not everything in the world was ugly. But these black and white prints of Kit's touched something inside him that he didn't expect. Without the vibrant greens of the forests and the multicolor images of the Tetons to charge the pictures with life, the feeling that emanated from them was one that Hank recognized only too well. It was the loneliness that drew his gaze and held it, tightening the knot in his throat.

"Like them?" Kit's voice was soft, almost shy, when she came to stand beside him.

He cleared his throat and said, "Don't you take anything in color?"

"Sure. I'll develop those when I get back to New York. These I did . . . oh, I don't know, for myself, I guess."

"You're very good."

"Thank you."

She was standing so close that he was almost afraid to turn to her. He willed his attention to remain on the prints and tilted his head this way and that to view the photographs. But the loneliness of the mountains and the warmth simmering from the woman at his side began to converge on Hank. Gradually he shifted his gaze to her, though he had no idea why he did it. Without thinking, as though it had been planned far in advance of that moment, he reached out and curled his fingers around a strand of auburn hair. He wasn't thinking of the consequences; he simply wanted to touch it.

The gesture surprised Kit, but she didn't pull away.

His touch confirmed what his eyes already knew: her hair was soft. He searched her face. He found the absence of makeup uniquely disturbing. But he didn't want to be disturbed by this woman. When he was this close to her, the defenses he'd spent years in building were dangerously close to being shattered. Just looking at her, Hank could think of a dozen ways he'd like to make love to her. He wanted to start here and now.

Kit knew that if they stayed like this, things would get complicated. His look was contemplative, assessing, not entirely friendly. He wouldn't be an easy man to love; that much she knew instinctively. Something in his eyes warned her that he was the kind of man who didn't show his emotions easily, yet who would demand it of her in return.

He was not a man to become personally involved with, she told herself. He would overwhelm her, and she knew there'd be no turning back. Nevertheless, she ignored the small voice at the back of her mind that told her to move away.

Their mouths met greedily. Kit's body heated up so rapidly that the room seemed to catch fire about them. A small sound issued from her throat. She entangled her fingers in his hair, thrilling to the silky softness of it. She wanted more, despite her own heated warnings. Hold me, her body seemed to cry. She moved, not away, but closer still. She could feel the tension in his body, the restraint he was trying desperately to maintain.

Hank realized that there seemed to be no pretenses about her. Her mouth was warm and soft, eager for his. Her body was tempting. Her scent enveloped him, clouding his senses, muddling his logic. For the first time in a very long while, Hank found himself wanting to give—regardless of the consequences. He held himself back nevertheless, making love only to her mouth, when she—and he, too—wanted much more.

Lips opened, invited, accepted. Fingers clung. He tilted his head to hers and, with a tender urgency, deepened the kiss. She tasted hot and sweet, and she made him burn. He had to hold back, he thought, or she would sear a scar on his soul, and he already had enough of them. Hank knew better than most that life wasn't as sweet as a first kiss between two young lovers. He allowed his lips to linger on hers a moment before retreating with a quickness that spoke of sudden regret. He drew away, satisfied that his self-control was still intact. Perhaps his pulse wasn't steady, but at least he was thinking clearly now.

Kit was reeling. She'd known his kiss would drain her. Even now she felt unsteady on her feet as she waited desperately for her equilibrium to return. There it was again, she thought, that look of regret on his face, as if he were waging a battle within himself, one side wanting to come closer, the other battling to the death to stay away. The by now familiar impenetrable veil fell over his eyes as he dropped his hand to his side.

Hank saw the look on Kit's face, the soft look any man would be hard-pressed to resist, combined with confusion. He turned away from it. "We ride out at sunrise," he told her as he strode to the door. "If you're there, you're there. If not..." The challenge was unspoken but nonetheless blatant in the arrogant shrug he gave as he let himself out.

Chapter 3

"Pete told me I'd find you here," Kit said, squinting into the dark stable at the figure moving among the shadows in one of the stalls.

She watched Hank look over his shoulder at the sound of her voice. In his hand dangled the bridle he'd been about to slip over the nose of a pretty chestnut horse. The horse's ears pricked forward, and its dark eyes regarded Kit with an easy but wary look as she approached.

Hank could barely make her out in the predawn darkness, but there it was again, the scent of fresh-cut flowers that he'd noticed the day before when he'd been with her. It had rushed into the stable ahead of her, heralding her presence. Today, as before, it made his nerves tingle. But in this place of leather and horseflesh, it had an even stronger effect upon him. It was like the appearance of a blossom in a dried-up garden.

He'd had all night to think about her. Only after he'd closed the door of her room behind him and stepped out into the air had he allowed himself to take the deep breath he'd needed. He'd tried to tell himself that it had been a tough few days, what with delivering that foal and dealing with not only Quint's insubordination, but Pete's infernal nagging. Hank knew it was more than that which had shaken him up yesterday, leaving his lungs thirsty for air. Any day at the Chaparral was a long, tough one. From the moment he got up until the time he fell into a fitful sleep at night, it was all routine—an arduous routine of sweating, straining labor that Hank thrived on. Without that to fill up his time and consume his thoughts, he'd be left with no escape from the memories burning inside him.

Looking at the photographs Kit had taken of the mountains had shaken him up more than he cared to admit. It was stupid, he knew. They were only pictures. And yet it was as if she had taken a picture of his very soul, for in those pictures he'd gotten a glimpse of himself, of his own loneliness, and he hadn't liked what he'd seen. Nor had he liked the apparent ease with which this woman saw right through him.

And then there was Kit herself. Into the midst of his routine had come this woman, disrupting the machinery of his mind and making him remember things he'd struggled to forget. She intrigued him, not just with that stirring beauty but with how she'd challenged him that day in the study, and later, when she'd shown no fear or trepidation in helping to deliver the foal. Frankly, she baffled him.

She moved toward him now in graceful, uncomplicated motions. Her long legs were clad in washed-out jeans that were frayed at the knees. A blue denim shirt opened to the waist revealed a white T-shirt with a faded logo. Her hair was caught up in a ponytail that swung from side to side as she walked.

Hank had known she'd be back. Still, it was with a note of mocking humor that he said to her, "I didn't think I'd see you this morning."

"That's because you don't know me," she responded cheerily. "He's beautiful." She indicated the proud-looking horse.

Hank smiled and went back to work. "His name's Dakota," he said, then slipped the bridle over the white-blazed face and fitted the metal bit into the horse's mouth. "We've won a few trophies together, haven't we, boy?" He ran a strong, sun-browned hand lovingly over the horse's shoulder. The animal uttered a deep neigh and turned its head to nuzzle Hank's sleeve affectionately.

Kit noticed that Hank seemed particularly at ease this morning, not nearly as hostile as he'd been that first day, nor as perplexing as yesterday. She used what she sensed was a rare moment of serenity in this volatile man to indulge her curiosity, not only about her assignment but about the man himself.

"Why do you do it?" she asked.

Hank removed a saddle blanket that had been slung over the door of the stall and placed it over the horse's back. "Do what?"

"Keep the wild horses here at the Chaparral. Are you paid to do it?"

He followed the blanket with a saddle of deep brown whose hand-tooled leather bore a rich patina from years of use and which squeaked when Hank adjusted the stirrups. "Hell, no!" he answered.

"Why, then?"

He shrugged carelessly and reached under the horse for the cinch. "About ten years ago, a guy from the Bureau of Land Management came out to ask some of the ranchers in these parts if we'd let them corral the captured mustangs on our land. I figured sure, why not? It seemed like a good idea at the time.'' Tightening the cinch, he explained, ''Sometimes when I was riding the range I'd come across one of them caught up in a snaggle of barbed wire. I'd shoot the ones that were still alive—and those were the lucky ones. It seemed to me they deserved better than that.''

''I wasn't aware that you did the actual rounding up yourself, though.''

''I didn't at first. The first couple of years the guys from the BLM rounded them up and brought them in.'' He remembered how it had been back then. He'd watch from off to the side as the families converged upon the Chaparral and excited children picked out their pretty little colts and fillies to take back home. Of course, all that had changed in a single night, a mere moment, and in the years since then, it had become desperately important for him to ride out after the mustangs himself. He told everyone that it was for the excitement, the closest thing to victory he would experience outside the rodeo arena, but while Hank thought he'd fooled the others, he wasn't able to fool himself. He knew why he rode out year after year in search of the wild mustangs. For one thing, it was a necessary diversion, a chance to get swept up in an emotion other than bitterness or pain. For another, it was the stallion. Always the stallion.

''Tell me about the mustangs,'' Kit prodded him. ''What are they like?''

Hanks thoughts came back to the present. ''The mustang's a scrub type of horse. Small, inelegant, lightweight and as intractable as hell. They were once used as cow ponies, but they've mostly been replaced by animals of better quality, like Dakota here. Every once in a while I break one to use for range work.''

''I'll bet you're very good at it, too,'' she remarked.

"And how would you know that?" he asked. "Don't tell me you used to break horses on the farm, too."

"No. I judged how good you are simply from the number of trophies you've won. That's quite a collection you have there. Why'd you stop?"

The question, although innocently asked, bristled in the sudden stillness that gripped the air around them. "You can't ride the rodeo circuit and run a ranch at the same time," Hank replied stiffly. "Besides, I got all that wild stuff out of my system years ago. Now whenever I get the urge to ride a bucking horse, I go out and catch a wild mustang and break him for ranch work. I don't need the crowds anymore, and I sure as hell don't need the trophies. Other things are more important." Forcing a lighter tone, he added, "Anyway, I'm thirty-eight years old, and these old bones can't take much more of that rough stuff."

The soft thud of Dakota's hooves etched through the quiet stable as Hank led the horse outside. Kit followed, her eyes glued to the fluidity of Hank's gait and the suppleness of his muscles. Old bones? she thought, unconvinced. Somehow she knew old bones had nothing to do with it.

A faint pink light hovered just beyond the treetops as the sun slowly rose in the east. Kit felt a distinct tenseness about Hank now, and even though his face bore an implacable look, she sensed she'd touched a tender nerve with him. She could not deny that she was curious, yet Kit's curiosity was tainted by an explicable fear. It wasn't him she was afraid of; it was the danger that lurked all about him. There was something hot and impulsive in him that, combined as it seemed to be with a good measure of pain, made him more than a little bit frightening.

Again she found herself thinking that he would not be an easy lover. There was no patience in him. He was a walking powder keg. But she knew there simmered beneath that rough exterior a kindness and a tenderness that even he seemed unaware of. Indeed, it was almost imperceptible except to one who'd stood in his arms as she had yesterday, and to one who looked closely, as she was doing now.

She decided not to press the subject of the rodeo circuit. Everyone was entitled to his secrets and aches, she reasoned, and she wouldn't tread where she wasn't wanted. How could she have foreseen the reaction that awaited, however, when she inquired, "And the piebald stallion? Where does he fit in?"

Hank froze in his tracks and turned sharply to look at her. His eyes blazed like two blue flames in the thin morning light. "What do you know about that?" he demanded.

Kit shrank inwardly from the menace in those eyes, the stance that was suddenly on the verge of anger. "Nothing," she admitted. "I heard it mentioned yesterday in town, but—"

He cut her off sharply. "Forget about him. The piebald's just another wild mustang, that's all."

"So there you two are," rang out a male voice behind them. Hank and Kit turned in unison to see Pete approaching, leading a saddled horse by the reins. "Here she is, Hank, like you asked." Turning to Kit, the older man smiled and said, "Morning, Missy. Here you go. Bayberry's a little sweetheart. You won't have any trouble with her. Course, I wanted to saddle Frisco for you. I figured anyone who can handle herself the way you did the other day with that mare and her foal can ride a horse as rambunctious as Frisco, but Hank said to saddle up Bayberry for you." He held the reins out to her.

Kit stepped forward and took them. She patted the pretty, docile mare and said, "That's all right, Pete. Thanks anyway. She and I will do just fine. We girls understand

each other, don't we?'' she said to the horse. Turning to
Hank with a look of annoyance, she asked, ''If you didn't
think I'd be back, why'd you bother to have a horse saddled for me?''

He glared irately at her in answer to the challenge in her
tone. ''You know something, lady? You ask too many
questions.'' He thrust one booted foot into the stirrup and
mounted. With a subtle tensing of the knees and a smooth
pull on the reins, he set the chestnut stallion in motion.

When Hank had trotted off, Pete turned to Kit and
asked, ''What's got into him this morning?''

Her eyes were still fixed on the rigid back of the retreating man. There was an air of unflinching pride about him,
which, Kit was discovering, could be infuriating. ''Don't
ask me,'' she grumbled. ''All I did was ask him about the
piebald stallion.''

''Whoa, Missy,'' Pete exclaimed, ''you sure do know
how to stir up a hornets' nest, don't you?''

With a look of exasperated innocence she asked, ''How
was I to know I'd said the wrong thing?''

He smiled kindly at her. ''No, you couldn't have known,
could you?''

In her attempt to steer around one obviously painful
subject, she'd run smack-dab into another. First, his quit-
ting of the rodeo circuit and now the obsession with a
spotted horse. Were the two somehow related, connected by
a slender thread stretched nearly to breaking, inside Hank
Reardon? It provoked in Kit a crazy curiosity that went
against her better judgment. ''Pete,'' she began. ''About
the stallion—''

''Why don't you run and get your things and pack them
into your saddlebags?'' Pete suggested, cutting her off. A
little too quickly, Kit thought. Evasion seemed to be the
fare of the day around here. She let it go. What did it mat-

ter? She was here to take pictures, not to penetrate the inner sanctum of a faded rodeo rider who had a vendetta against a horse. Besides, she told herself again, Hank Reardon wasn't the kind of man you got close to, not if you had all your wits about you. She gestured toward her rented car that was parked not far off and said, "I'll go get my stuff."

It took only a few minutes for Kit to retrieve her things from the car and pack them into saddlebags. Pete nodded approvingly at the sweater she'd brought, commenting, "It can get pretty cold up in the mountains at night, even in the summer."

"Don't I know it," she said with a laugh. "I grew up around the Adirondacks. Not quite what you have here," she said, gesturing to the towering, jagged peaks that rose up in the distance all around them, "but there are some formidable back trails up there. My dad and I used to ride up into the mountains and go camping. It gets pretty cold up there, too."

When she finished packing her gear, Pete said, "Come on, I'll give you a boost up." Cupping his hands, fingers entwined, he received Kit's boot and hoisted her into the saddle. He was not surprised by her agility, which made her feel lighter than she actually was. "You trot on over to the corral. I'll be along in a few minutes."

At the corral Kit found half a dozen men already assembled. An uneasy silence fell over the group. From under the brims of their hats they studied her, some with curiosity, others with suspicion. One, a good-looking man astride a fancy palomino, eyed Kit with typical male lust that he made no attempt to disguise. Pete performed the introductions when he arrived.

She met the camp cook, a red-faced Irishman named Tom O'Reilly, and the hands, Randy, Jim, Bill, Ramon and

Dan Quint. The man named Quint continued to stare at her in a way that made her uncomfortable. She recalled the snippets of conversation she'd overheard between Hank and Pete the other day and Hank's disparaging comments of yesterday. So this was the man whose style Hank didn't like. There was something about the cocky way he sat in the saddle that Kit didn't like either. She endured his lazy smile and lecherous stares until Hank rode up. After speaking a few quick words to the men, Hank turned Dakota's head toward the north.

The sun was up, and an early-morning mist settled like dust over the tranquil valley in the bend of the Snake River as the party of eight men, one woman and assorted pack-horses filed out of the valley. The men paired off for quiet conversation as they rode at a leisurely pace. Hank took the lead, riding alone, making conversation with no one, occasionally extending a gloved hand to pat the sleek neck of his mount.

Kit and Pete rode side by side at the rear of the column, chatting amiably as they began their ascent into the hills. Bayberry proved an easy horse to ride. There was no need to worry about the inclines, for the sturdy little mare was a hunter, the kind sometimes used by outfitters, Pete explained, because they were sure-footed on steep, muddy trails and strong rather than fast. The mare turned at the flick of the wrist and started with the barest nudge of the toes. Pleased to have found a horse to her liking, Kit relaxed and luxuriated in the sights around her.

A tidal wave of rock broke over the horizon, filling it with gargantuan beauty. There were other ranges with taller summits, but the Tetons were still adolescents, not yet smoothed over by eons of erosion. They were spectacular in their raw and rugged youth. To Kit the mountains looked like a stage designer's backdrop, lowered from the heavens for the performance of some epic production.

Pete pointed out the sights and helped Kit distinguish the myriad fragrances of white and lavender columbine, wild vetch, lupine and Indian paintbrush. Pete, she learned, had been born and raised around the Texas panhandle and had migrated to Wyoming, where a lifetime of cowpunching, harsh summers and wicked winters had left their grit permanently etched on his face. It was hard to tell precisely how old he was. Sixty, maybe? But there was a liveliness in his dark eyes that offset the deep seams in his face. He was an easy talker, amusing Kit with bits and pieces of past and present as they rode on into the lengthening day. It was Pete who filled in much of the background on the wild horse roundup and adoption, although he was careful to avoid conversation about Hank.

"There certainly doesn't seem to be any love lost between Hank and Quint," Kit noted.

"Those two never did get along much," said Pete. "You know how it is between men sometimes. They're both strong-willed and pigheaded." He seemed eager to let the matter lie. Wisely, Kit did the same.

A few miles later the group crested a divide. At some points the trail was nearly vertical, and they had to stop often to rest the straining horses as the valley slipped away rapidly below them. As their mounts clambered up the hillside, Kit gave Bayberry a few appreciative pats for the extra effort. As they rode along, everything was silent except for the click-clack of the horses' hooves and the echo of bird song from the treetops. Because it was midsummer, most of the animals were hidden in their shady dens, but Kit occasionally glimpsed a deer bounding into the breaks or a muskrat swimming in a stream. It was easy to lose track of time out there, to feel small and insignificant in the shadow of the mountains that cut the sky all around them. For long stretches they rode without speaking, feeling the moisture gathering at the backs of their necks and trickling down between their shoulder blades in tiny beads of wetness as the sun inched higher in the cerulean sky.

"Where are we going?" Kit asked Pete after a while. She was beginning to wonder if they weren't just wandering around in aimless circles in the hope of stumbling across some wild mustangs. "Are there really any horses up here?"

"Don't worry," Pete assured her. "If anyone knows where to find them, it's Hank."

She glanced up ahead to the front of the column, where Hank rode in solitary silence, and quipped, "Is he always this antisocial?"

Pete gave a half shrug and said, "Hank's a lot like that piebald stallion. Both of them are loners."

"Oh, I don't know about that," she said with a sigh. "Everyone needs someone, no matter how hard they try to hide it. Whether it's a rogue stallion or a stubborn man, there's something deep down inside of us all that longs to be touched by another of our own kind. I suspect Hank Reardon and that stallion are no different."

"You're right about the stallion," Pete confided. "He's got himself a mate. White as snow, she is. Saw the two of them together once when I was tracking elk."

"And Hank?" she ventured. "Why's he like this, Pete? So...so...oh, I don't know."

In a gentle tone he said, "Tell me something, Missy. Did you ever get madder at something than you should have when it was really yourself you were mad at?"

"Sure," she admitted. "But not to the point of alienating other people."

"Some of us just hurt harder than others, and when we do, we get madder."

"What's Hank hurting over?"

For a moment Pete seemed to be making some sort of decision. He looked earnestly into Kit's green eyes and opened his mouth to speak, but the sudden appearance of Hank at their side chased away whatever Pete had been about to say.

Hank fixed his blue eyes immediately upon Kit. "We'll be stopping for lunch soon. Pete, why don't you ride on up ahead with Tom and find us a suitable spot to make camp?"

"Sure thing, Hank." The older man trotted off to the head of the column, spoke a few quick words to Tom O'Reilly, and the two of them moved on ahead, disappearing over the top of a rise in search of a campsite.

Kit felt a distinct tension in the air all around them. It seemed to follow in Hank's footsteps like a shadow. They fell into a silence that was broken after a while by Hank's deep voice. Gesturing around them, he said, "They're something, aren't they?"

Kit expelled a breath of awe in the direction of the vast Teton range, and agreed, "I've never seen anything like them."

"Compared to, say, the Rockies, they're just babies. A mere ten million years old." He swept his arm in a wide arc, motioning far below them to the forty-mile stretch of land that was Jackson Hole. "The earth's crust cracked along there and the mountains sprang from the fault. Some geologists think the process is still going on."

With a slight reddening of the cheeks Kit inquired, "How'd they get their name?"

"They were supposed to have been christened by French Canadian trappers in the early 1880s. I'm not so sure about that story, though. It's hard to imagine that the trappers named these rugged peaks after something as round and smooth as a woman's breasts.'' As he said it, he glanced at Kit's breasts, which bobbed lightly beneath her cotton shirt as she rode. ''Most likely,'' he went on, swinging his gaze back to the scenery, ''the name originally referred to a trio of softer peaks on the Idaho side of the range.''

Kit could easily tell from the way Hank's eyes caressed the terrain as he spoke that he loved this place like no other. ''What happened after the trappers left?'' she asked.

''Jackson slumbered on for another half century or so,'' he said, growing more relaxed in the saddle. ''After a while the Indians left. The first homesteaders arrived in the late 1880s, but most of them turned tail after one winter. This country's not much good for crops. The growing season's too short to be worth the hardship.''

In a way, she mused, he was much like the land he described; intractable, owning a primitive quality that belonged to this vast and wild place. ''Your family must go back a long way in these parts,'' said Kit.

''My great-grandfather was one of the first settlers in Jackson. In my grandfather's day it was just a cow town.''

''And the Chaparral? Is that part of the family heritage?''

''No. The Chaparral's mine. My father had a spread not far from here where he raised cattle. The place was practically bankrupt when he died. I sold what was left and raised the rest of the cash to buy the Chaparral by riding rodeo.''

''No cattle, though,'' she observed.

Hank shook his head. ''Too much trouble. Besides, there's something about raising an animal only to slaughter it that bothers me. Horses—that's what we raise on my spread.''

The dry summer air carried aloft the sweet fragrance of the shaggy-leafed trees. Though it was hot, the air was crisp and clear. Kit breathed it deep into her lungs, filling herself up with the mountain aroma. She felt strangely at ease riding beside Hank. Then, from very high in the sky, came the screech of a bird. Glancing skyward, squinting in the glare of the sun, Kit spotted a lone hawk circling, its wings spanned. The bird soared higher, arcing across the blue sky on currents of air, then disappeared behind the crest of a peak.

Hank saw the hawk, too, and was about to say something about it when Kit silenced him with a gasp and pointed to something up above. Hank turned in his saddle and looked to the top of a summit that rose more than two hundred feet over their heads. There, at its peak, a horse was watching as the riders below filed past. A mountain breeze played with its mane, flicking up the ends along its proud, arched neck. The sun reflected in blinding flashes off its coat, which shone alternately white and black. A chill ran down Kit's spine.

Kit felt the tension of his muscles as she and Hank rode in taut silence. She looked around. No one but them had seen it. She ran a nervous tongue over her lips and dared to ask, "That was him, wasn't it? That was the piebald stallion."

Hank's voice scratched painfully at the back of his throat. In a tone of contempt, he said, "Yeah, that was him." With a swift kick at Dakota's flanks, Hank galloped to the head of the column.

A short time later, the party stopped to rest and water the horses at a stream that trickled down from higher up, where snow still clung tenaciously to the uppermost ridges in saw-toothed patterns. Kit was happy to see that Pete and Tom had chosen a picturesque spot to make camp for lunch.

Unable to resist the magnificent storybook scenery, she got her camera out and began to click the shutter furiously as she captured nature at its most sublime. Later Pete handed her a sandwich that he'd pulled from his pack. Kit nibbled at it, but she wasn't very hungry. Maybe it was the mountain air, which she could feel growing thinner the higher they climbed. Or perhaps, she dared to think, it was the occasional glance from Hank Reardon that swung in her direction every now and then.

He sat with his back pressed up against the trunk of a tree, one leg stretched out, the other bent, his Stetson tipped back on his head. He ate slowly, thoughts seemingly a million miles away except for those periodic looks in Kit's direction that told her he was very much aware of what was going on around him. A shiver ran like ice water down her spine whenever he fixed his eyes on her. They seemed to be telling her something. It was almost as if they were warning her not to come any closer, to keep her distance. From what? she wondered. What was he so afraid that she might see?

After lunch they packed up their gear, mounted and continued on into the afternoon, cutting deep into canyons, slicing further into the mountains. Giving Bayberry her head, Kit dropped the reins, took out her camera and began to shoot. When she'd had her fill of the Technicolor world of the mountains, she snapped on a telephoto lens for some tight close-ups of the men.

By now the men were used to the mechanized click-click of the shutter and for the most part paid her no mind. Because Kit's work was often a direct result of her own emotions, her pictures reflected the variety of the men she was riding with, as the camera's telescopic eye penetrated their intimacy and brought each into sharp focus. The camera noted the cockiness with which Dan Quint sat his horse.

He's a good rider, all right, Kit thought as she focused on him. And a consummate show-off, too. He was undoubtedly a good-looking man, although not her type. More interesting was the way Quint's eyes strayed often—with a look of contempt, it seemed—in Hank's direction.

As Kit moved her camera from face to face, each view was rendered radically different by virtue of its subject. Yet written among those varying features was the common denominator that had brought them all together: a love for the work they did.

It was, ultimately, one face in particular that drew Kit's attention, one hard, implacable expression that commanded her camera's eye.

She liked the way its owner sat his horse, not quite at ease, but ready, remote. As unobtrusively as possible, Kit urged her horse to move a little faster so she could get closer to the front of the column where he rode. At that angle, she could see the fine lines and details of his face. He was staring straight ahead, the color of his eyes matching the crystal intensity of the sky. A breeze whipped up the dark tips of his hair at his collar. Through the lens Kit traced his profile; the thick sweep of lashes; the firm, straight nose; the lips, which were tightly pressed yet full enough to be beautiful; the strong line of his jaw, which was set with stubborn determination. There was something rocklike and unrelenting about his features, she thought, something hard and uncompromising in his eyes, but also a softness so deeply ingrained that it was all but invisible to the human eye. Through the magnifying lens, however, Kit saw it, felt it, sensed its presence keenly. And just then, when she felt herself drawing closer to the unspoken vulnerability, those eyes suddenly turned in her direction.

Kit gasped inwardly. Now she was the focus of his attention; only seconds before it had been the other way around.

She lowered the camera and fiddled with it while a host of chilling sensations rippled over her. There it was again, that warning look, that premonitory sign of danger lurking deep in his eyes, and accompanied by something else, something she could not put her finger on. It seemed almost as if he were challenging her, not with words or actions but by his look alone.

She'd never been a very aggressive person, but this man tapped in her a need to prove herself. If she had to travel in close company with someone who so obviously ruffled her feathers, perhaps it was best to deal with the matter directly. Urging Bayberry into a trot, Kit brought the mare close beside Hank's big chestnut stallion. "Does it bother you when I take pictures of you?" she asked.

Hank assessed Kit with his cool blue eyes. He would have expected someone like her to be harder, more aggressive, glossier. Instead, she looked like the girl next door, although he couldn't recall any girl next door ever looking like her. Her shoulder-length hair, which was pulled back in a ponytail, was rich and dark and deep, with crimson sparkles that reminded Hank of the sun when it set between the tall peaks of the range. Her eyes were green like the hills in springtime, almond-shaped, fringed with heavy lashes that had a way of falling with a delightful flutter. She certainly wasn't vain about her appearance. The other men appeared to take her presence in stride and, with the possible exception of Quint, who seemed to have set his sights on her, much to Hank's annoyance, she'd get no trouble from the men. Hank shrugged noncommittally and replied, "I can't say I like the idea of having that thing pointed at me. I thought you were here to take pictures of the horses."

"I'm here to take pictures of the horses *and* the people," she told him. "The ones who come to adopt the horses and the ones who round them up."

"I see. Well, I'm sure the other guys would be much better suited for it. They're regular hams when they get going."

Kit looked forthrightly at him and smiled, causing Hank to narrow his eyes and focus on her face. The curve of her lips, the flash of her teeth, the easy, relaxed way she smiled at him, all combined to pack a punch he hadn't expected. "And you?" she asked. "Is there even the tiniest bit of a ham lurking somewhere beneath that grim exterior?"

He gave a derisive snort in reply, prompting Kit to add, "Or are you afraid that the camera might see what the others can't?"

For one moment she thought she'd gone too far. Her breath caught in her throat when the smile died upon his face and his eyes flashed at her. Her only answer was a mouthful of dust from Dakota's hooves as Hank dug his heels into the horse's flanks and took off down the trail at a gallop.

Chapter 4

The stars were arrayed against the ebony sky like a host of fireflies. The horses stood quietly, munching feed from their nose bags as the flames of a campfire crackled and sputtered, illuminating the camp with a ring of warm light.

After a dinner of hamburgers, baked beans and hash browns whipped up over the open flames by Tom O'Reilly, the men, with the exception of Hank, who went off into the darkness alone, sat down to a game of five-card stud. When the horses had been unloaded earlier, out had come several six-packs of beer that had been cooling since then in a nearby stream. The men drank beer and laughed among themselves as they played cards, occasionally swearing at a bad hand.

Kit used the last few hours before turning in to jot down on a pad her impressions. The notes—words, snippets of sentences, whatever struck her as worth recording—often helped when the prints were developed and she had to choose among them. But mostly they were to satisfy herself. Her pen drifted across the page as she logged the day's journey into the Teton wilderness. She paused, then penned a single word, a name that seemed to write itself without volition on her part. *Hank*. Then an assessment that, as she read it, frankly shocked her. *Bold. Arrogant. Obsessed. Sexy. Vulnerable. Dangerous. Handsome. Blue eyes. Strong body.* Kit slapped the pen down. She didn't like where her thoughts were taking her. She stuffed the notebook back into her bag and rose from her spot before the fire.

She wandered to where the horses were tethered for the night. Seeking out Bayberry, she ran her hand along the mare's neck and stroked the pink, fleshy muzzle. The mare responded with a playful nudge.

"You're a sweetheart, all right," Kit whispered to the horse. "But I bet you'd run your heart out if you had to." The mare gave a soft, concurring whinny as if she understood. "Yeah," said Kit, "I know it and you know it, but they don't, do they?"

"Do you always talk to horses?"

She jumped at the voice, which had come from the shadows. Its deep tone was instantly familiar, but when he emerged from the darkness, Kit caught her breath. He came forward in long, deliberate strides to stand beside her. His nearness reminded Kit of that day in her motel room, the unexpected kiss and its earth-shaking repercussions. There was a stirring scent about him, a subtle mingling of leather and male musk that combined with the fragrant midnight breeze to create a heady effect upon her senses. The moonlight slanted through the branches, falling softly upon his face, tempering his rugged features, mellowing the look in his blue eyes.

Kit moved away from him, uncomfortably aware of his proximity. She already knew what the heat of his touch was

like, and how the strength of his kiss could reduce her to
liquid. Her body was still resounding from the way he'd
kissed her in the motel room. There had been a tenderness
in his lips that seemed to run contrary to everything else
about him, and in spite of every inner warning, she felt
herself drawing inexorably closer to this enigmatic man.
She replied in a soft voice, "When I was a kid on the farm,
I used to talk to the horses all the time. Sometimes they
understand better than people do."

Hank gave her a careless shrug and said, "They don't ask
for much, that's for sure."

"No-frills affection, is that what you mean?"

"Something like that, I guess."

"Is that the way you prefer it? No strings? No attachments?"

"I've got nothing against attachments," he said. "I just
don't have the time for any myself."

"You must be a very busy man, then. Don't you ever
take time out?"

"Running the Chaparral takes up most of my time.
There's only one other thing I take the time for."

Kit held her breath for one precarious moment, for
through the darkness, his eyes were caressing her in the
most telling manner. When he spoke, though, Kit suddenly realized that she'd foolishly misread his thoughts.

Damn, Hank thought. He hadn't meant to say that. It
had just slipped out before he could stop it. Ah, what the
hell? Everyone knew about it anyway. It was no secret in
these parts. Flatly he told her, "I've got this horse to catch,
and until I do—" He moved his shoulders as if to suggest
that nothing else mattered, not even the ranch.

Earlier that morning, when Kit had mentioned the piebald stallion, Hank's reaction had been swift, a violent
flash of his eyes and retreat behind the impenetrable wall

he'd built up around himself. Yet it was he who'd brought it up just now, in a voice taut with emotion but barely above a whisper. "And will you catch him?" Kit probed.

"Oh, I'll catch him, all right. He and I have a score to settle."

From the conversation Kit had overheard in the coffee shop in Jackson, she had gathered that the piebald stallion had stolen other horses from Hank's herd. Could something like that produce the violent reaction she'd witnessed that morning at the mere mention of the stallion? Or was there more to it?

Hank was watching her through the darkness and wondering what it would be like to go further than a kiss with this woman. How would it feel to run his fingers through that thick mass of auburn hair, which now hung loosely about her shoulders? Was she as smooth and silky all over as he imagined? He thought for a moment that the other men must be wondering the very same things about her. How could they not? Something unpredictable and unwelcome jabbed at him. Hank was unwilling to name the emotion, but it had the distinct flavor of jealousy. He wondered, too, whether she had a lover, and it wasn't until he heard her gasp that he realized he'd spoken the thought out loud.

Kit managed not to choke on her surprise. "If that's an offer, I'm afraid I'll decline. Rude, arrogant men aren't my type."

Hank felt like the world's biggest jerk. Damn, what was it about this woman that had him saying the stupidest things? Despite his own embarrassment, however, he had to admit he liked her spunk. He laughed nervously, and in an attempt to make light of his blunder, said, "It's just that I, er, noticed the way Quint's been looking at you, and I thought..."

Kit was not amused. "I'm certain Quint can speak for himself," she told him. "Not that it would matter if he did, because if rude, arrogant men aren't my type, fancy peacocks aren't either."

"You haven't seen Quint in action," said Hank. "He's pretty good."

"With the horses or the ladies?" she quipped.

"From what I understand, both."

"No, thanks," said Kit. "I'm not a bronc that needs busting, nor do I have any intention of becoming a notch on Quint's belt of female conquests, so I'll just have to pass on him, if that's all right with you."

As far as Hank was concerned, that was just fine with him. He didn't like the idea of Quint scoring with a woman like Kit. She was too classy, a woman of too much substance for a man like Dan Quint. And anyway, she wasn't interested in Quint. For one thing, she'd just said so, and for another, Hank had seen her pretty green eyes stray often enough to his own to know where her interest lay. It both flattered and scared him. Of course, he wouldn't have noticed her stares had he himself not been looking at her so intently, and that was what scared him the most. He was beginning to feel something for a woman, for *this* woman, when he swore he'd never feel anything again.

He should have known she wasn't as uncomplicated as she appeared. She knew just which questions would provoke him, knew just how to coax to the surface things he'd buried deep inside. Hadn't he looked at her that very first day in the study and ached? At first he'd thought he was aching for something from the past, but now, standing this close to her, breathing in the scent of her, Hank knew it wasn't for a ghost from the past that he ached; it was for this woman. How could it have happened so fast? How could it have happened at all? His guard had been down for only a moment, and in she had slipped, just like that stallion, to turn his world upside down.

He wanted to soothe the ache. With the piebald that would come when Hank captured the stallion and evened up the score. With Kit Sloan, however, it could come only one way. The problem was he knew that if he made love to her the way he wanted to, once would never be enough. Instead of alleviating the ache, it would only intensify it, for she had the ability to undermine his control—and control was everything in his life. He'd perfected it over the years, learning that the calculated control he used to rope a steer or break a horse could also be applied to his emotions or, more precisely, to the memories that triggered the emotions.

Hank thrust his hands inside his pockets and said, "You'd better get some sleep. We'll be riding out just after sunrise."

It was useless to try to penetrate the shield he'd thrown up between them, at least for now, Kit decided as she bade him good-night and walked back to the campfire. She spread her blanket over the ground, curled up in it and forced herself to sleep.

For Hank, however, sleep would not come. Long after the others had drifted off, he sat by the fading fire, smoking a cigarette in silence, listening to the bullfrogs in a nearby stream, thinking and remembering.

What had he told Kit about the stallion? That it was just another wild mustang? Hank knew that was far from the truth. The horse had come to represent something that burned fiercely in his heart. It went beyond a thirst for revenge, although it had started out that way. It had become his reason for living, for getting from one day to another, from one year to the next, alone, without anyone...without Beth. Seven years after her death and he was still hurting, although for all the wrong reasons it seemed now. Somehow it had all come down to the stallion, until it was all that mattered—that is, until now.

Hank's gaze shifted to where Kit slept curled up in a blanket. The fading embers of the campfire threw a lambent glow across her face, tinting her flesh a deep bronze and sprinkling her dark hair with fiery highlights. Hank's thoughts drifted from out of the past to the present, to this moment, this heartbeat. Somehow she had awakened that heartbeat in him. Something deep in his soul was responding with a recognizable longing. In its own way it was just as strong as the bitterness that ran thick in his blood. For the first time in a very long time, Hank fell asleep with something other than the past on his mind.

The new day broke to a gleaming sun. Kit was awake before she even opened her eyes. She lay there, wrapped in the scratchy wool blanket, feeling strangely content, listening to the birds in the treetops. Into her nostrils wafted the welcoming aroma of coffee, pancakes and bacon frying over the open fire. The early-morning sun warmed her cheeks. What a difference from the cold nip that had chafed them during the night! This high in the mountains, June had little meaning when the sun went down.

Beyond Kit's closed eyelids the light grew stronger. Suddenly, everything went dark as though a huge black cloud had filled the sky. Kit's eyes flew open. The towering figure of Hank Reardon blocked out the sun, casting her into shadow. From Kit's perspective, his six-foot frame seemed to spike the sky. She squinted up at him, her hand going to her eyes to shield them from the glare that shot in bursts of brilliance from behind him.

He was dressed in a maroon cotton shirt, over which he wore a leather vest of weathered cowhide. Fawn-colored suede chaps were strapped over his jeans. His Stetson dangled from one gloved hand as he spoke to her in that deep and lazy voice that she had come, these past few days, to recognize so well.

"Good morning," he said. "Tom's fixing some breakfast. If you want some, I'd suggest you get your butt out of there."

Kit sat up and brushed the blanket aside, murmuring, "Good morning." She was unaware of the sight she presented with her hair tousled from sleep and her T-shirt twisted provocatively about her, the loose neck hanging off one shoulder to expose the soft skin that Hank knew must still be warm. Something inside him tightened.

When Kit saw his blue eyes fix upon her anatomy and linger, she was suddenly aware of her disarray.

Hank smiled broadly, adding to Kit's embarrassment by saying, "I didn't think you city women knew how to blush."

Her cheeks had indeed colored beneath his stare. Damn him, Kit thought with a sudden burst of anger. She couldn't let him shake her up this way. Forcing a negligent tone, she said, "I'm not from the city. I just live there." She pulled a clean shirt from her saddlebag and got up. "Is there someplace where I can change my clothes?"

Hank's smile turned decidedly sardonic. "You wanted to ride with the men, green eyes. I'm afraid you'll have to do it the way the rest of us did."

Wisely, Kit didn't ask in what manner that was, although she had a pretty good idea. Men seemed to feel no embarrassment about baring their backsides before one another, but she'd be damned if she was going to bare hers to them. She spotted a cluster of boulders some yards away. They'd have to do. With all the nonchalance she could muster, Kit turned her back on Hank and walked off, feeling his eyes still upon her.

When she reappeared a few minutes later, dressed in a fresh shirt and jeans, modesty still intact, Hank was gone. Reasons, Kit huffed to herself as she packed up her gear. Everyone seemed to suggest that Hank had reasons for being the way he was. Did they make it necessary for him to mock her as she sometimes sensed he was doing? Well, she had reasons, too, for not letting this dark, brooding, arrogant man bully his way into her heart. Number one was her cardinal rule never to become involved with her subjects. Number two... Well, that was enough for now.

After a quick but tasty breakfast of flapjacks, maple syrup and butter washed down with strong black coffee, Kit went down to the creek to brush her teeth and wash her face. The stream was clogged with beaver dams, but there was no sign of the flat-tailed creatures that had worked tirelessly to build them. She gazed wistfully at the water, wishing she could wade in with a bar of soap and wash away the grit and grime from yesterday's ride. With the possible exception of Quint, Kit figured that the men would respect her privacy if she took a bath in the stream, but she decided against it. If they could do without a bath on this trip, so could she.

When Kit returned to camp she found Hank at work saddling Bayberry. He was just tightening the cinch when she walked up and took the reins. "Thanks," she said as she slid her boot into the stirrup and mounted. "But I could have done it myself."

He had no doubt that she could have saddled Bayberry on her own, but her lack of gratitude despite her thanks irked him. Why was she making it hard for him to be nice to her?

Kit suspected that it was Hank's way of apologizing for the embarrassment he'd caused her earlier, but wouldn't a simple "Hey, I'm sorry" have been better? Tapping her heels to Bayberry's flanks, she trotted off.

Morning grew upon them. Kit rode at the rear of the column, pausing now and then to admire a pretty sight or take some pictures. They climbed higher into the mountains, sometimes following paths so narrow that they had to ride single file. They splashed through knife-bright streams and cut diagonal paths through fragrant forests of pine where the sun dappled the ground and played hide-and-seek among the branches. At a salt lick they spotted deer, moose and bighorn sheep. Eagles and ospreys dived from lofty heights to scoop fish out of the streams. Blue herons stood picket on creek banks. White pelicans dotted the ponds. Otters and beavers glided noiselessly through icy mountain lakes.

When the sun was directly overhead, they stopped for lunch. Kit passed up one of Tom's chicken salad sandwiches. She found a shady spot beneath an aspen tree, sat cross-legged on the ground and rooted through her bag for a candy bar.

"Candy for lunch?" Hank's voice spoke from overhead.

Too involved in taking a big bite out of the melting candy bar, she couldn't answer just then. She licked a dollop of chocolate from her lip with the tip of her tongue in a move that was completely unplanned but produced a predictable response in Hank. Looking up finally, she said, "Caffeine. It gets the juices going."

He had a hard time taking his eyes away from her lips. "I know what you mean. The air's thin up here. The lungs have to work harder and you get tired. I feel it myself." Oh, man, Hank groaned to himself, here he was, rambling on like a schoolboy. Face it, Reardon, he scoffed. It's not tiredness you feel; it's lust.

Kit looked at the vital, strapping male form standing before her with feet braced, showing not a hint of weariness, then down at the partially eaten candy bar in her hand and said, "Here, catch."

He caught it with a lightning-quick reflex. He took a bite and smiled broadly. With a tip of the hat and a polite "Thank you" he ambled off, polishing off the rest in one bite.

Some time later, when they were back on the trail, Hank reined his horse up and dropped into pace beside Kit. He slipped his canteen off his saddle and handed it to her. She took a sip of the cool, refreshing water and handed the canteen back to him. Their fingers touched briefly, unexpectedly, and although it was no more than a second, a spark of electricity leaped into the air, threatening to set the forest aflame. Kit pulled her hand back and turned her attention to Bayberry, patting the smooth brown neck with fingers that throbbed from Hank's touch.

Hank, too, did his best to ignore the charge that went through him. Forcing a laugh, he asked, "Are you saddle sore yet?"

As she'd been getting dressed that morning behind the boulders, Kit had noticed that while her hind end wasn't sore—thanks probably to the bicycle riding she did through Central Park—her reins-pulling muscles and back were indeed sore from the hours spent in the saddle yesterday. Maybe she'd been in the city too long, she reflected. Nevertheless, she smiled back at him and said, "Sorry to disappoint you, Hank, but I feel just fine."

The sound of his name on her lips jarred him. It seemed so natural, as if she should be saying it all the time.

Kit had indeed said his name so easily she wasn't even aware of it. She was beginning to relax, to settle back in the saddle. Stealing a peek at Hank, she saw that he, too, appeared comfortable, not filled with the usual nervousness that stood between them. He did not, she noticed, spur Dakota back to the head of the column but lingered at her side. After a while he spoke, and even his voice had none of its customary tense edge.

"What's Kit short for?" he asked.

"Catherine," she replied. "But my dad always called me Kit. He used to say that Catherine was too stuffy for someone who was always climbing trees and falling off rocks."

"I agree. Kit suits you better." What he didn't say, of course, was that he liked the way her name rolled off his tongue, or how it bounced off his thoughts in short, quick bursts, much the way his breathing did whenever she was near. "How long have you been in New York?" he asked.

"Eight years. It's funny how the place grows on you."

"Do you miss it?"

To her own surprise she answered, "No, not really, now that I think of it. I guess I'll always be a country girl at heart."

"Still," said Hank, "that's a cutthroat business you're in for a country girl. *Human Interest Magazine*. Man, it doesn't get much bigger than that."

"I've only worked there a short while," she explained. "Before that I free-lanced." She grimaced. "I never knew when the phone was going to ring. It used to scare me." Her expression turned thoughtful and she said, "Even though I have a certain stability now, somehow that uncertainty seemed more lifelike. I guess that must sound pretty silly."

Beyond the obvious physical attraction, they shared a passionate desire to choose their own work, to set their own standards and shape their own days; she as a photographer, Hank as a rancher. "I know exactly what you mean," he said. "You get up every morning, and you know there are certain things you've got to do. The same things every day. Yet no two days are ever alike. Of course, out there there's the uncertainty of the elements to deal with. Sometimes a winter storm will break from out of nowhere and you could lose five or six good horses on the range. One year I lost my two best brood mares to a viral infection. But we always managed to come out okay." He paused, then added through compressed lips, "Or at least we did until that stallion came along and ruined everything."

He reached forward to grasp Bayberry's reins and brought the mare to a halt. "Look, I dropped back here to tell you that we're going to ride up ahead and single out the mares and foals and head them back in this direction. I want you to wait for us here."

The abrupt shift in the conversation baffled Kit, as did his instructions. She looked at him blankly. "You mean you want me to wait right here?"

He nodded.

"Now?"

"Now's as good a time as any."

"But there aren't any wild horses around," she objected.

"Sure there are. They're just up ahead over that rise."

Kit looked in the direction in which Hank gestured, brows knit with skepticism. "How do you know they're there?"

"I don't," he admitted. He motioned to Bayberry. "But she does."

Sure enough, the mare's ears were flicked forward as if listening to something that human ears couldn't hear. "This won't take long," Hank said to Kit. Giving Dakota a touch of his spurs, he took off at a gallop and disappeared with the others over the top of the rise.

Bayberry fidgeted beneath Kit as they waited in the cool shade of the trees. A cloud of dust rose in the distance, and Kit could hear the far-off whistles and whoops and shouts as the men chased the wild horses. She resented having been told to wait. Surely she could ride as well as any of them. Besides, she was here to take pictures. Her chin tilted upward as it was wont to do when her ire was on the rise. She had a job to do, and she wasn't about to let an order by Hank Reardon prevent her from doing it.

Bayberry responded to Kit's sharp kick of the heels by sprinting forward and galloping toward the rise. At the top they halted as Kit scanned the terrain. From this vantage point, she had a view of the countryside for miles around. Below was a great gathering of dust as dozens of horses stampeded, trailed by eight men at varying distances. She had no trouble recognizing Hank's chestnut stallion in the lead as it zigzagged through the herd, singling out several horses and herding them back around with the skill of a seasoned cow pony. Hank had his lasso twirling in the air over his head, ready to loop any that sought to escape.

The other men worked similarly, although with not quite the skill that Hank seemed to exert so effortlessly. Not even Dan Quint, with all his boasting and potential, rivaled Hank's skill with a rope and way with a horse. What a contrast, thought Kit. One man trying so hard to look good; the other looking so good at what he did without even trying. A sensation of feverish excitement raced through Kit as she watched the action. There was something primal about it: man against animal, speed versus cunning. Set against the backdrop of the mighty Tetons, it had Kit standing in the stirrups. This was Hank's element, and she could not help but see once again, the bond that existed between the man and his domain.

Like the mountains, Hank was strong and sun-browned, but the rugged imperfection of his looks was startling next to the sheer perfection of nature. Kit's eyes blazed. Hastily she removed the camera from its bag. In seconds she was firing the shutter, catching Hank in action, the expression of grit and determination stamped on his face, the spectacular display of his muscles in motion. Caught up in the fever of the chase, Kit snapped off one lens and snapped on another. She swept the viewfinder across the terrain with the wide-angle lens, catching horses and riders in action, moving the camera to blur the images for effect. She was so absorbed in her work that she didn't see it at first, but when she did, the warm rush of excitement through her veins turned suddenly to ice.

About a quarter of a mile to the east was an abrupt drop that was invisible to the men below. The horses, she realized with horror, had run out onto a mesa whose sheer wall fell straight away. A look back at the stampeding horses wrenched a painful gasp from Kit. One group of about a dozen had broken away from the others and was galloping wildly toward the cliff, where certain death awaited.

Kit began to shout and wave her arms wildly in the hope of catching someone's attention, but the men were too busy to notice. Kit grew frantic. She had to do something. With no time to plan, she sprang into action, shoving the camera into her bag and putting her heels to Bayberry's flanks.

They tore down the hillside. The plucky little mare responded to her rider's urgency. Hooves flying over the ground, Bayberry raced across the open tableland with Kit crouched low over her neck, clutching a fistful of coarse mane, urging her faster, faster.

Dakota's coat was flecked with lather, but the big horse wasn't even breathing hard when Hank jerked suddenly on the reins, bringing him to a stiff halt as he caught a glimpse of something speeding past. "What the—!" It was Kit, galloping at breakneck speed after a bunch of horses. What was she doing? He should have guessed that her stubborn pride wouldn't allow her to sit quietly in the shade and wait. But whatever anger Hank might have felt at Kit's disobedience turned to something much worse when he spotted the cliff up ahead. A terrible dread welled up inside him, threatening to explode. She wasn't going to make it! He shouted her name, but the sound that emerged from his throat was nothing more than a strangled groan. He gave Dakota a savage kick and the horse lurched forward.

Kit had no idea she was being chased as she hunched low over Bayberry's straining neck. The mare ran her heart out, showing speed that no one would have guessed from just looking at her. Little by little she gained on the stampeding horses and gradually overtook them. She pulled out ahead of them, racing like the wind straight toward the precipice. With the drop only yards away, Kit reined hard, bringing the mare around in a sharp turn to head off the horses that would otherwise have gone over the edge.

Kit's heart hammered in her chest. Her knees shook from her close brush with death. Somehow, by the craziest stroke of luck, she had pulled it off, and the consequences she hadn't stopped to consider earlier suddenly overwhelmed her as she brought her horse to a halt and sat there breathing hard and trembling. The last thing she needed was to see Hank galloping hard in her direction.

Dust flew from Dakota's hooves when Hank brought the big horse to a standstill. He flung himself from the saddle and bounded toward Kit with a furious look in his eyes. Something told Kit to turn and run, but something else held her frozen to the spot. She expected him to be angry. What she didn't expect was for him to reach up, plant both hands tightly about her waist and pull her unceremoniously to the ground. She tumbled to her feet before him and with a gasp looked up into his arctic-cold eyes.

"Are you crazy?" Hank shouted. "You could have been killed pulling a damned fool stunt like that!"

Kit winced as his fingers bit into her shoulders when he gave her a hard shake. "They would have gone over!" she cried.

"You could have gone over, too," he said harshly. "I told you to wait for me up in the hills, and as long as I'm running this outfit, you'll do as I say. Do I make myself clear?"

She struggled in his grip, seeking to extricate herself not only from those bruising fingers but from that look that chilled her to the quick. "Let me go!" she demanded. "You're just angry because it wasn't you who saved your precious mustangs."

"Is that what you think?"

"Yes! Since the day I got here I've had to prove myself to you. Well, let me tell you something, Hank Reardon—"

He never heard the rest of her angry words. His arms wound around her like serpents, cutting off the rest of her protest, pulling her tightly into his embrace and forcing the air out of her lungs as his lips came down over hers. There was no tenderness in him now, no gentleness as his mouth overpowered hers. He kissed her savagely, hungrily.

How very different this kiss was from the other, Kit thought dazedly. The other had been tender, touching, tentative. This one was filled with bitterness and pain and a million other dark emotions she could not even guess at. She was mad to respond to him, she knew, but it was a madness Kit had no wish to be cured of. Her fingers tingled at the feel of the skin beneath his collar. Her lips parted further, allowing him to taste the warm, sweet wetness of her mouth.

Attacked by sensations and feelings she'd been unprepared for, Kit was oblivious to the whistles and shouts of the men and the high-pitched squeals of the horses reverberating all around them. There was a savage pounding at her temples. Her nipples hardened against his chest. Her hips brushed against his bursting body, and the feel of his throbbing, swollen arousal between their bodies pulled her deeper into a whirlpool of passion that threatened to drown her.

For several fierce minutes, they clung to each other, lips melded, bodies pressed together in urgency. And then, during that moment of suspended reality, it was as if the curtain suddenly went up all around them. The sounds of the chase roared in their ears, the ground shook with the thunder of hooves, and the two people who only moments before had been caught up in a dream now were plunged back into the real world.

Suddenly the passion was gone, having burst like a bubble. In a swift motion Hank released Kit and took a half step back. He was breathing hard. In spite of the red-hot heat emanating from him and the hunger still written in his eyes, there was a look of cold, stinging regret on his face.

He hadn't meant to feel passion, not *real* passion. He'd meant only to scold her for scaring him half to death. But then he'd seen her eyes, large green orbs filled with fear, and had felt her body tremble. The sight of her lips, slightly open, quivering, had touched him more deeply than he could ever admit. Something had happened to him. He'd suddenly wanted to possess her for reasons that had nothing to do with anger but everything to do with the feel of her soft, warm body pressed to his. Even now, with her cheeks flushed, her eyes showing a mixture of fear and anticipation, her lips reddened by his angry kiss, even now he wanted her. He was a fool for letting himself be trapped by her beauty, and if it were only that, he could have turned and walked away. Furiously Hank held on to his anger, but it kept slipping, for it was far more than her loveliness that attracted him.

Kit's hand flew to her mouth to catch a sob. She turned away, not understanding the distance that was suddenly once again between them and the recognizable look of regret on Hank's handsome face. Hank took a step forward and put his hand out to touch her, but he pulled it back, not daring to, afraid she might bolt like a frightened filly. His breathing was still a little ragged and his voice emerged as a low sound that scratched at the back of his throat. "Kit, I...I don't know what to say. I'm sorry."

She whirled to face him, eyes glassy with tears and wide with fury. "Sorry?" she echoed. "For what, Hank? For kissing me?" With a look of disgust, she swished past him and stalked back to her horse. Hank followed in long strides behind her. She mounted and looked down at him from the saddle. "Let me give you a little bit of advice," she said coolly. "Never apologize for kissing a woman, Hank. It only makes her feel like a fool for having kissed you back."

He reached up to grab the reins before she could turn the mare's head away. "That wasn't what I apologized for," he said, blue eyes searing her.

Kit's own eyes stuck bravely to his. "What was it, then?"

He uttered a low expletive through clenched teeth. "Dammit, Kit, you're one of the most desirable women I've ever met. I'd be a fool and a liar to say I don't want you. I kissed you, and I'm not about to apologize for that. I only meant..." How could he explain about the past, about Beth, and how Kit's close call had brought the memories surging back? Where could he even begin to explain? He let go of the reins. "It's not you. It's me. There are certain things..." He gave a helpless shrug. "I just can't forget them."

The anger drained out of Kit as she sat there astride the mare looking down into his tortured blue eyes. There was so much she didn't know about him, so much she didn't understand. One thing seemed certain. Something haunted him from his past. It had to do with the stallion; that much she knew. Looking down at him, she said, "Sometimes, Hank, we never forget. The trick is in learning to live with it."

Chapter 5

It was hot. Heat rose from the ground in waves making the land look as if it were moving. The Chaparral sat under a dust cloud in a valley in a bend of the Snake River, a frenzy of activity. Tempers flared as the mercury climbed. Husbands quarreled with wives. Two of the local citizens became embroiled in an argument. Even the horses in the corral were tense and anxious as the adoption proceedings went on into the afternoon.

Kit wandered through the crowd that had converged upon the Chaparral for the event capturing on film the faces around her. There were the beleaguered expressions of the parents, some of whom were obviously wondering what had possessed them to think adopting a wild horse was such a good idea; the bemused faces of the tourists who had driven the eighty miles out from town to watch; and the knowing grins of the locals, who watched the visitors plunk down seventy-five dollars for a horse that little Janey or Timmy would probably never be able to ride. Mustangs, they knew, made lousy riding pets unless broken in properly. It was doubtful that any of the out-of-towners had the means or the skill to do so.

The only ones unaffected by the heat and the pressing crowd were the children who raced wide-eyed along the perimeters of the corral where the colts and fillies were penned. One red-haired little boy in overalls caught Kit's fancy as he gazed longingly at the frisky pinto colt that pranced about the corral. She focused in tight when the colt was brought before the crowd. The boy tugged furiously on his father's sleeve. The man looked down at his son as if to ask, "Is that the one?" The boy nodded vigorously and then beamed from ear to ear when his father stepped forward and bought the pinto colt.

Kit felt a small surge of joy for the boy. Having grown up on a farm, she knew just how important and exciting it could be to have your very own horse to follow you around and nibble carrots from your back pocket. She smiled at seeing the boy's dream come true.

Hank, too, was watching, but his face bore only a serious, disapproving look. It wasn't hard to figure out who had sired that colt. If he turned out to be anything like his sire that family was in for trouble. But Hank kept silent. He knew nothing could dissuade that boy from having his colt. Just as nothing could dissuade Hank from having his own wild mustang, he swore to himself, features hardening as he turned away from the corral.

It was in that moment, when Hank's thoughts were on the stallion and least prepared for it, that their eyes met. Their careful avoidance of each other all day was suddenly in jeopardy.

Kit felt her heart slam against her chest for a second before she summoned the strength to tear her gaze from his and return to work. She moved off, working smoothly, efficiently, the cool professional on the outside, while inside her emotions were in conflict. It had been two days since Hank had kissed her atop the cliff after she'd saved the horses from going over. They'd returned to the Chaparral without speaking to each other, Hank riding up ahead busy keeping the horses herded, Kit staying purposefully behind, preferring coughing on the dust raised by all those hooves to risking his arrogance again. They'd parted without a word of goodbye, each wary and tense from the foray into the mountains and its unexpected repercussions.

That made twice now that he'd kissed her—once tenderly back at the motel, once harshly atop the cliff. The first time had aroused in Kit a sudden, unexplained need to give to him; the second time had stirred in her a desperate desire to take from him. And each time it had gotten more difficult for her to turn back. Why, even just now, staring into his cool blue eyes across the dust-filled distance, she'd felt a tremble clear to her fingertips. Damn, she thought angrily, why did she have to be so undeniably attracted to a man who seemed to regret his own attraction to her? With that dismal thought she went about her work, trying in vain to put him out of her mind.

Beads of perspiration slithered down Kit's back and between her breasts dampening her tank top. Her usually buoyant hair hung heavy at her shoulders. In an attempt to get some relief from the heat, Kit swept it all up into a mass atop her head and secured it there with a large barrette pulled from the back pocket of her shorts.

The motion served to create a heat of its own, however when viewed as unconscious seduction by the man who watched her from a safe distance.

Hank's eyes stung from the heat and dust. The smell of the horses was thick in the air. But as the crowd pressed in on all sides and the noise grew to one constant roar, Hank was strangely oblivious to the discomfort around him. Usually these events sent him inside, behind closed doors, until it was over and the crowds had gone. But today Hank lingered on the perimeters of the crowd, feigning a lack of interest, while inwardly all his senses were attuned to the tall, slender, green-eyed woman moving through the crowd. He experienced what had become a predictable tightening in his gut at the sight of her.

Even dressed in a pair of khaki shorts with bulging pockets, loose-fitting tank top, her hair piled on top of her head in a disarrayed mass, with perspiration trickling down the sides of her face—even now she was beautiful. Hank shook his head in wonder. What was it that made a man hungry for one particular woman? All he knew was that when it hit, it hit hard, no matter what you said or did or told yourself to the contrary. Suddenly, the defenses Hank had spent years in building were in danger of crumbling, for as he and Kit had stood there looking at each other, he'd felt a joyous surge. It had been brief, though, chased away by a resounding sense of the guilt he was beginning to think would never leave him. He'd seen the look of disappointment just now on Kit's face as she turned away. He wanted to tell her that it wasn't her; it was him. But he'd tried that once before, the other day on the cliff, and it hadn't worked. How could he expect her to accept that without an explanation? She wasn't the kind of woman you gave half truths to, but how could he explain what it was like to carry a guilt that your mind knew to be illogical yet which gnawed year after year at your heart? He hated himself for what had happened back then, even though it hadn't been his fault. If Kit knew, would she hate him, too? he wondered. It was a risk he couldn't take.

But all the guilt and uncertainty in the world mattered little when a spark of jealousy flared within him, burning away every other emotion as he watched Dan Quint make his way toward Kit. It was obvious by the way Quint strutted that he was on the prowl and just as obvious from the look in his eyes that Kit was the prey. Hank's muscles twitched as Kit talked with Quint. Hank was too far away to hear what they were saying, but he recognized all the signs of a man on the make. Kit had already made known her feelings about Quint. Nevertheless, Hank watched intently, ready to step in at the first sign of trouble. Hank hadn't exaggerated when he'd told Kit that Quint had a way with the ladies. Sometimes after a weekend off, Quint showed up at the Chaparral with a bruised lip or a sore jaw, and Hank had suspected on more than one occasion that some irate husband had caught Quint sneaking out through the back window. Hank had never cared for the way Quint used to look at Beth, but after all, you couldn't stop a guy from looking. As long as he didn't touch.

Hank watched the couple in the distance. He wasn't aware of it at first but as the feeling grew upon him, it startled him to realize that he was thinking of Kit Sloan as his. Was he crazy? The first woman to touch something inside him since Beth, and here he was tripping over himself in the process. Get yourself together, Reardon, he ordered himself. He raised a gloved hand to his eyes and rubbed them, hoping the couple would be gone when he opened them. But they weren't. With a tired sigh, Hank turned around and headed for the house where he spent the next few hours locked in his study.

The crowd and the noise and the heat eventually took their toll, and Kit wasn't sorry to see the last of the tourists pile back into their campers and leave the valley. The day's activities ended; an almost unearthly calm settled over the ranch. The sun was on its way down. Above the peaks, a purple sky signaled the approach of dusk.

Kit sat with her back against a fence post, taking her usual care to label every canister before dropping in the spent roll of film to await processing back in New York. Adeptly she dismantled the camera, packing each lens away in its leather drawstring pouch, fitting the lens cap over the camera and storing it away in the leather bag that was worn smooth from use. Her eyes were weary, her throat was parched, and her arms ached from having held the camera at all angles to get the shots she wanted. It had been hard work, not the least part of which had involved keeping up a brave front in Hank's presence.

After packing her gear in the trunk of her rented car, Kit went up to the house for something to drink before the long ride back to Jackson. Inside, she darted her eyes about, hoping to catch sight of Hank. Her heart sank a little when he didn't appear. She accepted a glass of lemonade from the housekeeper and headed for her car. On an impulse, she changed direction, thinking that she could use a few minutes to come down from the day before starting back. And having always found a sense of calm around horses, Kit headed for the brood mares' corral.

As the sun sank, patches of fiery light sparked the western sky. Kit stood with her arms resting on one of the fence posts, watching the horses. One came over to her and poked an inquisitive nose through the fence. Kit patted the soft, fleshy muzzle and spoke in a low, calm tone to the animal. The horse responded with a gentle nudge.

"She doesn't usually take to strangers."

Kit tensed. She hadn't heard him come up behind her, but suddenly Hank was there, his voice soft at her ear. "You have a way with horses. They trust you."

She managed an elegant shrug. "There's no reason they shouldn't. They have nothing to fear from me. I'm not going to try to ride them if they don't want to be ridden, and I'm not going to try to catch them if they don't want to be caught.''

He detected the ring of disapproval in her tone, and he knew she was referring to the stallion.

"You have quite a way with horses yourself," she said. "That was some fancy riding you did, rounding up those mustangs."

It was the first time either of them had dared to bring up the subject of the other day. Leave it to Kit to be the one to do it, he thought. "I've had lots of practice."

He also had quite a way with kissing, Kit mused. Did he have lots of practice at that, too? "I didn't see much of you today," she said. It wasn't true; she'd been aware of where he was at all times.

Hank shrugged. "I don't much like crowds."

"Crowds? Or mustangs?"

"Maybe a little of both."

Kit turned back to the horses.

"You're looking at the bread and butter of the Chaparral," Hank said of the dozen or so horses in the corral.

"Is it true that half your herd's out there with the wild mustangs?" Kit asked.

If he was surprised by her question, he gave no sign of it. By now he must have come to expect her directness as par for the course, she thought. He snorted derisively at her observation and said, "If half my herd were out there, I'd be out of business."

Pointedly, Kit observed, "It looks as if you practically are."

Hank kicked at a pebble with his boot. "Yeah, I guess the place has gotten a little shabby."

"How come?"

"The money isn't coming in the way it used to. Between what we made selling stock and what I brought in from the circuit, we weren't the richest outfit around, but we did okay. At one point I even thought I might introduce some Arabian stock into the herd, but...well..." He hedged. "There doesn't seem to be much need for that anymore."

"Why not?" asked Kit. "It sounds like a good idea to me."

"Look around you, Kit. You said it yourself, only I'll say it plainer. We're on the brink of bankruptcy."

"But surely you could change that."

"Yeah, how? Like Pete says, horse-breeding isn't worth a damn if you don't have the horses to breed."

"So get them."

"With what? It takes money." He was beginning to sound more like Pete, and he hated himself for it.

"Can't you get a loan from the bank?"

"Using what as collateral? A run-down ranch that the bank already owns?"

She looked up at him forthrightly and said as if it were the most logical thing in the world, "You could always take up the rodeo circuit again."

Now *she* was beginning to sound like Pete, and Hank wasn't sure he liked it. His eyes shifted away from hers. "No, I...I couldn't do that."

"Why not, Hank? If you need the money—"

"Because I stopped competing years ago. I told you that."

"Yes, but—"

"Besides, I'm too old. You should see some of these younger guys. Like Quint. I saw you two talking earlier. Did he tell you he's got a good chance to win number-one spot this year in the finals?"

"Yes, he did. Several times, in fact. But I wasn't talking about Quint. I was talking about you. Too old?" She chuckled as she swept her gaze over him in an assessing manner. "Not from what I saw the other day. He doesn't like you, you know."

"Did he tell you that?"

"No, but it's not hard to tell. He's not nearly as good as you are, and I think his pride may be suffering."

Hank saw that Kit assumed that Quint's obvious disdain for him was due to the usual competition between men.

"I asked Quint if he knew why you'd stopped competing," she told Hank.

"What'd he say?"

"Nothing. He's only interested in talking about himself."

A tremor of relief passed over Hank as he realized that Quint knew but hadn't told her. "Does it matter so much why?" he asked her.

"It does if you stopped for all the wrong reasons."

The last rays of the setting sun shot orange light across the land, tinting Kit's face a deep bronze and setting the strands of her hair on fire with light. If he lived to be a thousand years old, Hank would never forget the sight of her at that moment, green eyes fixed upon him, her face half bathed in shadow, skin matte soft in the evaporating heat of the day. She was looking at him with eyes that had a way of seeing past whatever fences he threw up, as if to say, "Never mind about all that. I know what you are." Here she was again, doing it to him, drawing out of him things he didn't want to think about, making him say things he never thought he'd hear himself saying.

"I don't know," he offered with a shrug. "Who knows? Maybe after I catch the stallion I'll think about going back on the circuit." It was something he'd toyed with in his dreams, and here he was telling it to her.

"Why is it so important for you to catch him?" Kit wanted to know. "Is it because he's stolen from your herd?"

Hank began to grow impatient. She was asking too many questions. Still, he heard himself answer gruffly, "He's stolen more from me than he should have."

Kit watched him. Only minutes ago he'd been guarded and defensive when talking about rodeo competition, but at the mention of the stallion, he was on the brink of anger. "Why is he so hard to catch?" she asked. She refused to be intimidated by the spark of fury her questions provoked.

Hank swallowed hard. How could she know how her painfully honest questions affected him? "He's like the wind. There one minute, gone the next. He's sly, too. There's something more than just horse inside of that horse. If you ask me, he's got some fox in him as well."

"Perhaps. But even a fox can be caught."

"Are you suggesting I haven't tried hard enough?"

"Goodness, no!" she exclaimed. "From what I've heard, if anyone's tried hard enough, it's you. No, I only meant that if it's so important to you to catch the horse, there must be some way—"

"Forget it!" His deep and angry voice silenced the rest of Kit's words. "You don't understand!"

"I'm trying to, dammit!" she shot back.

"Well, do you have to try so hard at everything you do?"

"I don't know how to do it any other way. I never learned how to be a quitter."

"Is that what you think I am?"

Kit was undaunted by his menacing stance and the chill in his blue eyes, which bored down at her. "I know that you've quit the rodeo circuit, and you've quit this place, and it looks to me, Hank, like you've quit on yourself."

It's not what you think, he wanted to say. But the words stuck in his throat. There were no guarantees in this world. Still, she was right; he deserved a better chance than the one he was giving himself. Maybe, just maybe, this woman could give it to him. He opened his mouth to speak, to attempt an explanation, when the untimely interruption of Quint paralyzed the words in Hank's throat and drove him back behind a wall of stony silence.

"The horses are all bedded down and I'm headed into town," Quint announced as he approached.

Hank turned away from the look on her face, unsure whether he was angry or glad of Quint's interruption, knowing only that the other man's appearance further complicated an already complicated situation.

Kit felt frustration at Hank's behavior. Why did he draw so near one moment, only to draw away the next? Did he think he could manipulate her emotions like this and get away with it? Knowing how much it would bother him, Kit turned deliberately to Quint and smiled. "What's in town?"

"The rodeo. I aim to give the tourists their money's worth. Wanna come along?" he asked Kit.

"No thanks," she replied. "You go ahead. Some other time perhaps."

"How about tomorrow, then?"

She wished Hank would say something, *anything*. A forceful "The lady's taken" would have done nicely, but she was being presumptuous to think Hank's feelings for her ran along that route. Still, anything would have been better than his tight-lipped silence while Quint made his play. "Tomorrow?" Kit repeated. "You mean the Jackson rodeo?" She knew from her research that tourists in Jackson were entertained by the rodeo five nights a week.

"Naw, that's kid stuff. I'm talking about the one over at the Lazy J. It's a spread about fifty miles west of here. Once a year, the hands from the Lazy J challenge men from the other outfits to see who can ride and rope the best."

"I see." And in a tone cool enough to mask her interest, Kit turned to Hank and asked, "And will you be at the Lazy J tomorrow?"

Hank had been observing the exchange between Kit and Quint in controlled silence. Why should he care who she went out with? "I don't think so. Someone's got to work around here."

The remark, obviously meant for Quint, elicited a laugh from the other man. "You know what they say," Quint scoffed. "All work and no play makes Hank a dull boy."

Hank lifted a dark brow and said, "Is that what they say? Well, we've got a saying around here, too, Quint. All play and no work gets Quint fired."

Quint smiled. "Firing me won't change anything. I'll still be number one."

Hank smiled, too, but the expression didn't reach his eyes, which were as hard as ever. "You're good, Quint; I'll give you that. But it takes more than fancy riding and fast roping to get to the top. It takes guts." He saw Quint's eyes widen, and he added, "Not the kind it takes to get on a Brahman bull. I'm talking about the kind it takes to lose."

Quint's whole body tensed. "I don't plan on losing."

"Maybe not tonight in Jackson. And maybe not tomorrow at the Lazy J. Maybe not at Cheyenne or Calgary or the national finals this year. But one day, Quint, you'll lose. You can count on it."

Resenting Hank's arrogant confidence, Quint sneered. "Losing is something you know all about, isn't it, Hank?"

Hank didn't answer. His look alone said it all as it ripped into the other man.

Quint began to grow nervous under that glare. Pulling his gaze away, he turned back to Kit and said, "So, whaddaya say, Kit? Want to go tomorrow?"

Kit hesitated. She could feel the air sizzling between Hank and Quint. It was like the meeting of two tomcats in an alley. Was this what competition did to men? Or did the enmity that ran thick between these two particular men go deeper than that? She looked at Hank. Say something, she pleaded with her eyes. But Hank remained silent, and Kit acted on impulse. Feeling angry and confused, she said, "Sure, why not?"

Quint smiled triumphantly. "Great. I'll pick you up at your motel around nine. It's about an hour's drive, so we should get an early start." He sauntered off, leaving Kit and Hank to sort out the damage that had been done.

There was a tense, expectant silence between them. Kit already regretted her impulsiveness and wished she hadn't agreed to drive out to the Lazy J tomorrow with Quint. But what was done was done, and she'd make the best of it. She only wished there was some way to make the best of her situation with Hank. She looked up at him slowly, and something inside her lurched to a halt when she found his gaze upon her, eating her up with its intent.

Hank cleared his throat and said, "I figured you'd be leaving in the morning."

She turned away and headed toward the car. "Well, you figured wrong, Hank."

"Obviously," he muttered, trailing after her. "I thought you said Quint wasn't your type."

At the car Kit paused with her hand on the latch. "He's not."

"Then why are you going to the Lazy J with him tomorrow?"

She opened the car door and slid behind the wheel. "I can use the opportunity to get some final shots. You know, fill-in stuff. I'll be leaving the day after tomorrow." She started the engine. When she looked up at Hank she saw a handsome face partly hidden in shadow. The fading embers of sunlight tempered his rugged features to near perfection, causing Kit's breath to catch. Somehow she found her voice in the flurry of emotion that came over her. "After all, there's no need to stay beyond that," she said, trying hard to sound uncaring, but failing miserably. "Is there?"

Hank looked earnestly into her eyes. He wanted to touch her. Just to stroke her cheek with his fingertips would have been enough for the moment. Her softly spoken question resounded in his ears. He could tell by her look that she expected an answer. "Kit, I can't make any promises, not right now."

Maybe not ever, Kit was thinking glumly as she left him standing there in the twilight and drove away. Besides, she reminded herself, two kisses did not forever make.

Later, in bed, she lay awake thinking about him. About the way he'd said one thing about promises while his eyes had said something else. About his look of fury when Quint had made the remark about losing. She'd thought Hank would strike him. She'd sensed the iron-willed control Hank had exerted over himself. Control seemed to be very important in Hank's life, she'd observed. Yet where the stallion was concerned, it seemed that Hank was out of control. It made no sense. Questions sprang at her. Where had the obsession with the wild horse come from? Why had Hank stopped competing? Why did a once-thriving ranch stand dangerously close to financial ruin? What memories caused the ofttimes icy, impenetrable look in his blue eyes?

Kit's eyes misted over. So he could make no promises. Well, neither could she. She could not, for instance, promise that she wouldn't fall in love with him. Nor could she promise that she wouldn't become trapped in the mystery that surrounded him. She already felt like a beleaguered fly in a web struggling to be free of the silken threads that held it. More and more she was aware of the physical longings he aroused in her. More and more she wondered what it would be like to make love with him. He felt the same way, too. She sensed it in the way he kissed her. She could see it in the way he looked at her, claiming her with his eyes whether he spoke the words or not.

Kit fell asleep eventually, perplexed, on the edge between happiness and despair, wondering dismally whether anything could quench the terrible fire inside her, the fire that Hank Reardon had set with his rough appeal.

Miles away, at the Chaparral, Hank tossed and turned in bed, naked beneath the sheet. There was a hole inside him that he desperately needed to be filled. He told himself he wanted Kit Sloan because she was there; she was handy. What man in his right mind *wouldn't* want her? It wasn't the lust that scared him, though. What scared him was that even as his mouth had been on hers, his hands grasping at her soft flesh, he'd known it was more than simple physical desire. Smooth skin, soft breasts, warm lips, alluring body—many women fitted that description. But none had this woman's essence, the magic she cast over him by simply being who she was. What he felt for her was want and need combined until one was indistinguishable from the other. It was her that he wanted, with her beautiful green eyes sparkling with challenge. It was the way she smiled. The way her womanly fragrance filled his senses. It was the sound of her voice, so smooth and beguiling that he almost didn't notice the impact of her questions or the directness of her remarks until it was too late and he revealed more of himself than he'd ever intended.

After a while Hank fell into a restless sleep that was filled not with brooding memories from the past or hazy images of a spotted horse but with a green-eyed woman who was forcing him to take a good, hard look at himself.

Chapter 6

A stiff summer breeze rushed past the open car window, rustling in Kit's hair, blowing russet strands into her eyes to tangle in her lashes. But Kit didn't mind. It was still early, but it was hot, and she was glad for the movement of the air past her face as she and Quint drove along the black-topped highway to the Lazy J, horse trailer in tow.

Rolling grasslands and stands of timber streaked past. There was an immensity of space out here. The sky was infinite, cloudless and blue. She sighed inwardly. How could she forget about him when there was so much out here to remind her of him, like the color of the sky and the strength of the mountains and the loneliness of the range?

Quint's voice interrupted upon Kit's thoughts. "So anyway, like I was saying..."

She pulled her eyes reluctantly from the window.

"Two judges each award from zero to twenty-five points for the rider's performance and the same for the horse's. That's why some of us like to draw difficult horses," he added with a boast. "It's a ten-second ride. If you stay on the horse the full ten seconds, don't change hands on the rein or touch the horse with your free hand, you'll score points. Of course, bareback riding is a lot tougher. You gotta be strong to stay on a horse using only one hand to hold the grip that's attached to the strap around the horse. That's my event. I don't know anyone in these parts who can beat me in bareback bronc riding—except, of course..." He paused with a disapproving look, then went on. "Now, bull riding, that's a dangerous event. A bull will..."

Kit slipped in and out of a daydream as Quint went on about saddle bronc riding and bareback bronc riding and bull riding and steer wrestling and calf roping. He recited scoring procedures and explained about quarter-finals and disqualifications, all the while boasting of his own particular prowess in the arena. And yet she noticed that Quint did not breathe fire and life into the sport the way Hank did whenever he spoke about it—which, she admitted wasn't very often. She'd seen them both in action, and it had been Hank, not Quint, who'd impressed her the most. Quint was a showboater. To him, being good meant the acclaim that went with it. For Hank, being good was a way of life. She honestly didn't think Hank could do it any other way. An act that came as naturally to Hank as breathing was riddled with calculated moves and cunning on Quint's part.

"The suicide circuit," Quint was saying. "That's what they call the rodeo tour. It goes all year, and you have to travel around a lot. You pay your own way, too—entry fees, room and board, stabling for your horses. You get your share of injuries, too. Last year I dislocated a shoulder in Jackson and tore up the ligaments in my foot at Cheyenne. But it's all worth it."

"Ah, yes," Kit remarked. "The pot of gold at the end of the rainbow."

"Something like that. And a chance to show my stuff, of course."

Wryly, she muttered, "Of course."

"Hell, last year two riders tied for the title, and each won more than ninety thousand bucks."

"And you aim to break that record?"

"That's not the record. Back in seventy-six, the all-time money mark was a hundred and twenty thousand."

"Who won it?"

His look soured. "Hank Reardon." In his tone was the ring of hostility that usually accompanied the mention of Hank's name. "I figure this'll be my last year as an amateur. I'm gonna turn pro next year. By then I'll have enough money to pay my way through to the national finals in Las Vegas."

"When is that held?" she asked.

"In December. This year the purse is over a million. The top fifteen money winners in each event qualify for nine days of hard competition. At the end of that is all those big bucks and the world championship title. I aim to be there next year. Then it's watch out, Reardon!"

Kit was also thinking of Hank and of what a shot in the arm it would be for the Chaparral if he could only win a portion of that purse. She looked at Quint. "Why is it so important for you to beat him? He's not even competing anymore. Why not just go out there and do the best you can? Hank should have nothing to do with it."

"That's where you're wrong," he told her, rejecting her logic. "Reardon has a lot to do with it."

"If you mean because he used to be number one—"

"I mean because I'm sick and tired of watching the winning come so easy to him. It used to be rodeo riding. Before that it was—" He stopped himself. "Look, I've got my reasons for wanting to break his record. Besides, records are meant to be broken, aren't they?"

"Why do you dislike him so much?"

The directness of the question made him take his eyes from the road to flash a look at her. "What do you mean?"

But Kit could tell he knew exactly what she meant. "Doesn't he pay you enough?"

"Sure, he pays me fine."

She studied his profile. There was something tentative in his look. He seemed to exhibit all the signs of a man who had something to hide. She recalled the day Hank had come into Jackson to pick up the feed Quint was supposed to have gotten. "Does he work you too hard?" she asked, even though she knew that wasn't the case.

Quint snorted derisively. "I do my share. Besides, that place won't be in business much longer. Hank's down to his last dozen brood mares." He paused to consider something, then smiled, just twitching the corners of his mouth. "It would be a damned shame if anything happened to those horses, wouldn't it? Why, it just might drive Hank out of business."

"What would happen to them?"

He answered with a shrug. "Beats me. But Hank's stock does have a habit of disappearing."

Surely he was referring to the stallion, and the stallion, Kit suspected, was somehow tied in with Hank's disappearance from the rodeo circuit. She knew she was taking a chance with her next question, but she asked anyway. "Quint," she ventured, "why'd Hank stop competing?"

Kit watched as Quint considered the question. She couldn't help but feel disappointed when he said, forcing a casual tone, "Hey, have I told you how great you look today?"

Kit groaned inwardly. Here it comes, she thought. She'd been wondering when he'd get around to making his play.

"That sure is a pretty dress you're wearing." He gave a thorough, appraising look to her thin-strapped green sundress, with its bare back and hem of peekaboo eyelet lace. "I like the way it matches your eyes."

What a rogue he was, she thought, blushing nevertheless.

"Yeah, I sure do have a thing for blue-eyed women."

She looked at him in surprise, wondering if he was teasing her. Kit frowned. How could he look at her so intently and as often as he did and not really see her? She supposed some men were like that. With a sigh she turned her gaze back to the window to watch the terrain slip by.

Kit was more than a little relieved when they reached the Lazy J. She jumped out of the car and sprinted off with her camera before Quint could extract from her more than just a vague promise that she'd see him later. Kit was glad to be out of his company. She didn't like him, although she still wasn't sure exactly what it was about him that bothered her. Still, she could easily see how the ladies would fall all over him. His good looks undoubtedly blinded many women to the self-centered man underneath.

But it was more than Quint's preoccupation with himself that disturbed Kit. It was his hostility toward Hank. Until today she had assumed it had to do with the competitive spirit. The rodeo was like any other sport where the participants were trained athletes and the will to win was fierce. But now Kit wasn't so sure. As she looked around, she was struck by the camaraderie among the men, which seemed to survive the competition, no matter how stiff. Behind the chutes she heard one man telling the next how a particular horse bucked and turned, and another advising a competitor about the erratic twists of a certain bull.

They were part of a brotherhood, sharing any piece of knowledge that would help the other man. The real competition was not between men, but between man and animal. Which all served to make Quint's behavior even more baffling.

But excitement at the Lazy J was high this afternoon, and Kit didn't dwell too long on Quint's misguided competitive spirit. The dust was thick in the air as it flew in every direction from the corrals. Calves bawled when they found themselves roped and tied in a matter of seconds. Steers were wrestled to the ground in displays of strength and skill. Barrel racing drew the female competition, each contestant galloping her horse around three large oil drums in a cloverleaf pattern. There was trick riding and fancy roping as the participants primed the onlookers for the more dangerous events, yet to come.

Kit spotted Pete in the crowd and made her way to him. His face lit up upon seeing her. "Well now, Missy, glad you made it. Whaddaya think of our little shindig?"

"It's terrific," Kit exclaimed, obviously caught up in the excitement. "How about you, Pete?" she teased him. "Are you going to show the boys how the men do it?"

He chortled with mirth. "Damn if I couldn't show them a thing or two in my days. Nowadays, Missy, I'm just an observer."

"Speaking of observers, is Hank here?" She hoped her voice didn't betray more than a casual interest.

He looked at her kindly. "Sorry, Kit. It would take a miracle to get him here today. When I left him this morning, he seemed dead set against coming. Told me to mind my own business, like he usually does."

"Does he always make it a point of staying away?"

Pete went to a nearby cooler and pulled two cold cans of beer out of the ice. He handed one to Kit and said,

"Sometimes he comes, sometimes not. I wouldn't count on seeing him here today, though. Naw, there was something about the way he said it." He shook his head. "Like I said, it would take something pretty special to get Hank here today." He grasped her hand and spun her around. "Enough of old Hank. Come on. Quint's about to come out for the steer-wrestling event. This should be interesting."

They found an empty spot alongside the corral and waited for the gate to swing open. The steer burst out and then dashed across the arena with Quint galloping after it. Another rider raced on the opposite side to keep the steer running straight. When Quint drew level with the steer's head, he flung himself from the saddle. He grabbed the steer by the horns and planted his boots in the dirt to get a firm hold. Locking his grip on the steer, he wrestled the animal onto its side. The deciding factor in this event was time, and Quint impressed the crowd with his speed.

Kit looked at Pete to see his reaction. The older man nodded with grudging appreciation. "Not bad. Not bad at all," he said with a ring of disappointment in his tone.

"Do you think he's better than Hank?"

"I think his best can't equal Hank's worst."

She smiled at him. She felt the same way. "Think he'll ever compete again?"

Pete took his hat off and scratched his head. "Did anyone ever tell you that you have a knack for asking the damnedest questions?"

From somewhere behind them a familiar voice said, "I told her the same thing myself."

Kit turned with an intake of breath. Pete, too, whirled. But his look of shock turned to one of sly understanding when he saw how Hank's blue eyes focused on Kit. "See?" Pete said to her. "I told you it'd take something special." He walked off, chuckling to himself.

"What was that all about?" Hank asked when he came to stand beside Kit at the fence.

She looked up at him. In spite of her own height, he seemed to tower over her. Determined to show no surprise at his unexpected appearance, she said, "He said it would take a miracle to get you here today."

"He did, did he? Pete likes to think he knows me better than he really does."

"Maybe in some ways just better than you know yourself," she suggested.

He fidgeted beneath her stare. "Anyway, there's no one left back at the Chaparral, because everyone's here, and seeing as how I can't do all the work myself, I figured I'd drive over and catch a bit of the action."

Despite his resolve to stay away, he'd been lured there that afternoon not only by the promise of action but by the opportunity to see her again, maybe for the last time. One look at her and he wasn't sorry he'd come. The sundress she was wearing matched her green eyes, and its straps were so thin he could break them with a flick of the wrist. He noticed that her shoulders were tinted pink by the sun, and tiny droplets of moisture dotted the soft flesh that disappeared into the bodice of the dress. Her back was bare, begging for his touch. Yes, he'd had to come. The thought of her auburn hair clinging seductively to her neck in the heat, the chance to breathe her fragrance and hear her voice again no matter how mad her questions made him…all that and everything else about her had drawn him like a bear to honey.

He nodded at the can in her hand and said, "Can I get you another one of those?"

"Sure," she said, tilting back the can and finishing the last of its contents.

So far so good for the small talk, Hank thought as they walked to the cooler. But even as he inquired, "How's it going? See anything good?" he knew it was just a matter of time before the small talk turned to things that mattered.

"I just saw Quint wrestle a steer," Kit announced.

He lifted one dark brow in a gesture of mild interest. "And?"

"And he's good."

"Tell me something I don't already know."

"Does it bother you that he might one day break your record?"

He laughed. "Hell, no! Records are meant to be broken. Even mine."

"That's what Quint said."

"Yeah," said Hank, "it sounds like something he'd say. What else did he say?"

"Other than a whole lot about himself, he said that back in 1976 you won a hundred and twenty thousand dollars on the circuit." She raised her can of beer in a gesture of salute. "I'm impressed."

Hank grinned. "They still talk about that in these parts."

His pride was showing, and it was good to see, Kit thought. With his features softened by an easy smile, he was a strikingly good-looking man. "What did you do with the money?" she asked.

"I put it into the ranch. Bought some stock, made a few repairs, paid off some loans, bought my wife that four-wheel drive she'd been wanting."

"You're married?" She'd never considered...never imagined... She knew he must have had women in his life, but a wife? Kit's throat went dry, and she prayed desperately that the disappointment tearing through her didn't show on her face.

He hadn't meant to say that, Hank thought. It was just that she had a way of coaxing things out of him. Strangely, though, now that it was out, he was glad of it. He pushed his Stetson back on his head and said, "I used to be. I'm a widower."

As sorry as Kit was at the death of his wife, she was just as relieved to know there was no Mrs. Reardon waiting in the wings. Simply and sincerely she said to him, "I'm sorry."

Hank shrugged beneath his calfskin vest and muttered, "It was a long time ago."

There was something in his voice that told Kit the memory still pained him. "What do you say we go catch some of the action?" she said. Slipping her arm through his, she steered him toward one of the corrals where a cowboy lurched this way and that atop a bucking horse and eventually fell facedown in the dirt.

"I can't believe they do that," exclaimed Kit. She was amazed by the perseverance of the men, who got back on every time they fell off.

The frenetic atmosphere of the afternoon had infected everybody. Between the laughter and the gasps of excitement and the snapping of pictures, Hank explained to Kit about the gear the cowboys used and how the horses were selected by lottery. He grasped her hand and led her behind the chutes. "Come on. Let's go see who's up next." He was like a child at the circus, and his enthusiasm was contagious. "See there," he said when he brought her close to the chute and they peeked inside at the horse. A cowboy climbed the chute and prepared to lower himself onto the horse he'd drawn. "You have to get that rope securely wrapped around one hand," Hank told her. "Then you signal for the gate to be opened." The rider in the chute did just that. The horse bucked out into the ring. "You're required to place your spurs on the horse's shoulders at the start," Hank shouted over the roar of the crowd, "and use them on the first jump out of the chute."

The ride ended with the cowboy sprawled on his back in the middle of the corral. Despite his loss he received a rousing cheer from the onlookers, most of whom had themselves been up or were about to be.

"That's got to be the longest ten seconds in the world," said Kit.

"I see you've done your homework."

"Not exactly. Quint told me."

Hank made no comment.

They moved on to the next corral, where one of the Chaparral hands was roping a calf and doing a fancy job of it. But Hank seemed suddenly uninterested in the action. "What is it with you and Quint?" he asked.

"Nothing," Kit asserted.

"Have you told Quint that?"

She was beginning to resent his line of questioning. "I see no need to tell Quint anything. Besides, he's been a perfect gentleman."

"So far," he cautioned her.

"Which is more than you can say, isn't it, Hank?"

"I'm just saying watch out for the guy, that's all. Are you so stubborn that you can't take a bit of friendly advice?"

"If that's all it is, no. But when you're too pigheaded to admit you're jealous, that's another story."

"Jealous? Me?"

"I may have been born and raised on a farm, Hank, but I know a jealous man when I see one. Go on. Deny it. Why not? You deny everything else."

With her own ire mounting, Kit didn't notice the tensing of his features or the careful, almost deadly, way he was looking at her. "You're dying to get into that arena," she went on, "but you won't admit that either."

"What are you talking about? I told you, that's all behind me."

She gave him an exasperated look as if to say, "Oh, no, not that again."

"Dammit, Kit, what do you want from me?"

"I want you to go out there," she said, jabbing a finger at the corral. "You *should* be out there. It's where you belong. It's where you want to be."

"Did Pete put you up to this?" Hank asked accusingly.

"Of course not. I don't need Pete to tell me that rodeo riding is in your blood. I can see it in your eyes and hear it in your voice. It's too bad you haven't taken a good look at yourself lately, Hank. You might see it, too." She turned and walked off, feeling like a fool for her efforts to draw him out.

Some time later, still cursing her attraction to the most pigheaded man she'd ever met, Kit ran into Pete.

"I've been looking all over for you," he said. He grabbed her by the hand. "Come on Missy. There's something you're gonna want to see."

He led her to the corral where the bareback riding was about to begin. The first few riders exhibited promise and some skill. A couple even made it through the eight seconds allotted for the event without being unseated, but the horses they'd drawn had been unimpressive. On the whole, scoring was low. When Quint came out of the chute, astride a troublesome horse, the crowd perked up. No wonder this was Quint's favorite event, she thought. He was good at it. When his ride was over, Kit turned to Pete and said, "It'll be hard to beat him."

Pete smiled. "Hard, but not impossible."

He looked about as sly as an old fox as he stood there with his eyes riveted on the center of the corral. What was he up to? Kit wondered. When the gate swung open and the next rider burst from the chute, she knew.

It was Hank. A wild roar went up from the crowd. Kit's own heart palpitated in her chest.

Dust and dirt flew in every direction as the horse made a mighty protest, bucking and lurching, twisting this way and that in an attempt to toss the man from his back. But Hank stuck to his back like glue, just as determined to stay on.

With the camera at her eye and a precise twist of the lens, Kit focused on the scene. Hank's hat flew off his head and landed on the ground. The sunshine bounced off his head, sparkling off his dark hair like gold dust. Kit tightened the shot, calling it into sharp focus.

With the rein gripped in one gloved hand, the other arm swinging free, Hank held his position. There was a rhythm to his movements, a grace that was almost balletic despite the dust and dirt and the occasional obscenity shouted from the onlookers.

The buzzer sounded and the pickup man rode in to aid Hank in dismounting the still-bucking horse. Hank moved across the corral with the long, confident strides of a winner to retrieve his hat. He swept it up off the ground and used it to beat the dust from his jeans.

The voice over the loudspeaker announced Hank the winner in the bareback bronc riding event just as he emerged from the corral. Pete and Kit were waiting. Pete slapped him soundly on the back. "Great ride, Hank. I *knew* you'd be back."

"Hey, Pete," laughed Hank. "Take it easy. It was only one ride." But even as he lent modesty to his win, he was smiling from ear to ear, scarcely able to contain his own excitement. It had been such a long time since he'd felt that rush, he thought. Breaking a horse for range work at the Chaparral was one thing, but this was something else. Kit was right. This *was* where he belonged. He sought out her eyes, which were shining with pride, and he was stunned by a feeling stronger than winning. It had been even longer since he'd seen that look in a woman's eyes. With a jolt, he realized how much he'd missed it.

Hank and Kit and Pete were soon enveloped by a crowd of well-wishers, and no one noticed that there was one among them who didn't share the excitement of Hank's ride.

Quint stood on the fringes of the crowd. Only a few minutes ago it had been him they'd been cheering. He didn't like the swiftness with which his limelight could be stolen, nor did he like having it stolen by Hank. Feeling cheated, he waited until the crowd dispersed before doing anything about it.

Pete had gone off to get another beer, leaving Hank and Kit alone. There had been no exchange between them since the flurry of words they'd fired at each other earlier. What need was there for words when now, as then, their looks said it all? Hank thought. He was thanking her with his, for making him so angry that he'd forgotten about the guilt.

Kit was certain he could see right through her to her erratically beating heart. He thrilled her in a way no man ever had, and her look could not help but tell him so. But the moment was brief, shattered in the next instant by the approach of Quint. His voice filled with acrimony, he said, "Well now, let me congratulate the winner." But no hand came out to shake Hank's hand when he came to stand beside them. "Not bad, Hank. You planning on a comeback?"

But Hank neither confirmed nor eased Quint's obvious apprehension. "I've got a ranch to run."

"Then maybe you'd better run it," suggested Quint, "and leave the fancy riding to others."

"Others? You mean to you, Quint?"

Quint shifted from foot to foot beneath Hank's cool stare. "Me, for one. And to the others who haven't given up either."

Hank's muscles tensed beneath his shirt. He kept his voice low and controlled. "You don't know anything about it."

"Well, I'll tell you what I do know," drawled Quint. "I know that I don't like sharing the attention."

"Sharing it, or sharing it with me?"

"Both."

"Sorry, pal," Hank laughed, although it was a harsh and bitter sound, "there are just some things we have to live with."

"Who would know better than you, Reardon?" said Quint.

Just then, Pete returned with a cold beer, and Kit, who'd been observing the exchange, turned a fearful look on the older man and said, "What's with them? Have they always been this way?"

Pete's face assumed a worried expression. "I've seen it getting worse over the years, but lately it's gotten bad."

"Pete, maybe you'd better stop them before it gets out of hand," Kit suggested.

He gave her a hapless look but took her advice. "Now, Hank," he said stepping forward, "what do you say we go on over to the west corral, where they're about to start the bull riding?"

Hank's eyes never left Quint's face. "Sure, why not? It's been a while since I've been on a bull, but it's kind of like riding a bicycle—once you learn how, you never forget."

Quint looked as if he hadn't counted on more competition from Hank. "I gotta warn you, Reardon, bull riding's my best event."

Kit spoke up without thinking. "But Quint, didn't you say that bareback bronc riding was your best event?"

She realized her blunder when he flashed a heated look at her. "You must have misunderstood me," he said. "But now that I think of it, to hell with the bull-riding event. There's something else I'm even better at. Come on, let's get out of here."

His suggestion was both blatant and embarrassing to Kit. "Why don't you go on ahead," she told him. "I'll find my way back to Jackson."

"What do you mean? I drove you here; I'll drive you back."

"I'm not ready to leave just yet," said Kit. It was obvious to her that he was just using her to get to Hank. She hadn't misunderstood what he'd said earlier about bareback bronc riding being his best event. Losing to Hank must have been a bitter pill for Quint to swallow, but it didn't give him the right to use her as a weapon against Hank. Hank knew it, too. "Leave Kit out of this, Quint."

Quint turned his temper on Hank now. "Stay out of this, Reardon. It's none of your business."

"You're only using her to get to me," accused Hank.

"I told you, it's none of your business."

Hank took a menacing step closer. "I'm making it my business."

"Yeah? Then why don't you do something about it?"

The challenge was answered in less than a heartbeat when Hank lunged and sent his fist into Quint's jaw.

Kit screamed and jumped out of the way.

Quint staggered back. His hat had been knocked off his head by the impact of Hank's blow. Ignoring the fury blazing in Hank's eyes, Quint regained his balance and dived for him.

They came together in a flurry of fast-flying fists. Each landed some good blows as Pete and Kit and a dozen others circled the two men, helpless to prevent them from going at each other. Kit was oblivious to the sound of her own voice as it tore from her throat, beseeching them to come to their senses. She watched as Hank's fist drew back in what seemed like terrible slow motion. It hung there for one incomprehensible moment, curled into a tight ball of whitened knuckles, then surged forward in a burst of power and fury.

The sound that accompanied the blow wasn't the soft thud of flesh striking flesh. It was the sound of one hard object crashing against another, and it sent chills down Kit's spine. She shut her eyes tight, but she could not block out Quint's awful grunt of pain.

The impact knocked him back several yards, to the ground, and his legs went out from under him. He lay there for a few seconds, looking confused and stunned. When his eyes stopped rolling, he looked up at Hank, who stood over him in a combative stance, legs braced apart, chest heaving, fists curled and waiting. Quint didn't move. "Collect your wages and be off the Chaparral by morning," said Hank, then pivoted sharply and strode away.

Behind him Quint's voice came after him like a dagger. "One ride doesn't make you a hero, Reardon."

The victory of Hank's ride was painfully short-lived. The look of pride in Kit's eyes had turned to fear, and whatever good had come out of it was washed away by a flood of regret. On his way past Pete, Hank said without looking up, "See that she gets back to Jackson," and stalked on to his car.

Hank drove back to the Chaparral in a mist of blinding dust and harsh recriminations. He knew it wasn't Quint, who'd been a troublemaker from the start. Hank had only himself to blame for not having fired him years ago. It wasn't Kit either. How could she have known the need she aroused in him? She couldn't have guessed how intensely lonely he'd become, how desperate he was for the fundamental values she represented: honesty and pride and a belief in yourself, and the courage to face the truth, no matter how painful.

It was dusk when Hank arrived home. He headed straight for the stable, where he threw a saddle on Dakota and galloped off in the direction of the mountains. Maybe there he would find solace from the memories, relief from the guilt, and an easing of the fever that had burned within him since the intrusion of Kit into his life.

Later that night Hank lay, unable to sleep, by the light of a campfire. His thoughts drifted back to the past. It was ridiculous, he knew. After all, he wasn't responsible for Beth's death, not really. Certainly no court of law would ever convict him. But Hank was his own judge and jury and had pronounced himself guilty in his own heart. If only he'd been there, instead of off riding the circuit. If only... And now, seven years later, all that remained were the regret, the guilt, and an overriding desire for vengeance that would never be satisfied until he caught the piebald stallion and evened the score.

Hank allowed the fire to burn down to a few smoldering embers and pulled the blanket tighter around his shoulders to ward off the night chill. His eyelids began to droop, and eventually he slept in a silence so deep that it had a sound of its own.

Chapter 7

Kit stood at the entrance to the barn, scanning the dim interior, which was vast and low-beamed, shadowy even in the noonday brightness. The scent of oats and fresh, sweet straw mingled with the smell of leather and horseflesh. A shaft of sunlight cut a diagonal path to the ground from the loft window. Someone was moving around in one of the stalls. Maybe it was Pete, she thought. But an unexpected sight greeted her.

At the sound of Kit's gasp, Quint jerked his head up. When he saw who it was, he frowned and went back to stuffing his belongings into a duffel bag.

She was surprised to see him there. Hank's order for Quint to be off the Chaparral by morning had left little room for argument, and here it was, nearly noon.

His curt voice filled the silence. "I didn't expect to see you here," he said without looking back up.

"I'm leaving in a few hours," Kit explained. "I just came to say goodbye."

He snorted derisively at that. "Not to me, that's for sure. If it's Reardon you're looking for, forget it. He's gone."

Kit felt seized by a small sense of panic. "Gone? Where?"

"How should I know? Wherever it is he goes when he rides off."

Hank's absence explained the reason for Quint's lingering. But still, the warning had been implicit. "You're taking a chance, aren't you?"

He cocked a brow at her from over his shoulder and said, "Your concern is touching."

"I only meant that Hank could walk in here any minute."

"Oh, I get it," Quint drawled. "The concern is for him. Afraid I might give him a taste of his own medicine?" His hand went up to his still-swollen jaw for emphasis. "Besides," he scoffed, "he's not likely to be walking in here anytime soon. When he goes off, usually it's for days."

Days? Kit's heart sank. Trying hard not to let her disappointment show, she said, "Actually, I came to say goodbye to Bayberry."

"Why don't you just go on down there and do it, then?" Quint snapped, obviously annoyed by her presence.

She understood his bitterness and wounded pride, which must hurt as much as his jaw, but what did it have to do with her? "Quint," she began, "about what happened yesterday, I—"

"Forget it. I was wrong to use you the way I did. For *that* I'm sorry."

Aside from the fact that his sarcastic tone made a mockery of the apology, Kit looked at him curiously, for he seemed to be implying that there was something for which he *wasn't* sorry.

Quint slung the duffel bag over his shoulder and turned to face her. He gave her a long, appraising look and said finally, "He doesn't deserve you." A hard look came over his face that he tried to cover with an unconvincing laugh. He turned away, and as he did, he said half to himself, "He didn't deserve *her* either, and look what happened to her." Shaking his head, he walked off. She heard him start up the engine of his car outside and drive off in a spray of dirt and gravel.

Kit found Bayberry in her stall munching from a pail of oats. Hitching up the hem of her calf-length denim skirt, Kit climbed to the top of the stall, the way she had done as a child. The wall separating the stalls was high enough to keep the horses from nipping at one another, but not so high that they couldn't see one another for company. "Horses are just like anyone else," her father used to say. "Sometimes they want company; sometimes they just want to be left alone." Like the stallion, Kit thought, running free and wild up there in the mountains, wanting only to stay that way and not be under relentless pursuit by some man whose emotions were out of whack. She sighed. Oh, well, it looked as though she'd never learn the truth of that matter.

Being in the barn brought back childhood memories of her father's barn, of playing hide-and-seek in the loft. This one looked similar, but the feelings it evoked were very different. The only other time she'd been there was the day she'd arrived at the Chaparral. She had little recall of actually helping to deliver the foal. In the aftermath of that first meeting, all she could really remember was the heat of Hank's hands on her waist. She had to admit she'd come unhinged that day. The funny thing was, Hank wasn't even here right now and she still felt the same way. It was as if all her connecting threads had come unraveled. As she sat in the dim, quiet barn thinking about him, she could feel her heart tripping over itself. She'd never met a man who made such an impression on her. The sad irony was that she probably never would again.

In a few hours she would board a plane bound for New York, and all of this would become a part of the past. But not even the thought of putting it behind her was soothing, for she knew that if she never saw this place or Hank Reardon again, a piece of her would always remain in the Teton wilderness. The place and the man had inflamed too many emotions for her to ever be the same.

The sound of the barn door opening brought Kit's head up from her wistful daydream. She turned to look down the length of the barn, thinking that Quint must have forgotten something and returned.

Two figures were silhouetted against the yellow sunlight outside. Kit's heart skipped a beat when she recognized one of the forms.

Hank entered the barn, leading Dakota on a loose rein. In his dusty and worn jeans and a day-old growth of beard on his face, he looked like one of the ranch hands.

Hank was feeling tired and sullen, in no mood for surprises, and certainly not prepared for the one that awaited. His ride into the mountains had done little to ease the frustration that was tearing at him. Nevertheless, last night *had* been different from the countless others he'd spent beneath the stars. The old feelings of guilt and irresponsibility over Beth's death were there, sure, but they'd been overshadowed by a stronger emotion. Need. Last night Hank had come to grips with his need for Kit Sloan. A hell of a lot of good it did him today, he was thinking as he walked with heavy steps through the scattered hay toward Dakota's stall.

Kit watched him approach. His effect on her was always the same. It began as an intense sensation in the pit of her stomach, like being on a roller coaster in a downward swoop, and was followed by a tingling that spread clear to her fingertips. She sat there mute, unable to say or do anything.

The big horse pricked up his ears when her scent alerted him to her presence, but Hank, walking in front, was too absorbed in thought to notice Kit sitting atop the stall. When they were practically upon her, she nervously cleared her throat and said, "Hello, Hank." She was grateful that her voice betrayed only a glimmer of the apprehension she was feeling.

Hank looked up. He scanned the dim barn and found her perched on top of the stall, her hair hanging loose about her shoulders. He could see the roundness of her breasts pressing against the soft fabric of her white chambray shirt. Her full skirt was gathered up above her knees, and her long, lean legs dangled on either side of the stall. Her feet were bare. He spotted one sandal peeking out of the hay where she must have let it fall. She hadn't been expecting company, if the deep blush on her cheeks was any indication. It served her right, thought Hank. What did she expect, sitting there like that, driving him crazy with unrehearsed seduction?

He tore his gaze away and led Dakota into the stall. Not trusting his voice, he said nothing as he slipped the bridle off the horse and hung it on a peg on a post outside the stall. Kit watched his muscles flex when he reached under the horse to unfasten the cinch, then bunch with strength as he pulled the saddle from the animal's back. His hair fell over his collar when he bent to examine a front hoof. Kit could see the dark stubble that spiked his chin.

Hank began to rub down the big chestnut horse trying hard not to glance in Kit's direction. But he was painfully aware of her. His weariness had fled the moment she'd uttered his name; now he was filled with a nervous energy. Get hold of yourself, friend, he told himself. It's only sex. And then he remembered last night, the realization and acknowledgment of his need for this woman, and he knew that anything he told himself was a lie. He'd been cursing himself over having let something so good get away, never dreaming that he'd ever see her again, much less have her within arm's reach.

His pulse began to pound, first at his temples, then moved slowly, steadily downward, invading his limbs and his belly, throbbing without mercy. He closed his eyes and willed his body to stop before it was too late. But the sound of her name was already spilling from his lips before he could prevent it, and in its deep tone Hank heard his own urgent, aching need.

"Kit . . ."

He was there beside her, looking up at her, his blue eyes dark with emotion. His hands were strong yet gentle as they closed on either side of her waist and lifted her from her perch. She placed her hands on his shoulders for support. The power that surged beneath her fingers made her feel weak. He let her slide slowly down the length of his hard, tensed body and held her there, suspended above the ground. Neither spoke. They were face to face, eyes clinging, breath mingling. She could feel the hardness of his desire pushing against her.

"Kit," he whispered, "you have such brave eyes. Can you make me forget, for a while at least?" As he held her, he could feel the wild beating of her heart.

In that deep and vibrant voice that made Kit's heart sing, he said, "Kit. Kit. I want to make love to you. I've wanted it from that first day.'' His breath was hot and quick against her ear, mingling with the thunder in her blood.

He swept her up into his arms and carried her out of the stall and into another across the way where the straw was freshly spread. Not until he'd gently laid her down upon it did Kit realize that her feet had never touched ground.

They sank into the bed of straw, and Hank covered her body with the weight of his. Two impulses ran through him, battling for supremacy. One was to take her lingeringly, savoring the impact and making each moment last forever. The other was to possess her with savage intensity. He was dangerously close to losing control over the choice.

He'd known her such a short time, yet it seemed as if he'd been waiting for her forever. If ever a woman was worth waiting **for**, it was the one beneath him now. Words couldn't describe the softness of her skin beneath his palms as his hungry hands ripped her blouse away.

She didn't know how her blouse had come to be lying in a heap off to the side, or how the buttons of her skirt had come undone, the garment slipping easily away. She knew only that in a matter of heartbeats she lay naked beneath his hard, still fully clothed body. The friction of the fabric of his clothes on her sensitized skin sent waves of pleasure through her.

He closed his fingers around her soft, pliant breasts, kneading, touching, teasing, making her flesh tingle. He lowered his head and kissed the vulnerable undersides and tickled her nipples erect with his tongue before returning to her mouth to graze her lips with his and murmur, ''I need you, Kit.''

His words, uttered simply and honestly, thrilled her in a way she'd never known before. There were so many things he could have said to convince her that what was about to happen was right. Another man might have told her how much he wanted her. But for Kit, wants weren't enough. Needs were different; they were stronger, deeper. She wasn't surprised by his need, for she'd already seen it in his eyes. Still, she knew it had taken courage for him to say it.

She opened her eyes to look at him. His face, only inches from hers, was agonizingly handsome, with its desire-narrowed blue eyes and dark stubble. A one-night stand wasn't what Kit wanted. She took love far too seriously for that. Yet she remembered what he'd said to her about not being able to make any promises, and she wanted him to know that at this moment there wouldn't be any. So, putting aside her doubts, she summoned her own courage and said softly, "It's all right, Hank. No promises." She lifted her hands to his face and brought his mouth to hers. Eyes open, they shared a long, quiet kiss. It was the last either of them knew of reality.

In the ensuing minutes, every rule was broken, every promise forgotten. All that remained was the incredible passion between them.

She wanted him, wanted the triumph of hearing him catch his breath, the weakness that followed losing her own. She slid her hands from his face to his shoulders, and from there to the front of his shirt, where, with fingers fairly shaking, she tugged at the buttons until the last one popped free. She pushed the shirt from his shoulders and slipped it down his arms, feeling his flesh heat up along the way beneath her palms. His upper body was strong and brown, well defined from the physical rigors of ranch work. In spite of the calluses on his palms and the rough stubble of his beard, which rasped her flesh, his skin was incredibly soft and smooth. She knew it would be even softer in places as yet undiscovered and felt an impatience building within her.

She wanted the thrill of letting herself go, of giving herself up to him. Take more, she encouraged him with her lips. Still more, she pleaded with her hands. She ran her palms along his bare back and down to his taut waist and finally into his jeans, where she filled her fingers with the firm flesh of his buttocks.

Hank could not endure much more of the slow torture she was inflicting. Lifting himself up, he discarded his jeans and the rest of his clothes until he was as naked as she was. With half-closed eyes she watched him undress and felt herself grow warmer as more of his vital, strapping form was revealed to her. He dropped back and poised atop her, looking at her an arm's length away, just looking. With her hair spread in dark waves against the straw, her beautiful eyes filled with desire, body all naked and warm, he couldn't remember when he'd ever seen anything more arousing. She was so slender and so smooth. The sunlight slanted in so that he could see where her tan gave way to paler skin. She was sexy and tempting, and he was powerless to resist her. Maybe it was the sound of her moaning that made him linger there when he was driven to hurry on.

The tension was mounting all about them now as Hank mercilessly explored every inch of her, driving them both beyond the brink. He demanded of her and she gave; he gave to her and she took. She moved quickly, eagerly, demanding when he'd expected surrender. It all happened so fast, too fast for him to brace himself against it. She seduced him thoroughly, irrevocably, and not just his body—that he gave freely, for it was the easiest to give—but his mind and his emotions as well. What kind of spell had she cast on him with her clean, hot, strong loving?

Energy and passion raced neck and neck as Hank and Kit drove each other even higher. Tangled legs, teasing tongues, fingers wrapped in and around intimate places. Masses of emotion swirled around them, mingling and colliding as she sought his tongue with hers, inviting him farther into the warm, wet hollow of her mouth. She touched him, enticed him, enraged and weakened him. She drank in the sweet-salty flavor of his skin, with its traces of healthy sweat.

They were both hurrying now, hurrying toward the moment of surrender. He shifted his position. In compliance, she opened her legs, welcoming him into the space, then closing around him. She clutched him tightly, feeling his need in every savage thrust, in each desperate kiss, and matching it with her own. They were one, if not forever, then at least for now, and whatever promises they'd dared not speak were spoken by their bodies in the wordless language of love.

Kit's skin was still flushed from their lovemaking. Hank's was still damp. It was Sunday, and as most of the hands were off visiting families and friends, there was little chance of their being discovered lying naked in each other's arms.

They were careful, neither wanting to say anything that might be misunderstood. They had made love, and for each it had been more intense than anything they'd ever experienced. They knew they'd made rules and broken them and that someone had mentioned something about promises. But all that seemed far off now as they lay beneath the sun's warming rays, which streamed through the door.

Kit rested her head against Hank's chest while he traced a lazy pattern up and down her arm with his finger. She raised her eyes to look at him. He seemed to be a million miles away. Yet his expression, although thoughtful, bore no sign of regret, and for that she was glad.

She'd been right about him; he wasn't an easy lover. He demanded and took as much as he gave with a fierceness that both excited and frightened her. Beneath the whisper of her name she'd heard a chord of obsession ringing loud and clear from within him. Funny how she'd closed her mind to it while they'd been making love, only to remember it now. And then she remembered something else, something he'd said, and the warm glow of contentment faded in the harsh glare of reality. "Can you make me forget?" he'd said. "For a while, at least?" Was that all she was to him, a device with which to forget? A temporary relief? She'd been foolish to think there was a place for her in his life, crazy to mistake his lovemaking for anything other than pent-up frustration. It wasn't her he wanted; it was that damned horse.

Hank looked down at her. The light struck her face in such a way that the shadow of her lashes fell long against her cheek. He could see that she wasn't smiling. "What's the matter, green eyes? Regrets?"

Kit tilted her face up at him. "That would be a switch, wouldn't it, Hank?"

He hadn't expected such coolness when her skin was still so warm to the touch. Was that just a lucky guess, or was she beginning to know him too well? "Does it show that much?" he asked.

"Sometimes. I just wish I understood it better."

"What's to understand?"

His voice was calm, but she knew she'd touched something sore inside him when she heard his heartbeat accelerate beneath her ear. "You," she said.

He laughed. "Why would you want to understand me?"

She shrugged a slender shoulder against him. "I don't know. Maybe you intrigue me."

Hank mumbled an expletive and looked at her as if she'd gone insane. "You find me intriguing? Why, Kit? Because there are things I have to deal with in my own way, in my own time?"

It was Kit's turn to be surprised by a quick reaction she hadn't expected. "For starters."

"What the hell's so intriguing about that?" he demanded, sitting up abruptly and causing her to roll over into the hay.

"Great!" Kit groaned. "Some men smoke a cigarette afterward. *You* like to argue, I see. All right, damn it, what I find so intriguing about that is..." Thinking of the conversation she'd overheard from the window that first day, she blurted out, "Don't you think seven years is long enough?"

His eyes widened with disbelief. Her, too? "Seven years, twenty years or a hundred. As long as it takes." He grabbed his pants from the straw and began to dress.

Kit scrambled to her feet and went in search of her own clothes. She dressed with her back to him, unable to bear the embarrassment her nakedness was causing at this moment. "What is it with you and that stupid horse?" she complained to the thin air. "Why do you hate him so much?"

Hank pulled up his jeans over his slim flanks and said, "Hate him? I don't hate him. Not anymore." The hatred had eased, he thought, the way that most painful things do with time. He respected the stallion's courage and admired his cunning, but he also resented the animal's hold on him. Again he found himself agonizing over how he could possibly explain to Kit, who he knew had every right to be angry. He turned back to her to find her buttoning her shirt. When she was through, she came forward and began to move past him. He stepped in front of her, blocking her path out of the stall, and spoke in a low, teasing voice.

"You never did say what you came here for today."

"And you never did say what brought you down out of the mountains so soon. Quint told me you usually don't come back for days."

His ploy to tease his way out of explaining backfired as her remark fanned the flames of jealousy. "Quint? When did he tell you that?" he wanted to know.

"I...uh..." Kit stammered. It was best, she knew, not to tell Hank that Quint had been there earlier, yet she didn't like lying to him either. Opting for an explanation that was not exactly a lie, although it was short of the truth, she said, "Once, when I was talking to him."

"Yeah? Well, Quint's got a big mouth. I wouldn't listen to a whole lot of what he says."

Unlike you, Kit was thinking, who don't say a whole lot at all. "What is it between you two?" she said instead. "Why the hostility?"

Hank let out an impatient sigh and moved aside for her to pass, saying as they walked toward the door, "Who the hell knows? I could never figure it out. The guy just rubs me the wrong way, I guess."

"That wasn't exactly what I meant. What is it with *him*? Sometimes he looks at you with such...such..." She could've picked any number of words. Jealousy. Resentment. Bitterness. But Hank summed it up in one: "Hatred."

Something inside her shivered. Yes, that was it. But why? she wondered. Just one more in a long line of unanswered questions about Hank Reardon.

They emerged from the barn into bright sunshine and walked to her car. A dry summer breeze picked up the ends of her hair and flicked them about. He glanced down and smiled. She was barefoot. He hadn't noticed until now that she was dangling her sandals from one hand. At the car he reached out to pluck a piece of straw from her hair and said, "You'd better put your shoes back on now. You're headed for the big city."

It was the first either of them had spoken of her leaving, and though he'd said it in a soft, teasing voice, she could see from the look on his face that he was not unaffected. She bent over to slip her sandals on. "I'll send you some pictures of yourself," she said, "so you can see yourself as you used to be." She glanced up to see his reaction. "And still are."

By now he was accustomed to her pointed observations and the pluck with which she verbalized them. She had guts, he thought, and he liked that about her, even if her remarks did hit home and her questions did provoke him to anger.

They lingered, she with her fingers toying with the door latch, he kicking at the dust with his boot.

Looking down at the ground, he muttered, "So, uh..."

"Yes?" she said, a shade too eagerly, she thought with an inward gasp.

"Maybe I'll, uh, call you."

Her heart fluttered. "Do that."

"If I ever get to New York, that is."

Her heart sank.

An hour later Kit was on a plane bound for New York City. As the Teton range sank from view, Kit's spirits went with it. What did she expect, she asked herself, when it was she who'd said "No promises"?

Chapter 8

Kit's third-story loft was on a narrow, cobbled street in Manhattan's SoHo district. Once a factory, like many others along these crisscrossing streets, the building had wide windows and elevator doors that had to be pushed up to open and that served as the entrance to each dwelling.

The open space of Kit's loft was divided into a living area and a studio by strategic deployment of the furniture. Kit had lost count of the hours she'd spent in the makeshift darkroom in the back, or at the light table, hunched over slides with a magnifying glass. At least she didn't have far to go for something to eat or a place to put her feet up and relax. A few steps away was the kitchen, neat and compact against one wall. The living room was bright and airy, with one brick wall that ran the length of the loft. On it was hung an assortment of prints, including a few of her own that she'd liked enough to frame. The bed, the brass poster she'd brought from home, was hidden behind two silk screen room dividers that Kit had found in a local antique shop.

In the eight years she'd been residing there, Kit had grown fond of this quaint and quirky neighborhood. The art galleries, the boutiques filled with odd wonders, and the Sunday street-corner flea market were her favorites. But in the three weeks since she'd been back in the city, none of them pleased her anymore. The art galleries seemed lonely places to her now; the boutiques failed to lure her in. She'd taken to working extra hours in the darkroom, as if the obscurity could somehow erase the memories of her stay in Wyoming. It was foolish to think she could ever forget when one look at his picture brought it all rushing back as if it had been only a moment ago.

Spread over the coffee table were the prints of the Wyoming shoot. As she'd done dozens of times before, Kit picked up one in particular and stared at it. It was the close-up she'd taken of Hank the day they'd ridden up into the mountains in search of the mustangs. It was a tight shot, the focus crisp, the colors true. She moved her eyes over it, tracing every line, every pore, committing it to memory all over again. Her throat went dry at its impact. There was a rugged beauty to his handsomeness, combined with a primal quality that drew Kit's attention again and again. Something primitive lurked inside him, showing itself in the flash of his brilliant blue eyes. Even from a photograph those eyes had a way of reducing her to liquid.

With a groan Kit looked down at her watch. If she didn't hurry, she'd be late. Sid Burns, the photo editor at *Human Interest*, had called that morning and asked her to meet with him. He must have another assignment for me, Kit thought as she stared at the picture. Good. That was just what she needed—more work. Maybe this time he'd send her someplace far, far away where those cursed blue eyes would not follow her.

An hour later she was sitting in his office on the thirty-ninth floor of the building where *Human Interest Magazine* had its editorial offices.

"That's what I like about you, Kit," Sid told her after they'd exchanged the usual good-mornings. "I send you out to take pictures of families adopting cute little horses for their cute little children and you come back with something I didn't even know was there."

She wasn't sure she understood. Looking across his desk, over which were spread pictures of Hank Reardon shot from every conceivable angle, she said, "If you're not satisfied with the shots, Sid, I—"

"Not satisfied? Kit, they're great! How'd he ever let you get close enough for something like that?" He pointed to the same close-up Kit had been staring at that morning and said, "From what I've heard about the guy, he doesn't let anybody in, if you know what I mean."

Yes, she thought glumly, she knew exactly what he meant.

"I didn't want to tell you that before you left," he added. "I didn't want you to think I was sending you into the lion's den."

"Then why did you? Send me into the lion's den, I mean."

He shrugged and pushed his shirtsleeves up past his elbows. "Call me old-fashioned. Call me a chauvinist. But it worked, didn't it?"

"Oh, I get it. Send in a woman, huh?"

"Correction. Send in a *beautiful* woman."

Kit blushed. "Thanks for the compliment. And thanks for not warning me in advance," she added sardonically. "I like to do things on my own, even when it comes to making mistakes.''

"Mistakes? Honey, these photographs are no mistakes. You've captured something here. Something big.''

"Big?" She laughed. "Sid, they're only mustangs.''

"Not the mustangs. *Him*. Reardon. Haven't you heard?''

Kit's body tensed. "Heard what?''

"Reardon's started competing again. An editor friend of mine at the Cheyenne *Herald* called to tell me. He thought I'd like to know, seeing as how I recently sent someone out to cover the roundup. No, on second thought, I don't guess you would have heard. That sort of thing doesn't get much coverage on the six o'clock news in these parts, does it? Anyway, I decided not to run the mustang piece in the October issue. I'm running it as soon as I can. The timing is perfect, coinciding as it does with Reardon's comeback. Which is what I wanted to speak to you about. I think the mustang piece will be a perfect segue for the other one, don't you?''

Kit was trying hard to assimilate everything she was hearing. Hank was making a comeback? Could it be true? Weakly she asked, "Other one?''

"The one on Reardon's comeback.''

"Oh. Of course. Well, uh, yes, I think it would.''

"Good. Do you think you can leave in the morning?''

"Me?" she uttered.

"Of course *you*. I want you to cover Reardon's comeback.''

Kit felt as if she'd been punched. She was thankful that Sid was too busy scribbling notes on a yellow legal pad to notice that the blood had drained from her face. "Sid, I can't do it.''

"This stuff is big bucks," he went on, apparently not having heard her. "Reardon could be a leading contender."

"Sid, I said I can't do it."

He looked up. "Sure you can."

"No, really. Couldn't you put somebody else on it?"

He laid his pencil down and thought for a moment. "I could put Williams on it, or Horowitz, but that's not who I want. Besides, you've already been there. You've glimpsed something inside this man that no one else has. It's right there in the pictures, Kit. You can't hide it. And there's more." He hedged before going on. "He won't consent to it without you."

Kit was so stunned by the knowledge that Hank had started competing again that she didn't think there could be much more of a shock in store for her, but she was wrong. Her confusion and outrage were echoed in a single exclamation. *"What?"*

"He says you take good pictures."

"Really?" she replied stiffly. "When did he tell you that?"

"Yesterday, when I phoned him to talk about doing a story on his comeback. He rejected the story idea outright."

Yes, she thought, that was like Hank, fiercely private, unwilling to give up bits of himself without a fight. She knew it only too well.

"But he did go for the idea of just photos. The only condition is that you be the one to take the pictures. Sure, I can always send someone out there to cover the events, but only you can get close to the man, and that's what this piece is all about. Obviously he feels that way, or he wouldn't have asked for you."

Kit walked to the water cooler, where she pulled a paper cup from the dispenser and took a drink. Beyond the glass partition of Sid's office people rushed about like bees in a hive, putting together the stories and features that made the magazine one of the nation's most popular. One of the staff writers waved to her from across the office. Numbly, Kit waved back.

"Wyoming's so . . . so far away," she said.

"Not by plane it isn't."

"And hot."

"Kit, don't tell me you consider eighty-nine degrees and ninety-five percent humidity hot!"

She'd returned from Wyoming to find Manhattan gripped by a heat wave. Three weeks of electrifying heat combined with high humidity had indeed gotten to her, but Wyoming? And Hank? It was too soon, she thought frantically. No, she wasn't ready to see him again. Maybe if he'd called. A single word from him these past weeks would have changed everything. But Hank's silence had led Kit to a sad conclusion, and all her doubts about him had been confirmed. "I don't know, Sid. I'll have to think about it." But even as she said it, her mind was made up.

"Okay," he said. "There's just one thing. Could you let me know by tonight? If I'm going to juggle layouts, I've got to tell Nicholas about it. You know how he likes to stay on top of things. I planned on telling him about it tonight at the party. You'll be there, won't you?"

Kit hadn't forgotten about the black-tie party being given by Nicholas Costas, the wealthy and controversial newspaper publisher and owner of *Human Interest Magazine*. Nor had she forgotten that invitations by Costas were not to be turned down. "I'll be there. And yes, I'll give you my answer then."

* * *

Why me? Kit thought dismally later that evening as she dressed for the party. Of all the photographers on the face of the earth, why did it have to be her he wanted? Why couldn't he just leave her alone?

Maybe she should quit before they had a chance to fire her when she told them tonight that her answer was no, she considered rebelliously. She knew that was what they would do. Sid would be against it, of course. He liked her work too much to let her go over something like this. But Costas was another story. If he liked the idea for this piece enough, he would lay it on the line. He hadn't made his fortune by giving in, Kit knew. She'd seen heads on the block before. Now it would be hers. Free-lancing wasn't so bad, she reasoned. At least it was preferable to being ordered about by Nicholas Costas. But even as she thought it, Kit knew it wasn't really Nicholas Costas's powerful influence that she was rebelling against; it was her own emotions.

She'd been on edge for weeks, ever since she got back. Her eyes would stray at odd moments to the telephone, as if she could somehow summon its ring by sheer will. When it did ring, she'd fly out of her seat to answer it, hoping against hope that she'd hear Hank's vibrant voice on the line. But not once had it been Hank. Her expectations melted away, and her spirits went into a decline. She certainly was in no mood for a party. Black-tie affairs were not her cup of tea, anyway. All that pretension left a bad taste in her mouth. There was no way she could get out of it, though. The magazine had recently won a prestigious award in publishing, and Costas had invited his staff to his home for an evening of celebration. Word had trickled down from higher up that he expected everyone to be there. And one didn't say no to Nicholas Costas—unless, of course, one was prepared to quit or be fired. And it was with precisely those intentions that Kit hailed a taxi to take her uptown.

The cab dropped her off in front of a classic Manhattan apartment building. A uniformed doorman helped her out of the cab and ushered her into the lobby, where a security man checked her name against his list and told her to go on up.

In this, as in many of the posh, older buildings, each story held only one apartment, so when the elevator stopped at the top floor, Kit wasn't surprised to walk into a beautifully furnished foyer that was as big as her loft.

The lights were low, sending reflective shadows across Nicholas Costas's penthouse overlooking Central Park. His strong, striking tastes were dominant throughout, from the elegant chrome and glass furnishings to the plush hand-woven Oriental carpets and priceless Ming vases.

Conversation was subdued, barely rising above the tinkle of ice cubes in the guests' glasses. Kit accepted a goblet of white wine from the tray of a passing butler and mingled, saying hello to co-workers, who were soon to become her ex-colleagues. Costas himself was standing beside a huge, gleaming baby grand piano with his fifth, and very young, wife, greeting his guests as if he were royalty. Kit wandered over to them.

"Ah, Miss Sloan," said the publisher, "I'm delighted you could come."

As if I had any choice, Kit was thinking. "It was kind of you to invite me," she said politely.

"Not invite my star photographer? Don't be foolish." He turned to his wife, who appeared to have no interest in anything to do with publishing or photography and said, "My dear, you should see the wonderful pictures Kit took for our piece on wild mustangs. Why, if it hadn't been for her, we might never have had this chance to do the piece on the cowboy. Remember I told you about it?''

Although Mrs. Costas's look was blank, she nodded. "Sure, Nicky."

"Uh, Mr. Costas," Kit began, "I'd like to speak to you about that. You see, for reasons that I can't go into, I would rather not—"

But Nicholas Costas had already turned away to greet another subject, cheating Kit of her chance. She turned away and spotted Sid Burns across the room. "Okay," she told herself. "Let's try it again."

Kit greeted Sid and his wife and exchanged small talk, then said, "Sid, if you don't mind, I'd like to speak to you about something."

Misreading the apprehension in her voice, he said, "I knew you'd come around. Sure, come on. Let's go get me something to drink." He left his wife with a group of friends and ushered Kit to the bar, where he ordered a drink for himself, and then into a quiet corner where they could talk.

"Did you tell Costas?" she asked when they were alone.

"Yes, and he loves the idea. All systems are go. You'll be traveling around a lot in the coming weeks, following Reardon on the circuit, but Costas will spare no expense. He seems to think this one could snag an ASP award. Who knows?"

But even the prospect of winning an award from the American Society of Photographers could not sway Kit. "Sid, that's what I want to talk to you about. There isn't going to be any ASP award, because there isn't going to be any assignment. Not with me, anyway."

Sid rolled his eyes and groaned. "You're not going to start on that again, Kit, are you? It's no hotter out there than it is right here," he argued.

PLAY
SILHOUETTE'S

LUCKY HEARTS

GAME

AND YOU COULD GET

- ★ FREE BOOKS
- ★ A FREE UMBRELLA
- ★ A FREE SURPRISE GIFT
- ★ AND MUCH MORE

**TURN THE PAGE AND
DEAL YOURSELF IN** →

PLAY "LUCKY HEARTS" AND YOU COULD GET...

★ Exciting Silhouette Intimate Moments® novels—FREE
★ A folding umbrella—FREE
★ A surprise mystery gift that will delight you—FREE

THEN CONTINUE YOUR LUCKY STREAK WITH A SWEETHEART OF A DEAL

When you return the postcard on the opposite page, we'll send you the books and gifts you qualify for, absolutely free! Then, you'll get 4 new Silhouette Intimate Moments novels every month, delivered right to your door months before they're available in stores. If you decide to keep them, you'll pay only $2.49 per book—26¢ less per book than the retail price—and there is no charge for postage and handling. You may return a shipment and cancel at any time.

★ Free Newsletter!

You'll get our free newsletter—an insider's look at our most popular writers and their upcoming novels.

★ Special Extras—Free!

You'll also get additional free gifts from time to time as a token of our appreciation for being a home subscriber.

FREE FOLDING UMBRELLA
You'll love this bright burgundy umbrella made of durable nylon. It folds to a compact 15" to fit into your bag or briefcase. And it could be YOURS FREE when you play "LUCKY HEARTS."

DETACH AND MAIL CARD TODAY

DETACH AND MAIL CARD TODAY

BUSINESS REPLY CARD

First Class   Permit No. 717   Buffalo, NY

Postage will be paid by addressee

Silhouette Book Club
901 Fuhrmann Blvd.
P.O. Box 9013
Buffalo, NY 14240-9963

NO POSTAGE
NECESSARY
IF MAILED
IN THE
UNITED STATES

"It's not that," she admitted reluctantly. "It's...it's him. It's Hank Reardon. I can't work with him."

He raised a brow at her. "Is there something about our champion you don't like?"

No, she wanted to scream. On the contrary. There was entirely too much about him that she *did* like. "He's so...he's difficult to work with."

"Come on, Kit, you're a pro. You know better than to let something like that get in your way."

"Wrong," she countered. "I *used* to know better, but that was before Hank Reardon. There's something about him that just rubs me the wrong way." Inwardly she cringed at her own words. Hank had said the same thing of Dan Quint.

Sid took a sip of his drink and eyed her over the rim of his glasses. "Say, you aren't in love with the guy, are you?"

"In love?" She laughed, but there was a strained feeling in her throat. "Of course not! The man is arrogant beyond belief, and rude, and... That's ridiculous. I could never love a man like that."

"All right, all right, don't get so excited. You don't have to love him. Just take pictures of him."

Tell him, Kit was urging herself. Tell him the answer is no, and be done with it. But in the next moment the door to Nicholas Costas's penthouse opened and Hank Reardon walked in, and whatever Kit had been about to say was lost forever.

All eyes turned in his direction. He returned the stares. For one furious moment Kit felt the full weight of those blue eyes upon her until they turned away. She felt her hands go cold.

Who would ever have guessed that the tall, handsome, blue-eyed man in the black tuxedo was the same rough-edged cowboy from Wyoming who was trying to win his way back into the record books? Still, there was something about him that set him apart, telling the others in the room that he was not one of them. It was a rugged individuality that was feared by most men and adored by most women. Kit herself found it hard to ignore his presence.

She moved away, wondering miserably why she turned to jelly every time he looked at her. What was he doing here? She tried to relax, but couldn't. She could feel his gaze following her around the room, seeking her out when she tried to hide, scrutinizing her whenever she pretended to be wrapped up in conversation with someone else. He still hadn't spoken a word to her, but there was no need to. His look said it all.

Kit struggled to look casual, to give the impression that Hank's presence was of little interest to her. Why should it be? Why should she care that he'd started competing again? Surely it had nothing to do with her. Hadn't he made that obvious by not calling? Still, she found herself listening in on his conversation with others, thrilling to the sound of his voice.

He was asked the usual questions, like how many seconds he had to stay on a bucking horse, and had he ever had any serious accidents? Kit cringed. People always liked to hear about that stuff. But Hank seemed to take it all in stride. "Sure," he told one pretty blond guest, "I was gored by a bull once, and I've got the scar to prove it."

Kit knew that scar. She'd felt it on his hip when they'd been making love. Oh, damn, why did she have to remember that?

"If that's the only scar you have, Mr. Reardon, you must consider yourself very lucky," Kit spoke up. But she regretted her impulsiveness when he turned in her direction.

"No, Miss Sloan, it's not my only scar. Maybe someday I'll tell you about the others. It *is* Miss Sloan, isn't it?" He smiled devilishly, as if he liked toying with her emotions.

He was enjoying this, Hank thought, provoking her ire until her eyes sparkled the way he remembered. He smiled in full appreciation of her complexity. If she'd been beautiful the last time he saw her, dressed in denim and cotton, her hair hanging loose, she was dazzling tonight. He raked his eyes over her. She was wearing an ankle-length black sequined *bustier* dress. The snug bodice, the slinky skirt slit a little in front and a lot in back, announced "Hello, I'm here!" Her crystal earrings reflected the soft lights. Her dark auburn hair was swept up off her bare shoulders and coiled loosely atop her head, held in place by a comb of black jet.

Kit grew uncomfortable under Hank's stare. People were beginning to notice. Nervously she moved off, leaving him to answer their questions while she sought some relief. She placed her empty wine goblet on a table and left the room. In answer to her whispered query, the butler pointed down the hall.

She followed his directions and entered a darkened study, moving across the plush carpet to the sliding glass doors that led to a rooftop balcony. She stepped outside into the warm night air. She grasped the wrought iron railing and tilted her head back, drinking in the air, filling her lungs with it to regain a bit of her strength. Many stories below, the city was alive with after-hours entertainment, but up here, so close to the sky, Kit was filled with a different kind of excitement, caused not by throbbing neon lights or pulsing traffic but by a single pair of blue eyes.

"It sure is something, isn't it?"

The male voice from behind her shattered the stillness. Kit whirled to find Hank's steady gaze on her as he stood in the doorway. He stepped onto the balcony, wondering when he'd ever seen her looking lovelier, and it was only with the force of will that he looked past her to the city below. "There's no place like it in the world," he said.

"So you decided to come east for a little sightseeing. Is that why you're here, Hank?"

"Not exactly. I was invited by Costas."

"I see." Her voice sounded strangely calm even to her own ears. "Well, I'm sorry to tell you that you wasted your time. There isn't going to be any assignment."

"Why not?"

He was suddenly too close, and she was having trouble thinking clearly. "Because I have other things to do," she lied.

"Cancel them."

Her eyes flashed up at him. "You're taking entirely too much for granted, Hank."

"You're wrong," he said. "I take what I want, but I take nothing for granted."

"And is that what you did that last day, Hank? Took what you wanted?"

"Why not? It was there. And unless I'm mistaken, you wanted it, too."

His arrogance was too much to bear. "Yes! I wanted it, too. And now I'm sorry for it and I'm trying to put it out of my mind. Chalk one up to experience," she said bitterly.

His hand flew out to grasp her by the arm. He gave her a hard squeeze. "What are you talking about? You can't mean that."

Stubbornly, she responded, "Why not? If a tumble in the hay is good enough for you, then it's good enough for me, too."

"A tumble in the—! Dammit Kit, look at me. Is that all it was to you?"

She struggled to twist free of his grip and evade the look of hurt on his face. "What difference does it make? You made your feelings clear by not calling."

Hank swallowed hard and released her. She had every right to be angry with him. He'd wanted to call her; had agonized over it. But these past few weeks had been grueling ones for him. It had taken more courage than he'd thought he possessed to get out on the circuit again. It was the only way he knew to put Beth's death behind him once and for all. It was Kit who, without even knowing it, had made him see that. He touched her again, except this time there was no harshness in his grip, but only enough pressure at the shoulder to gain her attention. "I wanted to call you, Kit. Honestly. I had to come to terms with something first."

Sullenly, she said, "Well, you seem to have done all right."

"I've won a few events and a couple of trophies, if that's what you mean."

Despite Kit's resolve to remain unaffected by him, into her nostrils wafted the familiar, arousing scent of him, his earthy, masculine aroma, which hinted of something half wild. Suppressing its effect on her, Kit said, "Congratulations." Her voice sounded oddly detached to her, having nothing at all to do with the emotions that were surging wildly inside her.

"Congratulations aren't in order yet," said Hank. "I haven't won them all, not by a long shot. Let's just say I aim to give Quint a run for his money."

He saw concern flash across her face as she said, "He won't like you for it."

"I'm not out to win any popularity contests," he scoffed. "Besides, what difference does it make? Quint doesn't like me anyway. I stopped trying to figure that out years ago."

Kit studied his face in the starlight, her brows knit with uncertainty. "Why the sudden about-face, Hank?"

He turned to lean his elbows on top of the balcony wall and fix his gaze on the city. "It's funny. Being up here is almost like being in the mountains. If you close your eyes, the traffic down there sounds almost like the rush of a waterfall. Go on, try it," he urged her.

She closed her eyes and listened. He was right, she realized. Maybe that was what she'd always liked about this place, with its steel- and glass-structured summits and subway caverns. Within these streets was a strength and vitality not unlike that of the mountains. She opened her eyes and looked at him. He was staring at her. Nervously, she pushed back from her face a strand of hair blown there by the midnight breeze, and asked, "What's your schedule?"

He ticked off the names of some of rodeo's biggest competitions, then shrugged as if to suggest that his fate was somewhere in the wind. "After that, who knows? Maybe I'll even make it all the way to the national finals at Las Vegas in December."

"It sounds as if you have your work cut out for you."

"Nobody ever said rodeo riding was easy. Hell, I've got the scars to prove it."

"Hank, that scar, the one on your hip. Tell me about it."

Hank scanned her face, trying to understand her. Rodeo riding wasn't always a pretty sport. Beth had been scared to death of it. She had never come to watch him ride and had begged him to quit. Kit, on the other hand, seemed unafraid of its ugliness, unintimidated by its violence. Instead of shying away from it, she only wanted to know more about it. He realized in that moment what it was about her that made her so beautiful, at least to him. It was her courage.

Scars. She wanted to know about his scars. He'd start with the physical ones. They were the easiest to explain.

He spoke in a low, soft voice. "It was about ten years ago," he told her. "At Cheyenne. Through the luck of the draw I pulled Old Number Seven. He got to be called that because that old bull was so mean no one could think of something evil enough to name him. I eased down onto him in the chute, and as I was getting a good grip on the rope, the gate suddenly swung open. There must have been some crossed signals between me and the gate handler that day, because the next thing I knew, Old Number Seven had charged from the chute with me only half hanging on."

Ten years hadn't dulled the memory for Hank. He could still recall the fear and confusion that had gripped him. He'd known the instant they hit the ring that he was in for it. "That old bull twisted and spun like nothing I'd ever been on before. And in the next minute I wasn't even on him anymore. I hit the ground hard. The impact stunned me. It was only a few seconds, but it was long enough for him to spot me lying there."

He paused to pull in a deep breath before going on. "If it hadn't been for the clowns, that bull would've done more than just put a gash in my hip. As it was, it took sixteen stitches to patch me up. That and a fractured collarbone laid me up for a spell." He smiled grimly. "Not one of my better days, I guess. Still, it could have been worse. The reason we called him Number Seven was that he'd crippled seven men. I could've been number eight."

He fell into quiet recollection after that. He thought of things half forgotten, like the way Beth had yelled at him at first and later pleaded with him to give it up. "I lay in bed for a week after the accident," he recalled, "wondering whether it was worth it. And after that I spent six weeks with my neck in a brace."

Kit's voice, tinged with challenge, floated like cool mist into the silence. "And was it?"

In the darkness she saw him smile. "I went on that year to win the national finals," he said with pride and triumph in his tone. "In those days they were held in Oklahoma. They've added a lot of glitter since then."

"And you plan to be in Las Vegas this year?"

He met her steady gaze with his own, unflinching. "That's right."

She tried to sound light and uncaring. "Well, good luck, Hank. I'm sure you'll go all the way."

"I want you there."

He said it so simply and plainly that it shocked Kit more than if he'd demanded it. "Me? But why?"

"Can't you guess?"

"If you mean because I take good pictures—" she began.

He cut her off with a wave of the hand. "I had to tell him *something*, and I couldn't very well say you make good love or—"

"Never mind!"

He grinned sheepishly, but Kit wasn't amused. "So what you're telling me, Hank, is that you want me there because I'm a warm body?"

"Dammit, Kit, do you have to make everything so difficult?"

Outraged, she cried, "*Me?* How about you? I notice you still haven't answered my question."

"All right!" he stormed back at her. "You want to know why the sudden about-face? The Chaparral needs money, and this is the only way I know to get it. And—" He stopped, suddenly unsure of what came next. "And . . . I don't know. I can't explain it. It helps me get rid of the ghosts. Or, more appropriately, learn to live with them. Someone told me that, right after I'd kissed her.''

The day atop the cliff Kit recalled. How could she ever forget?

Hank was thinking of the way she'd looked at him that day from astride her horse and told him that the trick was in learning to live with it.

He badly needed to hold her, to lose himself in her courage and her warmth. The night was warm, but he suddenly felt cold. His eyes pleaded with her. Enough questions for now. He moved almost imperceptibly closer to her. He could smell her sweet fragrance all around him, filling the night and his senses until he was aware only of her. This woman would not have begged him to quit. Even after what happened that day with Old Number Seven, this woman would have dared him to get back on and give it all it was worth.

He stopped himself from reaching for her, but his eyes probed her, touched and caressed her. He leaned toward her. "I meant what I said that day, Kit. I do need you."

Kit took a deep breath and raised her eyes to his. If she tried hard enough, she could almost imagine them back in Wyoming, with the Tetons rising all around them in sawtoothed peaks. New York City seemed a million miles away, yet the different surroundings could not diffuse the incredible tension strung taut in the air between them. His tuxedo could not disguise the familiar strength of the muscles beneath it, nor could his spicy cologne completely mask the essence of sagebrush and leather in his skin. And all the trophies in the world couldn't hide the need that still ached in his blue eyes.

She became liquid heat in his arms as their lips touched in a long, quiet kiss. She'd never dreamed it was possible to desire one man so much. His eyes were bright when he raised his head. "Come back to Wyoming with me, Kit."

She couldn't think when he was kissing her. She eased herself out of his embrace. "I . . . I don't know, Hank."

"No pressure. I promise. You can set the rules. Just come back with me."

She thought of the Chaparral and of sharing Hank's bed there, and she knew it was useless to deny that she'd love it. But was that all they would share? She might trust him to keep his promise, but would he ever trust *her* enough to share with her the dark secrets of his soul?

He bent his head to kiss her again, and this time her hot surge of response burned away all doubt. For the time being, none of that made any difference to her. What mattered was here and now and their desire for each other.

Chapter 9

"Can I get you something to drink?" Kit offered. She and Hank were in her apartment now.

"Sure. Do you have a beer?"

"I think so. I'll check." She left him standing by the elevator door and walked off toward the kitchen area. Hank watched the movement of her hips in the black sequined dress, and the curve of her calves showing through the deep black slit until they disappeared behind the counter.

He turned away and glanced around, nodding approvingly. The furnishings were simple yet elegant, just like her. A black leather sofa of Italian design was flanked by two matching armchairs and a coffee table in a butcher-block parson's design, all atop a mauve area rug. The lighting, he noticed, was soft and flattering. As a photographer, she'd know how to light a room to achieve the best possible effect. There was a feeling of space here, broken only by the supporting beams, which were painted white like the rest of the place, including the plank floor. The room's openness made him feel at home.

He noticed the silk screen room dividers and went over to have a look. He was surprised at what he found behind them. It was a bedroom reminiscent of Southern mansions and was quite unlike the living-room area, with its sparse furniture and straightforward simplicity. The brass bed was covered in pale rose with a flounce of ruffle on the pillows. Atop a mirrored vanity of white wicker was an assortment of leaded crystal perfume bottles. It was an oasis of femininity amid the structured look of the rest of the place and the professionalism of the built-in studio.

Hank smiled. What a paradox she was, and this place was just like her.

He wandered back into the living room and noticed some of Kit's own prints hanging among the others on the brick wall. He'd know her work anywhere. She had an instinct for capturing the heart of a subject in a way that was uniquely hers. He was surprised to see a print he recognized as one of those from the motel room in Jackson. It was a black and white shot of the mountains, the one that had moved him to speechlessness the first time he'd seen it. Apparently it had moved Kit as well, enough for her to have had it blown up, framed and hung with the others.

His gaze strayed to a photo of a well-known Broadway actress. Face half smeared with cream, she was seated at the makeup table in her dressing room, gazing into the mirror at her own reflection. The poised smile and traces of still-youthful beauty faded as the cream washed away the makeup, until what remained was just an ordinary-looking woman well past middle age. There was a sad, resigned expression on her face, but in her eyes was a look of unspoken relief, as if she were glad to be rid of the mask. The rhythmic click-click of Kit's heels on the bare wood floor broke into Hank's thoughts.

"Sorry I took so long," she said as she came to his side. She'd fussed in the kitchen as long as she could, wiping and rewiping the perspiration from her palms on paper towels and taking a drink of water to gather her wits. Being near to him always made her feel out of control, a condition Kit could not risk if she was going to stick to her resolve not to take the assignment. She handed him the can of beer and said, "What do you think?"

He was wondering if it was just a lucky guess or whether she somehow knew he preferred his beer straight from the can.

"The picture," she prompted.

"I like it. Did she?"

Proudly, she said, "She ordered a twelve-by-sixteen print for herself. And thanks. I like it, too. It helps me to remember what's real underneath everything else."

"You're very good at what you do," he told her.

"So are you."

Hank turned from the picture with a skeptical sigh. "I used to be. I guess the next few months will tell whether I still am."

"I have confidence in you."

She had a way of astounding him with even the simplest, most plainly uttered words. He looked at her in disbelief. What was it about her that gave her more faith in him than he had in himself? "Why?" he asked her.

"Because I've seen you in action. And I don't need to see a hundred others to know when I've seen the best."

Hank considered this as he took a sip of beer. "All right, if seeing is believing, then say you'll come back to Wyoming with me."

"I can't."

"Why not?"

"Because it's not that simple."

"Nothing is ever simple, Kit. We both know that. Is it that you're afraid I might not make it?"

"No!" she exclaimed. "Of course not!"

"You talk about confidence, but apparently you don't have the courage to show it."

The sheer physical presence of him was making it hard for Kit to maintain control over her emotions, and Hank's infernal arrogance, which fanned the flames of her ire, didn't make it any easier. "That's a laugh, Hank, coming from you," she said curtly. "And where, may I ask, did this sudden burst of confidence on your part come from? I distinctly recall that when I left Wyoming, you were dead set against ever competing again, although God only knows why. You never did make that clear. But come to think of it, you haven't made a whole lot else very clear."

"I've made one thing very clear," he said, growing annoyed himself.

"Oh, yes, that's right, we make good love together. And you want me to pack my things and go back to Wyoming with you based on that? What else?" she demanded. "Some good pictures? Maybe an ASP award?" She remembered what he'd said to her about not being able to make any promises and wondered bitterly whether she could settle for less. She fixed her eyes on his. "Why did you come here, Hank?"

He shifted from one foot to the other, fingers flexing involuntarily around the beer can. "I got a call from your editor asking me if I'd consent to a story," he explained.

"You could have worked out the details over the phone."

If he'd learned anything at all about her, it was that she went right to the heart of the matter. He knew he should tell her that he'd come because he *had* to see her, but he said instead, "I guess I could have done that, but I wanted to see you. I thought maybe I could persuade you to take the job."

If he felt persuasion was in order, then surely he must realize why, Kit was thinking.

As if he could read her thoughts he said with a guilty shrug, "I realize I haven't given you much to go on. And there's no reason you should go back there with me. Hell, it's a messy job. All that dust and dirt. I can't say I'd blame you for turning it down. Besides, who'd want to tag along after some former rodeo rider who got this crazy notion in his head that he could make a comeback?" He laughed at himself and shook his head.

What he didn't say was that she was the one who'd put that notion in his mind. It was something she'd said to him the day they'd parted. She had offered to send him pictures of himself in action so that he might remember himself the way he used to be. Even now he could hear the challenge in her tone when she added, "And still are." She knew as much as he did that rodeo riding was in his blood, but what she'd known that he hadn't was the impact the photographs would make on him when they arrived some days later.

It had made Hank think. Could this be a way to exorcise the ghosts that haunted him? Why not? Rodeo riding had gotten him into this morass of guilt; maybe it could show him the way out. The next day he'd stunned Pete by announcing that he was riding into town to register for some of the local events. Things had happened fast after that. In a matter of two weeks he'd competed in events across half the state. It was a grueling schedule, but Hank felt energized in a way he hadn't been in a long time.

There was something strangely arousing about him dressed in a tuxedo with a beer in his hand, Kit was thinking, something touching in the way he tried to explain his feelings. And yet she sensed an evasion, unwilling, perhaps, on his part but an evasion nevertheless. Kit knew the Chaparral needed money, but she had an idea that the reason for Hank's comeback had to do with more than that. There was something he wasn't saying.

Kit felt torn by two impulses. If she stayed here in New York, at least she'd be safe from his kisses. In time she'd get over him, but she'd never know the truth. On the other hand, if she followed him back to Wyoming, there was a chance that in time she might break through the walls of his defenses to the truth, although the damage to her heart would be much more severe than if she stopped right now. It had to be one or the other, for the truth was, she was in love with him, and love left no room for anything in between.

She felt her muscles go weak as he caressed the back of her neck. She should have moved away from him, she thought. She'd known what she was doing by inviting him here tonight. They'd both known. Certain things didn't have to be said. He couldn't promise her that he'd trust her with his secrets, nor could she promise him that she'd return to Wyoming with him, but at least they'd have tonight.

Hank's breath was warm against her neck. "Kit, I want you. You know that. You just can't know how much."

Her breath caught in her throat as she took his hand. Without a word she led him behind the screens.

It began as a slow seduction of each other, not a hungry devouring like that day in the barn. Tonight they had all the time in the world.

They stood beside the bed, facing each other but not touching. His hands were at his sides. He had already tasted the soft wonder of her, and, no longer impatient, he was content for now just to look at her and savor the impact. In a low voice he told her, "Take your hair down."

Like a puppet, she did as directed, his voice the force pulling her strings. Her hair tumbled to her shoulders before the comb even hit the carpet. The bare skin of her shoulders looked even paler and more vulnerable compared to the rich, deep darkness of her hair. He longed to crush it in his fingers, but held the temptation in check, so mesmerized was he by her that he was powerless to do anything but look.

Obeying his wordless commands, she began to undress. Slowly the black sequined dress came unfastened, then slid from her hips. She stepped out of it, paying no attention, her gaze fixed steadily on his. *Yes,* her eyes insisted. *Yes.*

Only when she was completely naked did he move. He removed his jacket. She went to him, her fingertips brushing his flesh as she pushed his shirt from his shoulders. She watched as he did the rest and more and more of his beautiful masculine form was revealed to her eager eyes.

She marveled at the way his muscles flexed and rippled as he moved, how the cords of his thighs were taut with vital energy. She heard his quick intake of breath as she closed her fingers around him, and experienced a surge of blood through her veins at the sheer power, the incredible heat that simmered within that wondrous male body. She ached for his power, his strength—to grasp it, hold it, taste it. To feel it inside her and all around her. With a moan she melted against him, lashes fluttering and lips parting. She rained feather-light kisses across his chest, brushing his hard little nipples with her lips and tickling the taut skin at his belly with her tongue.

He was breathing hard and his eyes were closed. He tangled his fingers in her hair as she moved her head over his body and drove him wild with her kisses. It was a sweet torture he would gladly die of, but no such relief was in sight, and so, unable to bear the agony of her intimate kisses, he grasped her by the shoulders and pulled her head back up to his.

He kissed her hard. She felt his hands seek the soft silk of her breasts, the firmness of her nipples straining against his palms. When his fingers moved over her belly to that place that burned like a torch, she thought she would go up in flames.

Fingers still probing and caressing, he lowered her onto the bed beneath him, his body half covering hers. Kit felt the throb of need from deep within her. She writhed under him, her mouth fused to his, her own hands moving with more urgency than before. She twisted provocatively against him, her mouth hot and persuasive under his, inviting him to possess her fully.

In the end they both abandoned any attempt to go slowly as they were caught up in a whirlwind of unstoppable passion. They clung to each other, tumbling about the twisted sheets in a tangle of arms and legs. He thrust into her, and the thrill of her release triggered his own.

She could feel the blood flowing through his veins. His need was hers. Her desire was his. Interwoven, body and mind, hearts aflame in a single blaze of passion, they drove each other higher and higher. It was the thrill of the moment, the desperate need that transcended the moment, and the setting on fire of two hearts.

The midnight heat evaporated the perspiration from their bodies, and the cadence of their breathing gradually returned to normal as they lay in bed, side by side. A ribbon of moonlight snaked across their bodies from one of the tall windows. In a corner of the loft the glow of a street lamp through the window cast a yellow luminance over the walls and furnishings. The low hum of the central air conditioning unit was steady and reassuring, and Kit felt strangely content in the wake of their lovemaking.

Hank, too, was relaxed. He lay on his back, staring up at the high ceiling. He wondered fleetingly what time it was. Sadly, he thought that in a few hours it would be dawn, and with the new day, he'd be gone.

"Hank?"

Kit's soft voice chased away the uncertainty of tomorrow. He looked down at the woman nestled in the crook of his arm, her dark hair spread against his shoulder, and murmured, "Hmm?"

She looked up at him with sleepy green eyes. "What's Hank short for?"

He knew by her question that the uncertainty of tomorrow was far from Kit's mind as well. Chuckling softly, he said, "Henry."

"Mmm, that's what I thought." She snuggled deeper in his embrace, pressing her slender body closer to his. Her eyelids fluttered with sleepiness. "I like Hank. It suits you better," she mumbled, then fell asleep.

But Hank remembered telling her the same thing about her name once. He pulled her closer to him, feeling so much a part of her that it scared him. He was a fool for wanting her so much. To want only meant he could lose, and he'd been through that already. As he lay there the tension came creeping back, troubling him even after he fell asleep. It darkened his dreams, making him remember things he wanted to forget. Tonight, as it had repeatedly in the past, the nightmare returned.

The piebald. Always it began and ended with the piebald stallion. Hank would never forget the first time he saw him. It was the first summer they'd brought the wild mustangs in for adoption. There were about fifty of them, mostly mares and foals. Hank had to blink his eyes to be sure the horse was really there, but sure enough, there he was, moving from light to shadow, the most incredible little colt he'd ever seen. He moved friskily around the corral, that incredible coloring of white against black acting as both camouflage and screaming declaration. But it was more than the colt's satanic coloring that captured Hank's fancy. Those pink-rimmed eyes seemed always to be watching and waiting; for what, Hank never did know. He had plans for that colt. This one he'd adopt himself. At breaking time, he decided, it would be his legs that straddled the yearling's girth. It would be his hands that would tame it.

The winter was a bad one. During one particularly harsh blizzard, which dumped six feet of snow on the ground, several of Hank's horses broke loose and got lost on the range. The piebald colt was among them. When the deep snows melted, later that spring, Hank rode solemnly over the range and shuddered when he found their carcasses—all except for the colt. The coyotes must have taken him, he figured.

The raids in the middle of the night began several years later. The first happened while Hank was in Denver one summer, competing. Word reached him late that night at his motel. Some of his best brood mares had been stolen from the corral. But the news was far worse than that. Beth, Hank's wife, had somehow gotten in the path of the stampeding horses and been trampled to death beneath them.

No one knew who'd stolen the horses, or why. In the wake of Beth's death, it didn't seem to matter. Several weeks later, however, something happened that changed the course of Hank's life even more dramatically.

He awoke suddenly one night out of a fitful sleep, eyes snapping open, fully alert. He got out of bed and went to the window, where from the second story he had a clear view of the brood mares' corral. What Hank saw amazed him.

A lone horse circled the outside of the corral at a measured gait, as if assessing its contents. With the moon behind a cloud, Hank couldn't see him clearly. The horse's actions, however, were unmistakable. It approached the corral, turned its rear to it, and kicked down the top post of a section of fence. In one fluid leap, the animal sprang over the downed fence into the corral. As noiseless as the wind, he moved among the herd, singling out certain mares and herding them out of the corral. He waited until the last one was out. Then he rose on his hind legs, front hooves thrashing the black night. In that moment, the moon reappeared from behind the cloud.

The moonlight struck the horse's coat, illuminating the pattern of black and white. Instant recognition seared Hank's brain. His blood pumped with outrage. He raced to the corral in his underwear, rifle in hand, crying, "You! It was you who killed her!" Blinded by his own rage, he fired at the stallion. Another time, with a cooler head, he would have hit him, but the stallion got away.

Hank did everything he could think of to catch him after that. He lay on his belly in the grass for many sleepless nights, hoping to catch the beast in the act of stealing his herd. He set traps. But the stallion was a clever son of Satan and managed to elude Hank at every turn.

The game of cat and mouse went on year after year, and Hank's dream was always the same: Hank heard the sound of the gunshot and a scream. He could never be certain whether it was Beth's or his.

* * *

"Hank! Hank!" Heart pounding, Kit shook him. "Wake up! Hank! It's a dream!"

He awoke from the nightmare in a feverish sweat. His hold on Kit was so fierce it bruised her arm, but Hank was oblivious to the strength of his fingers. She winced from the pain but kept talking to him. "It's all right," she kept telling him. "You're awake now. It was only a dream." She fought to keep her voice calm, but the glassy look in her wide eyes signaled her own alarm. "Try to relax," she said quietly. "I'm here."

The sheet was soaking wet. He felt himself gasping for air, his breath coming from his heaving chest in rapid bursts. Despite the comfortable temperature of the room, he felt cold. He could feel the warmth of Kit's skin beside him and heard her calm, quiet words. Closing his eyes, he muttered an epithet and dropped back down beside her.

She watched him for a few moments, then said, "I'll get you some water."

"No!" His hand shot out to grip her forearm tightly. "Don't go. Stay."

"Yes," she assured him. "Yes, I'll stay."

She sat beside him on the bed, reassuring him with her presence while his breathing slackened and he regained a bit of his composure. At length she asked quietly, "Feeling better?"

"Yeah. Thanks." His voice was calmer now, not filled with the terrible anxiety of minutes ago. He sat up and said, "I'll take that drink now, and make it something stronger than water, okay?"

She returned in minutes with a glass of Scotch, which she placed in his hand. He took a sip, then another. She waited until he'd taken a couple more, then touched him lightly on the shoulder. "Hank, tell me about it."

He couldn't. Not now. Not yet. But even as the refusal formed on his lips, the pressure of Kit's fingers increased on his shoulder. "You'll feel better if you let it out," she coaxed. "Nothing gets better if you keep it in."

And he was a pro at keeping it in, he thought. All these years he'd hidden it, refusing to speak about it, not letting others speak about it to him, even refusing to acknowledge it to himself. He didn't know whether it was the quiet understanding in her eyes, the soft reassurance of her voice or the touch of her hand on him, telling him that he wasn't alone, that made him begin to talk. In the quiet of the night, in a loft in lower Manhattan, far from where it had all begun, he told her about that terrible night seven years before, about Beth and the piebald stallion.

Kit closed her eyes in anguish. "Oh, Hank, I'm so sorry."

Hank braced himself for a flood of sympathy. But when she opened her eyes and looked at him, he realized it wasn't sympathy she was offering; it was understanding.

Now she knew, or thought she knew, why he'd stopped competing. "You must have loved her very much," she murmured.

"We were..." He shrugged. "Comfortable with each other, I guess. But I didn't stop competing out of grief over my dead wife. Grief doesn't last that long. Somehow you pick up the pieces and go on. But guilt... guilt is different. It eats away at you and never goes away."

"Guilt?" Suddenly she understood. "Hank, surely you don't blame yourself for her death!"

"If only I'd been there instead of off competing in Denver," he argued.

She searched his face for a sign that it was a joke. A grim joke, to be sure, but a joke nonetheless. The hard, cold look of self-damning in his eyes made Kit shudder. "It doesn't make sense to blame yourself. You weren't even there. And if you had been, who's to say you could have done anything? What was she doing out there in the middle of the night, anyway?''

It was a question Hank had asked himself a hundred times. Any number of answers came to mind, but the one that weighed heaviest in his thoughts was the possibility that there had been another man. Prior to the accident he'd never had any reason to question Beth's fidelity, and even now a part of him knew it couldn't be true. Still, the question lingered.

"I don't know," he said. "And I never will."

"Hank," Kit urged him, "put it to rest."

"I'm trying to, Kit. That's why I've started competing again. Maybe this way I can get rid of the guilt. Maybe I can convince myself that I wasn't really to blame for Beth's death."

"And the stallion?"

His eyes turned dark and filled with cold anger and frustration. "Like I've said before, he and I have a score to settle."

"But Hank—"

"Don't argue with me, Kit," he growled, his words cutting across hers. "Whether you like it or not, it's something I have to do. Whether it makes sense or not doesn't matter. It's just the way it is. Hell, nothing makes sense anymore. Like what the hell she was *doing* out there. And why, after that first raid, I never found a trace of the stallion's tracks. But it was him. It had to be. Those mares didn't just walk off by themselves—that's for sure."

He swallowed the last of the Scotch in the glass and ran a hand through his hair, sweeping loose strands from his eyes. He lifted his head to look at her. "Now you know what you're up against. And if you don't want to come back to Wyoming with me, I'll understand."

He got up and walked naked to the bathroom, where he bent over the sink and splashed his face with cold water. The mattress sagged from his weight when he returned to the bed. He reached for her.

"Hank—" she began.

"Not now. Tell me later. In the morning. Right now I want to make love to you."

Once again their bodies fused as he transferred his need to her, and she her desire to him, until they were one.

When he awoke the next morning, he felt for her, but she wasn't there. A sense of panic came over him. He lay still, trying to remember what he might have done or said to drive her away. Then he remembered the dream and telling her of it, and he shuddered. Suddenly, he became aware of a sound, a gentle humming, and he turned his head. It was Kit, sitting at the vanity, brushing her hair. Hank shuddered again, this time with relief.

She spotted his reflection in the mirror and turned to smile at him over her shoulder. "Hi, sleepyhead," she said. "You'd better hurry up and get into that shower. Our flight leaves in two hours."

He sat up in bed and looked at her, his hair all tousled from sleep. He was sure he hadn't heard her correctly. "*Our* flight?"

Kit had been up for a couple of hours. She'd spent much of that time just watching him sleep. Then she'd made the necessary phone calls to Sid Burns at the magazine, to a friend to ask that her plants be watered, and to her mother, to say she'd be in touch. In answer to Hank's vocal disbelief, she replied, "Of course."

He laughed, still not entirely convinced that he wasn't dreaming. But then he saw her bags, all packed and waiting by the door, and Hank knew that Kit had made her decision.

Chapter 10

They flew directly to Cheyenne and caught a connecting flight to Casper. From there they drove north and west, spending the night en route in a motel room. They arrived in Cody just as the streets were filling up and events were getting under way.

There was good reason for the rodeo's popularity. For one thing, the sport and its participants carried with them appealing shades of the Old West. Another was the sheer excitement and danger of it. Demanding superb timing, stamina and balance, it was a mixture of Buffalo Bill showmanship and plain old guts.

Something was going on in every corral and arena amid the pageantry. There were trick riding and fancy roping, barrel racing and team riding. The air was filled with the smell of horseflesh and the aroma of hot dogs and cotton candy. It crackled with tension as children raced about in the stands and the old-timers reminisced about their own glory days. The newcomers tried to appear cool and collected while they sweated under their collars. The veterans looked over the stock in preparation for the day of competition ahead. Music blared from a brass band, while over the loudspeaker a voice welcomed the visitors with a twang and announced the day's activities. Horses whinnied and calves bawled. Steers protested loudly, and big bulls sent warning snorts from their nostrils and pawed the ground in their pens.

It seemed impossible that in a crowd of ten thousand Pete would find them, but he did. He raced up to them, his face flushed with relief.

"Hank! I was beginning to think ya wouldn't make it!" He smiled at Kit and said, "Hi, Missy, it's good to see ya again." But business was business, and there wasn't time for small talk. Turning quickly back to Hank, he said, "They're getting ready to draw for the saddle bronc competition."

Hank glanced at Kit. His look was apologetic despite the edge of urgency in his voice. "I'd better get over there."

"Go on," she urged. "I have to check my equipment anyway."

But his eyes refused to retreat from her lovely face, and he was reluctant to give up his hold of her hand. "I'll be back as soon as I can," he said, but still he lagged at her side.

Pete watched the silent exchange of looks and experienced a few awkward and anxious moments waiting for Hank to tear his gaze away and sprint off into the crowd.

When he was gone, Kit delved into her bag and took out her camera to get everything ready. She looked back up to find a telling grin on Pete's face.

"I knew the minute I saw you that you'd be good for him," he said to her.

She accepted his prophecy with no embarrassment and said matter-of-factly, "I may be good for him, but sometimes, Pete, I wonder whether he's good for me."

"It ain't easy loving Hank, that's for sure," Pete agreed. "I've had a lot of practice at it. Why, I love that boy like he was my own son." He paused and added slyly, "I guess that's why I recognize it when somebody else loves him, too."

She cocked her head to one side and studied him thoughtfully. "You're a sly old fox, you know that?"

"Sometimes," he said, "ya gotta be."

Hank returned shortly after that and Pete asked anxiously, "What'd ya get?"

"Trouble," Hank replied.

Kit's face registered concern. "Hank, are you in some kind of trouble?"

He laughed. The sound of it was rich and vibrant and reassuring, and his blue eyes sparkled with good humor. "No. That's the name of the horse I drew."

Kit laughed at her own foolishness. "When do you ride?"

"I'm up third. Come on. Let's go have a look." He took her by the hand and the three of them went behind the scenes, where two men were loading a rangy-looking horse into one of the chutes.

Peering from a safe distance through the chute's wooden slats, Hank asked, "Well? What do you think?"

Kit looked disbelievingly at the buckskin horse in the chute. "That's Trouble?"

"He doesn't look like much, does he?"

She looked from Hank to Pete and back again to see if they were pulling her leg. Sure, she'd been raised on a farm, but she was a novice when it came to judging mustangs. She eyed the horse again, saying with uncertainty, "I don't know. He's kind of skinny. It seems to me he's got a long way to go to live up to his name."

Gesturing to the camera hanging from a strap around her neck, Hank said, "Is there film in that thing?"

"Yes. I loaded it while you were drawing Mr. Vicious over there." She jerked a thumb at the buckskin.

"Just have it ready," Hank advised her.

"Oh, I get it," said Kit, understanding, or at least thinking she did. "You're sure to get an easy win on a horse like that, is that it?"

The prospect of an easy win wasn't altogether unappealing to Hank, but to him an easy win came not from riding a lackluster horse; it came from beating lousy competition. He rolled his eyes and said to Pete, "Take this woman out front and see that she gets a good spot. Then do me a favor, would you, and teach her a few things about saddle bronc riding."

Pete cackled with laughter. "I think she's about to learn."

Kit and Pete found a spot along the fence and watched the first two riders. One made the ten-second ride, but the horse he'd drawn hadn't put up much of a fight. The other man hit the ground on the seat of his pants.

The loudspeaker boomed. "Hank Reardon aboard Trouble out of chute number three!"

The crowd went suddenly quiet. Those who'd been busy earlier, buying popcorn and talking, sat still in their seats in the stands, eyes glued to the arena.

Hank was oblivious to the crowd as he climbed down into the chute and seated himself in the saddle. It was a modified stock saddle, smaller and without a horn. The rein was merely a rope attached to the horse's halter. When Hank was seated, a bucking strap was tightened around the horse's flank to encourage its action. Carefully Hank wrapped the rope around one gloved hand, flexing his fingers to achieve the most secure grip he could. He waited a moment, nervously flicking his tongue over his lips, before he gave the signal for the gate to be opened. As soon as daylight appeared, Hank put his spurs to the buckskin's shoulders as required by the judges and the animal burst out of the chute.

The crowd raised a thunderous roar. To those who watched with experienced eyes it was poetry in motion, but to Kit, who watched through the lens of the camera, it was a heart-stopping surprise.

The lean little buckskin twisted and lurched with a frenzy, not only living up to its name but exceeding it. With an extraordinary display of balance, Hank clung bravely to the horse's back, holding on with one hand. The actual ride seemed to Kit an eternity. The easy win she'd been expecting had turned into a grueling battle, and she realized now what Hank had meant about learning about saddle bronc riding. She would remember in the future never to judge a horse by its looks.

The sound of the buzzer tripped a mechanism inside her, enabling her to breathe freely again. A pickup man galloped alongside the bucking horse to help Hank off. Hank slid to the ground like rainfall. He retrieved his hat, which he'd lost during the ride, and beat at the dust on his pants with it as he strode from the arena to the shouts and cheers of the crowd.

When news broke over the loudspeaker that Hank had scored first in the saddle bronc competition, Kit's heart burst with pride. He raced to her side to claim a swift but thorough victory kiss before dashing off for the next event.

The calf-roping competition was next. The calf was given several seconds' head start down the arena before Hank and Dakota galloped out of the gate in pursuit. The big chestnut's hooves thundered over the ground while Hank twirled his lasso in the air. With a rapid movement the rope sailed forward and landed cleanly around the calf's neck. In one motion Hank secured the other end of the rope around his saddle horn, threw himself to the ground and raced toward the calf. Dakota, trained to step back at the precise moment to keep the rope taut, did his job with equal skill. The calf restrained, Hank flipped it onto its side and tied three of its legs together with a short length of rope that he'd been holding in his teeth. Speed was the deciding factor, and Hank raced against the clock now as he secured the bawling calf and stood back for the required five seconds to make sure the calf didn't slip out of its ties.

The buzzer sounded, and the loudspeaker came alive with Hank's time. Another cheer went up from the stands for the crowd's favorite, but only when the final man had competed and Hank's time proved to be the fastest was the favorite also recognized as the best.

Hank's handsome face was streaked with sweat, but Kit saw that his blue eyes were sparkling with vitality when he rejoined her and Pete during a brief pause between events. The bandanna around his neck was soaked with perspiration. His shirt was sticking to his back and ringed with wetness. He drank beer from a can. Tilting his hat back on his head, he held the cold can to his forehead for relief from the July sun and the heat of competition.

Hank's pulse was already racing, but the sight of Kit, green eyes aglow with pride, made it pound. Eagerly he asked her, "What'd you think?"

She beamed at him, her joy evident. "I think you've got Cody all wrapped up.'

He shrugged and tried to look noncommittal, although even he could sense victory close at hand. "The competition's not too stiff," he offered.

"You're too modest," she told him.

"Yeah, well I might not be if Quint were here." He turned to Pete and asked, "Where is he, anyway?"

"Beats me. Maybe he just got so cocky he figured he'd pass up Cody and save it all for Cheyenne. A good showing at Cheyenne this year could mean that he turns pro next year," Pete replied.

"I think you're right," said Kit. "The day we drove out to the Lazy J, he told me he was saving his money to turn pro."

Hank didn't care to be reminded of Quint and Kit together and was sorry he'd even brought up the subject. In a disgruntled tone he said, "You don't buy your way to the professional circuit; you *ride* your way into it. If Quint was smart, he'd have been here today competing with the rest of us." What Hank didn't say was that much as he disliked Quint, the other man's presence here in Cody today would have made things a lot more exciting. Quint was good; there was no question about it. Beating a mediocre rider was one thing, but beating a good one was what it was all about.

Kit was determined that nothing would mar the excitement of this perfect day, not even Quint. Even she was beginning to believe that things might turn out okay between herself and Hank. All too soon it was time to say goodbye to him again. A desperate kiss, a flicker of tongues and a lingering of lips, and Hank was off for the next round of competition.

She saw little of him during the next few hours, but she had her work to do, and today it was sublime. Hank's handsome face filled the viewfinder of her camera. He looked rugged and implacable. She caught the fluidity of his muscles in action, the tension in his expression as he watched the others compete, the flash of triumph in his blue eyes each time he was proclaimed winner of an event.

While Kit was busy with her work, Hank was doing his. Yet in spite of the tension of competition and the rigors of riding, invariably he would search for her in the crowd, and she'd be there in the background, watching and waiting. When the bull-riding event was announced, however, he noticed the look of pride in her eyes change to fear.

Even Pete looked worried when he heard that the bulls were up next. There was something about those big hump-backed beasts that set even Hank's own hair on end. Bull riding, he knew, was a particularly perilous sport. A bull would chase and gore an unseated man, as he'd found out once already. Others fared much worse. So, when he returned to announce his draw, Pete grasped him by the arm and asked anxiously, "Who'd ya get?"

Soberly, Hank replied, "Dynamite."

Pete whistled softly through his teeth. "You've got your work cut out for ya. But look at it this way. It coulda been Old Number Seven. He's here today, you know."

Hank grimaced. "I know. Bill Peterson drew him."

Pete shook his head sadly and said, "Old Number Seven'll make short work of Bill."

"Yeah," Hank agreed, "and Bill knows it." He turned to Kit, realizing that their talk might have been upsetting her. "How are you doing?"

"Just fine," she answered, but Hank didn't think she sounded very convincing. He read the fear in her eyes and heard the uncertainty in her voice. He put his arm around her waist and drew her close to him. Softly he urged her, "Don't go weak on me now, Kit."

She looked into his earnest blue eyes and hesitated. "It's just that..." She grasped his arm and squeezed the taut muscles beneath her fingers. "Oh, Hank, please be careful," she begged.

She felt so slender and fragile in his arm, so breakable in the face of something she didn't understand, and it was his turn to be the one who offered support and encouragement. "Don't worry," he said. "I have two good reasons to be careful. I'm looking at one of them right now."

She felt the subtle tensing of the muscles in his arm around her waist. "And the other?" she asked.

Hank's smile stretched into a grin. He leaned closer and confided, "I have this thing about staying alive."

She sent him off with a quick kiss and the thumbs-up sign, glanced apprehensively at Pete and took her place by the fence, camera ready.

Dynamite proved to be as explosive as his name. Using only one hand, Hank attempted to stay on while the angry bull twisted and turned in his efforts to be rid of his rider. Hank's skill saw him through to the buzzer, but he'd have been the first to admit that while it was mostly skill, it was also a lot of luck that got him safely through.

The next rider wasn't so lucky. Midway through his ride on Old Number Seven, an erratic twist sent him to the ground, facedown in the dirt. The bull rushed forward and headed for the fallen rider. With its horns it dealt the man a vicious blow before the rodeo clowns could divert its attention long enough for several men to hurry into the arena and carry the wounded man out.

From where Hank watched by the fence, still breathing heavily from his own ride, he cursed and dashed off into the crowd. He returned ten minutes later to report to Kit and Pete that in spite of a fractured hip and some stitches, the man would be all right.

Kit's face reflected relief that flooded through her. Thank goodness the man wasn't dead. But it wasn't easy for her to dismiss the thought that it could have been Hank.

The day came at last to a close. It had been a long and exhausting experience for Kit, filled with the thrill of victory and the heart-stopping fear that accompanied this dangerous sport. She packed her camera away, tagged the rolls of film she'd taken and settled back with a cold drink while Pete loaded Dakota into the trailer and Hank got his gear together. Dusk was descending when the three of them departed, Pete in his car with Dakota in tow, Hank and Kit in the car they'd rented in Casper. They had agreed that Pete would go on ahead and get Dakota settled. In three days Hank and Kit would meet him in Casper, where the Central Wyoming Fair and Rodeo would just be starting up.

That night Hank and Kit stopped at a motel along the way. The man behind the counter looked askance at them, no doubt noticing the absence of baggage and their request for one room. But Hank and Kit didn't care—all that mattered to them was each other. Hank's blood still raced from the excitement of the day's victories, but even they were trivial compared with the victory that awaited in Kit's arms. He could barely control his already racing emotions, and no sooner had they closed the door to their room than he enclosed her quickly in his embrace and began to take fierce possession of her.

The feel of her under his hands, combined with the scent of her, drove him wild. He kissed her hungrily, unable to get enough of her sweet taste. Soft skin, warm lips, an alluring body—many women had those things. But none had this woman's essence. To him her skin was softer, her breasts lovelier, her kisses more arousing than any other woman's. He gazed at her, marveling at the beauty of the naked body beneath his. Just looking at her was enough to make him want her. Tonight it would not be over quickly. He would need hours of her, of filling her up with his own. Hours to quench his thirst.

Kit moved beneath him, her own desire pounding a fiery demand. She, too, was caught up in the excitement of the day and the incredible heat of the moment. She trembled to think how precious his life was to her. Having watched him risk it all day, knowing how closely danger lay all about men in his profession, she clung to him even more desperately, wanting him every bit as much as he wanted her.

"Hank," she pleaded, her breath warm in his ear. There was no need to say more; he felt her need, heard in her breathless tone that same urgent arousal that drove him to a frenzy.

They tumbled about in the twisted sheets, a tangle of arms and legs. Her mouth was hot and persuasive under his, inviting him further, deeper, faster. In the end, abandoning any foolish notion he'd had to go slowly, he thrust into her. The tension that had plagued him all day uncoiled when she was all around him like this, drawing him into her velvety softness and making him think of nothing but the exquisite torture of release.

His release triggered hers, and together they crested a peak of pleasure and intimacy that left them breathless and exhilarated.

Wrapped in the drowsy contentment of their lovemaking, they drifted off to sleep, each in a private dream but irrevocably a part of the other.

They arrived at the fair in Casper three days later, as planned. They met Pete at the agreed-upon place and time, but instead of the enthusiastic greeting they'd expected, the older man was uncharacteristically subdued. When Hank questioned him on his strange behavior, Pete just shrugged and said, "You know how it is, Hank. After this run, it's Cheyenne. I'm just nervous, that's all."

Hank looked at him skeptically. "What's the matter, Pete? Afraid I won't make it?"

"Hell no, Hank. If you don't make it, hey, there's always next year to go for the championship. I just mean that Cheyenne's the biggie, and this here fair and rodeo is sort of the lead-in to that. The records show that whoever scores big here usually takes Cheyenne, too. You know that, Hank."

Hank put a hand on Pete's shoulder and squeezed it with affection. "Yeah? Well, I also know that records were meant to be broken, Pete. Even mine. Being champion? Sure, that matters to me. But it's more than that. Do you realize that if I score enough points here in the next couple of days and even do moderately at Cheyenne, I could win enough money to buy some stock and fix up the Chaparral? Maybe it's time for somebody else to be champion. Me, I just need to get by."

"Sure, Hank. Sure, I understand."

They turned and walked to the registration area, where Hank signed his name in the book. As always, he scanned the page to see what other names were on it. Bill Paterson's wasn't, but he recognized most of the others. His eyes narrowed at the sight of one name in particular: Dan Quint.

Hank looked back up at Pete with a wry expression on his face. "Well, look who's here. Is that what this is all about?"

"Whaddaya mean, Hank?"

"I mean Quint is here today. Is that what you're worried about?"

Pete fidgeted under the scrutiny of those blue eyes. "Quint *is* good," he admitted.

Hank's eyes hardened. "Then I've got my work cut out for me, don't I?" He looked at Kit. "Your readers ought to love this," he said with thick sarcasm. "Former rodeo champion loses in comeback attempt to brilliant young newcomer. Maybe you'd better take a few rolls of Quint. Pete here seems to think he's worth watching."

He stalked off, uttering a muffled oath, leaving Kit and Pete shaking their heads. Pete winced. "I didn't mean to upset him like that."

Kit patted his arm reassuringly. "That's all right, Pete. Maybe he needs to be a little angry today." Anger, she knew, could be a big motivator at times. With Quint's presence obviously affecting Hank, his anger might be just the thing to give him the edge.

The competition did indeed come down to the two of them. As the afternoon heated up, so did the tension in the air. Quint put on some incredible performances to match Hank's, and by late afternoon the two men were running neck and neck.

The final rounds were just getting under way. The effects of the grueling competition showed on Hank. Kit noted that his clothes were dusty, his shirt torn at the elbow from a nasty spill he'd taken from the bare back of a bucking horse. His face was taut with emotion, his eyes bright with the anger that had gotten him through this day. Kit, too, felt the strain. She had photographed the action, drawing it into sharp focus through the lens of the camera and feeling almost a part of it. The heart-racing excitement flushed her face and left her muscles tense, her nerves on edge. She observed that Pete continued to be subdued. At times he seemed to be oblivious to the action. Something was obviously on his mind, she thought.

The steer wrestling event was the last for the day. When Hank had gone off to get ready for it, Pete turned to Kit and said, "Hang around, Kit, would ya? I think Hank might need to be with you after this one."

She looked at him quizzically. "Pete, is something wrong? You've been acting funny all day. I don't understand it."

He shook his head solemnly and predicted, "You will."

Despite Pete's tone of foreboding, it was hard not to get caught up all over again in the excitement from the arena. Quint came out first, dazzling the crowd with his skill and scoring high. Kit captured some of it on film, just as she did the crowd and the animals, all to serve as background to her photo essay on Hank. She worked smoothly and professionally to get the shots. But when Hank came galloping out of the gate astride Dakota, her emotions took over. She yelled and cheered with the rest of them as he took out after the steer. Another rider—a hazer, Kit learned he was called—raced on the other side to keep the steer running straight. When Dakota drew level with the steer, Hank flung himself from the saddle. He grabbed the steer by the horns, locked his boots in the dirt to get a firm grip and, using incredible power, brought the steer to the ground on its side.

In a matter of seconds it was over. When the loudspeaker announced that Hank had broken his own record, the place went wild.

He returned with triumph stamped all over his face. He wound a strong arm, whose muscles were still heated with energy, around Kit and pulled her close. He kissed her on the mouth, not caring who was watching, telling her and anybody else that he was a force to be reckoned with.

Hank hoped that from somewhere in the crowd Dan Quint was watching. You can have the damned championship, Hank told the other man in the privacy of his mind.

This is something you'll never take away from me. He tightened his embrace and kissed Kit harder.

They were both breathless when he released her at last. Kit's blood quickened in anticipation of the night's love-making. It would be fast and hard and dangerous, to match his mood.

Nothing, it seemed, could break the incredible tension between them or quell the fire. Nothing, that is, except for Pete, whose behavior cast a pall over the triumph of the day.

"Come on, Pete," Hank said, attempting to cajole his friend out of his mood. "All right, so I didn't win them all today, but I put on a damned good show. I'm also tied with Quint for first place. You aren't still worried about that, are you?"

Kit, who recalled Pete's request that she hang around, looked apprehensively at the older man.

Pete grew uncomfortable beneath her questioning stare and Hank's demanding one. He knew he couldn't avoid it any longer. He took a deep breath, then said, "Hank, there's something I've been meaning to tell ya."

"Tell it to me later, over dinner." Hank laughed. He was trying hard not to let Pete's behavior bother him, though something deep down inside him had suddenly come alert. "All this activity's given me an appetite. What I want to do right now is shower and change my clothes and sink my teeth into a thick T-bone steak."

"Uh, no, Hank, this can't wait."

Hank let the pretense go and looked him straight in the eye. "All right, Pete, what's up?"

Holding it in had been hard enough, but now that he'd been directly asked, Pete had no choice but to answer. "It's happened again, Hank."

At first Hank didn't comprehend. A question formed in his eyes that turned to slow recognition, wiping the smile from his face and replacing it with a cold and angry look. He knew exactly what Pete meant and demanded, "When?"

"A couple of nights ago."

"How many did he get?"

With difficulty, Pete answered, "Six."

Hank laughed. It was a bitter sound from deep inside his throat. "Six," he scoffed. "Precisely half my stock of brood mares."

Kit closed her eyes in anguish when she realized what they were talking about. Poor Hank. For the stallion to have stolen six of his remaining brood mares must have been a hard blow for him to take. She saw his muscles stiffen and knew he was fighting desperately to maintain control. She heard him ask Pete in a taut voice, "When did you find out about it?"

Pete hesitated. "This morning. Ramon called to tell me."

But Hank heard nothing about Ramon. His mind seized upon something else. "This morning?" he exclaimed. "And you're just telling me about it *now*?"

"I was gonna tell ya, Hank. Honest."

"When? When you were sure every damned event had been won? Your confidence in me is inspiring, Pete. Were you afraid I wouldn't finish what I'd started if I'd have known about the stallion?"

Kit stepped forward in Pete's defense. "Hank, that's not fair. Pete was only doing what he felt was best. Weren't you, Pete?" It must have been difficult for Pete to have kept his secret for so long. She sympathized with him for having to be the one to tell Hank.

"Really, Hank," Pete was saying. "I know how much it means for ya to win these events. I also know how stubborn y'are over that horse."

"You're damned right I am," Hank shot back. "Nothing's more important than that."

At that remark, Kit felt as if she'd been struck. When he heard Kit's gasp, Hank realized instantly what he'd said. "Kit, I didn't mean it the way it sounded."

He may have spoken impulsively, but Kit sensed he had spoken the truth. Bitterly she responded, "You could've fooled me."

"Please try to understand," he urged her.

Flippantly she told him, "Oh, I understand perfectly."

"No, you don't, dammit!" Hank yelled, startling her by the force of his reaction. "It's important for me to catch him. You know that!"

Kit gritted her teeth. How could a man be so stubborn? "This is important, too," she argued. "Right here. Right now. Not the stallion. The stallion will be there. He can wait. This can't." He said nothing, but she saw the muscles in his jaw tense, proof that much was going on inside him.

Hank felt trapped; had he escaped the bull's rage only to be speared on the horns of a dilemma? Should he stay here as Kit was suggesting and finish up the commitment he'd made to himself? Or should he head for the Chaparral and go after the stallion and risk losing it all—the stallion, the competition...and Kit? There was no question but that she filled in him a need that went deep. Now that he'd had a taste of it, could he ever live without it again? The lure of the stallion was strong, but Kit was right; the horse would be there when Hank got back. Then he'd go after the beast with everything he had. That son of the devil wouldn't elude him this time.

Kit watched as a look of cold resolution came over Hank's face, hardening his features and icing up his eyes. Finally he spoke. "You're right. First this, *then* him."

With Pete she watched him stalk off, knowing from Hank's tone of voice that whatever victory Hank had won in the day's battles at the rodeo was overshadowed by the desire for vengeance that ran as thick as ever in his blood.

Chapter 11

Cheyenne, a peaceful, prosperous community in the southeastern corner of the state, had been known as Hell on Wheels in the days of the Old West. That spirit was revived once a year, during the last week of July, at Cheyenne Frontier Days.

At Frontier Park, the nation's top cowboys called on all their skill and strength and daring to compete against one another in the big daddy of them all. Cheyenne's rodeo was one of the longest-running in the country. Having begun back in 1897, it was steeped in tradition. There were parades and free chuck-wagon breakfasts, where more than ten thousand people gathered outdoors on bales of straw for flapjacks, ham and coffee. It also ranked first in prize money; whoever won at Cheyenne went home ten thousand dollars richer.

The atmosphere in Cheyenne was one of tension. There was a sense of profound expectancy in the summer air, as if something wonderful and terrible were about to happen.

Hank had been competing with a vengeance since he'd learned of the latest theft of his horses. He'd finished up in Casper tied with Quint in points. They'd left Casper without ceremony, Pete having driven on ahead to Cheyenne with Dakota in tow while Hank and Kit followed at their own pace. At night he'd made love to her without his usual tenderness, seeking to sate his powerful hunger for her, hoping to drown in her passion and somehow forget about the stallion's latest conquest. But it was always there in the morning when he awoke.

Kit knew how much this theft was affecting Hank, but he'd cut her off whenever she'd tried to bring it up. It had been a tense ride to Cheyenne. They'd been there now for three days, and the competition had helped temper Hank's anger somewhat. The physical exercise provided a release for his heated emotions. Nevertheless, it was obvious that he was still bothered, for while he'd won the first round of the saddle bronc competition, he'd turned in a bad time in calf-roping, an event he usually won hands down.

As luck would have it, someone else noticed Hank's obvious distraction and was quick to turn it to his own advantage.

"Gee, that's too bad, Reardon," a familiar voice drawled behind Hank after he returned from his disappointing time in the calf-roping event. He turned slowly and looked over his shoulder. There was Quint with a big grin on his face.

The distance Quint had been keeping between himself and Hank in Casper and now in Cheyenne started to lessen as Hank began to lose in some events. "You're riding like a man with something on his mind," Quint observed. "Let me guess. I'll bet that old stallion came back and stole more of your mares."

Hank wasn't surprised that Quint knew. A man's misfortunes, like a bad reputation, preceded him. "What's it to you?" he asked.

Kit, watching, noticed that his face had paled in anger and his fists were clenched at his sides.

"It ain't nothing to me if you lose. I just know what it's like to be on the back of an angry bull. It takes hard concentration to stay up there, 'cause you know you're a lot safer on his back than you are on the ground. It would be a shame if he downed you. Dangerous, too."

Hank snorted derisively at Quint's attempt to unnerve him. "Thanks for the advice, but I've been at this a long time. I've been up on their backs and down on the ground and been caught midair in between, and I've always come out all right."

Quint conceded with a shrug, admitting, "I've learned a few things myself from watching you ride. Still, it's rough out there. The arena's no place to be thinking about anything else." His eyes shifted tellingly to Kit before he turned and walked off.

Like most predators, Kit reflected, Quint was quick to sense another's weakness and go for it. In Hank's case, it was his obvious preoccupation with the stolen horses. But it was easy for her to see through Quint, and as soon as he was gone, she grabbed Hank by the arm and said, "Don't listen to him. He's just trying to upset you." There could be no denying that Quint had succeeded in upsetting *her*, for she knew full well that the bull-riding event was up next. And despite her dislike of Quint, she had to admit he'd been right. Hank could afford no distractions.

As the days went by, Hank did his best not to let Quint's remarks—made out of jealousy, he knew—stoke the fire of an already inflamed anger. He tried hard to concentrate on what he was there to do. The rides were rough and the competition was stiffer than ever, but through sheer force of will, grit and determination, he managed to maintain his place in the standings.

By the next to the last day, the field of finalists had been narrowed down to only a few, Hank and Quint among them. Quint did everything possible to pull ahead of Hank, but Hank fought tenaciously to hang on to his slender lead. The last event of the day would be the bull riding, and the final rounds would take place the following day.

Hank was tense and on edge as he strode before the judges to make his draw. He looked down at the slip of paper in his hand. Something inside him went cold. The bull he had drawn didn't have a real name, only a number, and that number was seven.

Kit felt the cold, clammy fingers of fear at her throat when Hank told her the news. She tried to hide her anxiety from him, putting up a brave front, flashing him a pretty smile, trying hard for his sake. But she clung to him a little too long and kissed him a little too urgently when it was time for him to ride. His hands were strong and firm at her shoulders when he held her at arm's length and said, "Don't worry, green eyes. Everything's going to be all right."

Managing a stiff nod, she sent him off.

The stolen horses, Quint, none of it mattered to Hank right now as he climbed to the top of the chute. He didn't need Quint to tell him about concentration. Years on the rodeo circuit had taught him that lesson well. Not even Kit, whose sultry eyes turned him to jelly, was on his mind as he stared down into the chute at the bull, which waited with deceptive calm.

The sight of that brindled hump brought back memories to Hank of the last time he and this bull had met. Hank's spine stiffened. Today there would be no missed signals, no wrong cues, no unseen circumstances, to get in the way of his ride, he thought with determination.

The bull shifted when Hank's weight came down on him. Hank repeated his vow privately as he carefully wound the rope around his gloved hand. That done, he braced himself. Then he gave the signal.

The signals were right today, but something else was dreadfully wrong. Hank felt it the instant they broke from the chute: a movement in the cinch to which the rope in his hand was attached, ever so slight but keenly detectable to Hank, who was concentrating all he had on the bull. To him it felt like an avalanche of movement. He knew immediately what it was. The cinch was beginning to slip.

Hank felt the first shudders of fear slam through him. With a muffled curse, he held on for dear life, knowing he'd never make it for eight seconds.

Kit knew something was wrong the moment Hank broke from the chute. Through the close-up lens of the camera she had a tight focus on his face. Instead of its usual determined expression, she recognized fear in his blue eyes. An unspoken dread welled up inside her. She lowered the camera from her eye and looked out into the arena. Hank's movements were erratic. She saw him begin to fall, and what took in actuality only seconds to occur appeared before her eyes in torturous slow motion. She watched, helpless, as he slipped to the ground and the bull's hooves came down over him.

Hank hit the ground hard and rolled out of the way with a lightning-quick reflex. The rodeo clowns scrambled into action, but neither Kit nor the bull saw them. Both had their eyes riveted on the man who was just now struggling to his knees.

The bull charged. Kit screamed.

Things happened fast after that. One of the brave men with the painted clown faces and funny costumes dodged headlong in front of the charging bull. The beast came to a screeching halt just a foot away. Turning its vicious temper on the clown, the bull charged again, but the clever fellow already had things under control, allowing Hank to leave the arena alive and unhurt while he popped in and out of barrels to annoy the bull and delight the crowd.

Hank stormed away from the arena, his face filled with anger and confusion. What the hell had happened? What had gone wrong? A stroke of rotten luck? Hank wasn't so sure. But he said nothing, not wanting to alarm anyone until he was sure.

Kit rushed up to him, looking pale and anxious. "Hank! Are you all right?"

He closed his arms around her like two steel doors, and for a moment he just held her while he brought his simmering emotions under control. He could feel her trembling. "I'm all right," he assured her. "Are you?"

"Hank, I—" She looked up at him. Her eyes were glassy with fear, her voice quaking. "I thought...oh, Hank, I thought—"

With the palm of his hand, he stroked her silky hair to calm her and crooned soothingly, "Shh. It's all right. See? I told you it would be."

With Pete he wasn't quite so understanding, nor so collected. "Hank, what happened?" the older man exclaimed.

"What the hell do you think happened?" Hank snapped. "I fell off the damn bull, that's what happened!"

"But Hank—"

"Yes, yes, I know," he said with impatience. "That puts me a couple of points behind Quint. Thanks, Pete, but I don't need you to remind me of it."

Pete looked at Kit helplessly, as if to suggest that the sloppy ride Hank had just turned in wasn't going to do him much good in the competition. It was obvious to all concerned that Hank would have to work doubly hard next day, the final day of competition. Nevertheless, had Pete witnessed what Kit had seen through the camera, his first concern would have been for Hank himself and not the ride, and Kit sympathized with him for bearing the brunt of Hank's anger.

She wanted to ask Hank, to confront him with what she'd seen, but she dared not. Not just yet, Kit told herself as they walked from the arena in dead silence.

Though he said nothing of his suspicion, Hank left strict instructions that a man from his own crew was to be posted outside Dakota's stall that night. He was taking no chances.

The three of them packed up their gear and drove back to the motel, nobody speaking much. Kit knew Hank felt tired and tense, and he was deep in thought, remote and unreachable as he drove. Seated beside him, she was still too stunned by his narrow escape to have much stomach for small talk. In the back seat, Pete didn't bring up the subject of Hank's sloppy ride again.

When they reached the motel, Pete climbed out of the car and grasped Kit's arm to get her attention after Hank had gone inside. "It looks like those stolen mares have got to him," he whispered. "What happened today shouldn't have happened."

Inside, Kit showered, taking her time beneath the steaming-hot water. She stood beneath the stream without moving, letting the warmth and action of the water massage some of the tension away while she grappled with what had happened that afternoon and her reaction to it. Frankly, she'd been scared to death. Nothing had ever frightened her so much. The thought of something happening to Hank filled her with terror, and the notion that she might have been responsible for it, with agony. Hadn't she encouraged him to return to competition? Hadn't she dared him to do it? Yet she knew that if she had to do it all over again, she'd do it no differently. It wasn't in her to give up, just as she'd known that it wasn't in Hank to ignore a challenge. Besides, she'd been only the catalyst for Hank's comeback. The desire and the will had been there long before she'd ever come into the picture.

By now she also knew Hank well enough to be sure that it wasn't like him to let something get in the way of his concentration when he was riding. That's what worried her, for when he'd broken from the chute today, she'd seen in a flash that something was on his mind. What had caused the break in his concentration? Was Pete right? Had the stolen horses gotten to Hank? Was he worried about Quint? Was he regretting his involvement with her? She looked at him, through the dresser mirror as she brushed her hair. He seemed, even lying there in bed, a million miles away.

As Kit climbed into bed and snuggled against him, Hank opened his arm automatically to accommodate her. She smelled fresh and clean and softly scented from her shower. The effect worked subtly to lure him away from his dark thoughts. She was so warm and inviting, he thought, and when he was lost in her passion, it was easy to forget the things that troubled him, the ghosts that haunted him, and see and touch and know only her. He helped himself to what she offered, finding sweet salvation in her arms and a strong, driving need in her kiss.

Beneath the rattling hum of the window air conditioner, their moans of pleasure and gasps of delight faded eventually to contented sighs and whispered words as they lay in each other's arms after making love. Both were awake, each lost in a private reverie. They were two distinct parts, one very different from the other, who had come together in a frenzy of chemical reaction and mutual need.

Kit had never experienced such a feeling of togetherness. The effect of it left her quiet and thoughtful.

For Hank, Kit had become a necessary ingredient to life, like the air he breathed. She'd come along at a time when he'd been hungering for love without even knowing it. She'd made him recognize that need and she filled it. He'd been a fool to ever let her go or to risk letting something happen to her.

Hank's body tensed when he thought of all the dangers involved in rodeo riding, danger not just for himself but for Kit as well. This latest event proved it. What if someone had tampered with his gear? Would they tamper also with those he loved?

Instinctively, he pulled her closer for protection. If it weren't for him, she wouldn't be in danger, not just from some lunatic fan but from the everyday perils of rodeo riding. Was he crazy to ask her to be brave while he was carried out of the ring with broken bones? He knew what her answer would be if he asked her, but maybe it was best for them both if they ended this thing before it ever reached that point.

Kit felt the change come over him as they lay there. The subtle tensing of his limbs and the heat that suddenly flared from his resting muscles made her look at him. "What is it, Hank? Are you still thinking about those horses?" She heard his intake of breath and knew by the sound that he didn't want to talk about it. But it had to be confronted. "Please, Hank, don't shut me out."

She watched him turn his head on the pillow toward her. His eyes were like two blue flames from out of the darkness.

"I want you to leave, Kit. I want you to pack up and leave first thing in the morning." He saw her eyes widen with protest and urged her, "Forget this assignment."

Kit shrugged out of his embrace and sat upright in bed. "What are you talking about? I can't forget this assignment. Why would I even want to?"

He reached out and grasped her arm, squeezing it for emphasis. "Go back to New York City, where you belong. Where you'll be safe."

"Safe from what?" she demanded.

"You saw what happened today. It could happen again, only next time I may not be so lucky. A couple of years ago in Denver, a bull got loose and killed one of the spectators. Don't you understand? Too many things can go wrong—for me and for you."

She searched his face through the darkness, struggling to read the emotions underneath the words. "I came into this with my eyes wide open," she told him. "I don't quit assignments midway through. I'm sure that's one of the reasons Sid put me on it in the first place." The only thing that could make her pack up and go home would be his telling her he didn't love her, though he'd never actually said he did. Kit was silent for a moment. Was that what he was trying to tell her now? "What is it, Hank?" she pressed. "Something's bothering you. I know it is. Tell me."

Beautiful, brave Kit. How he loved her. He'd never told her; even now the words wouldn't come. But the feeling was there, and with it came the trust that goes hand in hand with love. She was asking him to trust her now. In her softly demanding eyes Hank saw courage and met it with his own. He released her and said self-mockingly, "Pete thinks I gave a sloppy ride today, doesn't he?"

"Can you blame him?"

"No. And is that what you think?"

Kit searched for a way to explain what she had seen through the camera, to express the indefinable feeling in her gut that something had been wrong. She said simply, "No. That's not what I think."

Hank swung his legs around to the side of the bed and sat there for many minutes, elbows resting on his knees, head bowed. At last he spoke. "There's something I haven't told you. What happened in the ring today was no accident. And it was no sloppy ride, dammit," he added defensively. "I have reason to think my gear was tampered with."

She scrambled over to him. "What makes you think so?"

"Because the damn cinch slipped beneath me. I didn't fall off that bull of my own accord. I know that's what everybody thinks, but I'm telling you I didn't."

"Hank, this is serious."

"I know, and that's why I'm worried about you."

"Me? That's ridiculous. Why would anyone do anything to me?"

"I don't know. I can't figure it out. Something doesn't add up. I'm telling you, Kit, I checked that equipment myself before the ride. It's like packing your own parachute. There are just some things you do yourself."

"What did you do after that?" she asked.

"What I usually do. I went to get something to drink. I watched some of the action. Mostly I just waited for my turn."

"How long were you gone?"

"Ten minutes at the most."

"Long enough for someone to mess with the cinch," she observed grimly. "But who?"

"Beats me. A misguided fan, maybe? Some of them come just hoping to catch a little blood and gore. The area's filled with people, from the handlers to the curious. It could've been anyone. Who knows? Maybe it was a sore loser." Or a desperate winner, he thought. One name in particular came to mind. Dan Quint. Quint had every reason to want him out of the way.

Hank thought about the man. Quint was rough with the horses. He was arrogant and boastful, a hotshot who relied on tricks and cunning to score with the judges and the ladies. But was he also the kind of man who would do something like this? Hank grappled with the uncertainty but ultimately dismissed it. Quint, he reasoned, had enough raw talent of his own not to have to resort to sabotage.

Kit sat beside him, her leg brushing his, and said, "I won't go, Hank. I'm staying."

He put his arm around her and pulled her down on the bed, crushing her slender body beneath the length of his. He was glad she was staying, but then, he'd never have the courage to propose it if he'd thought she would turn tail and run. He put his lips to hers and kissed her deeply, passionately. It was too late to turn back. They were in this thing together. They made love again, this time slowly, lingeringly, protracting the sweet torture until they fell asleep at last, spent and exhausted.

Something woke him. It was the sensation of being alone. He put his hand out on the bed. The place beside him was empty and cool to the touch. He sat up with a start, searching the darkness for her. Then he saw it, the red glow from beneath the bathroom door that signaled she was developing film, and he relaxed. He shook his head in wonder at her restless energy, which had her working in the middle of the night. He lay back and closed his eyes and soon drifted back to sleep, secure in the knowledge that she was still there.

The next day broke to a gleaming sun. Excitement ran high at Frontier Park, where the contestants and the crowds gathered for the final rounds of competition.

Hank extracted a promise from Kit not to say anything to Pete about their suspicions, not wanting to alarm him. Without telling Pete the real reason for his concern, he asked him to keep an eye on Kit, explaining, "You know how it can be at the end of these things. Things could get pretty wild." Pete assured him he'd keep a close eye on Kit, and it was with a slightly lighter heart that Hank prepared for the first event.

Having guessed that Hank would designate him as guard dog, Kit wasn't surprised to find Pete so attentive. But the older man's attention made it difficult for her to slip away and go in search of the answers she knew had to be out there somewhere.

She had said nothing to Hank about her middle-of-the-night work in the darkroom except to answer his query with a nonchalant "It went pretty well, thanks." She'd awakened with a strange sense of expectancy and had lain there, feeling edgy and restless, searching her mind for an answer to what had gone wrong in the arena. It wasn't a question of whether it had happened the way Hank had said. She believed him when he'd told her his gear had been tampered with. It was a question of why and, more important, who? Then it came to her. Maybe the pictures held a clue. She'd been all over that area taking pictures, and while it was doubtful that they would reveal anyone in the act of cutting the cinch, maybe she or Hank might recognize the faces. At least that would provide a basis with which to start. That hope in mind, she'd slipped from the bed, hastily set up her equipment in the motel bathroom and developed the film she'd shot that afternoon. She'd studied each print carefully after removing it from its water bath. Some faces she recognized; others she didn't. Since there wasn't much to go on, she decided against telling Hank. She'd tucked the prints into her bag, packed up the equipment and slipped back into bed before dawn.

Kit stuck to her resolve not to tell Hank about the pictures. The last thing he needed was something like that on his mind before the all-important final rides. Her opportunity to slip away from Pete came during the steer-wrestling competition while he was hopping up and down on the sidelines, shouting and cheering. In seconds she had disappeared into the crowd.

She searched for the people whose faces she recognized from the prints, but all her subtle questioning failed to turn up anything. No one seemed to have seen or heard anything unusual. After a while Kit got hungry. At one of the booths she ordered a hot dog with everything on it.

"Here, I'll get that," said a familiar male voice behind her. Before she could object, a hand darted past her to pay the vendor. "Make it two cold beers, too."

"Thanks for lunch," said Kit, taking a bite out of the hot dog as the two of them strolled on.

"Forget it," Quint said. "I owe you one."

"What for?"

"Let's just say I want to show you I'm not such a bad guy after all."

Kit couldn't resist a wry smile. "Why would I think that? What goes on between you and Hank is your business."

"I just thought he might have . . . well, you know . . . said some things about me."

Kit laughed. "You don't know Hank at all, do you?"

"What's that supposed to mean?"

"Only that Hank Reardon doesn't go around bad-mouthing people, and that includes you."

"You gotta admit, though, if anyone had a reason for doing it, it would be Hank. Me and him never did get along."

She didn't like the way he kept returning to this subject. It was as if he were trying to make a point. "Yes," she said dryly, "I've noticed."

Quint took a swallow of beer and wiped his mouth with the back of his sleeve. "It must be rough for old Hank. Champion once, trying to be again."

"Hank's not trying to be champion," said Kit.

"You could've fooled me," he replied.

She knew it was useless to explain to someone like Quint why a man like Hank did the things he did. Harder still even to make him understand the real reasons behind Hank's comeback. If a championship came out of it, fine, but that wasn't the fuel that stoked Hank's fires. "If you don't mind," she said, "I'd rather not discuss Hank."

"Sure. I can see you've got something on your mind, anyway. Wanna talk about it?"

She dared not trust anyone with her suspicions, least of all Quint, who might use them to taunt Hank and ruin his concentration. "It's nothing. Tell me," she said, changing the subject so obviously that he had no choice but to let the matter lie. "When that bull succeeds in maiming or killing somebody else, will they call him Number Eight?"

They were standing before the bull pen, in the center of which stood the formidable brindled bulk of Old Number Seven. "You mean that old bull?" Quint laughed. "I guess so. We almost found out yesterday, didn't we?"

Something in his tone made her look at him askance. "You sound almost disappointed that Hank wasn't hurt."

"You gotta admit it would narrow down the competition."

"That's disgusting," she charged.

"Maybe so, but that's the way it is. Cheating death's a part of the game. Reardon knows that better than most."

"And sabotage," she said bitterly. "Is that a part of the game also?"

He laughed—a little nervously, it seemed to Kit. "We all like to think it was sabotage that made us take a tumble, and not lack of skill or bad timing. Even your precious Hank Reardon."

"Still, it wouldn't be impossible to sabotage someone else's gear, would it?"

"Impossible? No. But I doubt it." He broke out into caustic laughter. "Has he fooled you into thinking that somebody actually sabotaged his gear? Is that how he explained his crummy ride?"

"He did no such thing!" Kit exclaimed. She realized too late that she had foolishly let her suspicions be known, opening herself up to Quint's ridicule and giving him more reason to come down hard on Hank. "It just occurred to me that somebody might have done something they shouldn't have."

"That's a pretty way of making a mighty serious charge," said Quint. "Who would do that?"

"I don't know. A jealous rival?" She turned away to deposit the empty beer can in a receptacle.

"Reardon's got lots of those," Quint pointed out.

"I'm sure he does. But not all of them were hanging around the chute yesterday. You were by the chute yesterday, weren't you?"

"Well, yes, but I—"

"Did you see anything?"

He rubbed his chin thoughtfully and said, "Now that you mention it, I did see this fella hanging around. I figured he was one of the handlers."

Eagerly she questioned, "What did he look like?"

"He was around five-ten or -eleven. Dark hair and eyes. Jeans. Blue shirt."

Dozens of men fitted that description, but none of the ones in Kit's photographs did. It was possible, of course, that a man who looked like that had been near the chute while she'd been taking pictures elsewhere. She was pondering the possibility when something clicked in Kit's mind. She looked quizzically at Quint. "Blue. You said the man was wearing a blue shirt."

"Yeah, that's right."

"But how would you know it was blue? Aren't you color blind?" She recalled the day they had driven to the Lazy J and he had mistaken her green eyes for blue. She'd realized later that Quint was color blind. She certainly hadn't thought much about it . . . until now. "You said blue," she repeated.

"So, I guessed. That's all. I figured it must have been blue."

She supposed it was possible. A man in a blue shirt, or maybe it was a green one. She bit her lip, pondering the clue.

"There's something I want to show you," said Quint. "Come on. I'll take your mind off all this mumbo jumbo about sabotage."

He led her away from the chutes to a quiet area where the spectators were not allowed entry. Here the animals were kept in pens and the contestants' trailers were parked. Pointing to the bulls, which were in a large pen, separated from one another by wooden slats, he said, "Look at them. Each one as mean as a hornet and a whole lot more dangerous. They'd just as soon gore you as not. It doesn't take a cut cinch to fall from one of those things. All it takes is an animal mean enough and angry enough."

"What?" Kit whirled to face him. "How did you know Hank's cinch had been cut?"

Kit saw something flicker in Quint's eyes, then he replied, "You said so."

"No I didn't. I never mentioned it." Instinctively, she moved away from him, but he put a hand out to stop her.

"Hey, Kit, you don't think I had anything to do with what happened to Hank, do you?"

"I—I don't know. I guess not." But even as she said it, she was far from convinced. Quint had been near the chute yesterday; she'd seen his face in her photographs. And now there was his mention of Hank's cinch being cut when she hadn't said anything about it. Her pulse quickened and her senses went on the alert, but the realization, once formed, slammed into her brain with the impact of a speeding train. Her hand flew to her mouth. "It *was* you!" she said with a horrified gasp. "*You* cut the cinch yesterday!"

Chapter 12

Now, Kit," he said to her in a placating manner, "don't you think you're overreacting?"

Not fooled by his friendly tone, she demanded, "Why would I be overreacting?"

"Because you have no proof of anything," he pointed out.

Stubbornly Kit replied, "I have all the proof I need."

Quint raised a brow at her and asked, "What proof?"

"For one thing, everyone knows you can't stand Hank."

He laughed caustically. "Enough to kill him?"

She bristled at his mocking tone. "How else could you have known that the cinch was cut? And don't try to tell me that it was me who told you, because I didn't."

Quint shrugged. "Your word against mine."

She detested that fulsome smile on his face, for she knew what guilt festered beneath it. Nevertheless, Quint was right. She didn't have enough on him to prove anything. Yes, his face was in her photographs, but so were hundreds of others. All Kit really had to go on was circumstantial evidence and her own gut feeling. In this case she chose to go with her instinct. In her mind Quint was responsible for Hank's accident yesterday. Let him think she had all the proof she needed against him. She looked him squarely in the eye, drew her shoulders back and said, "I have pictures to prove it." She held her breath for one precarious moment to see whether her lie would work.

This time Quint didn't have an easy answer. He watched her closely. Her complexion was flushed with anger, her eyes fixed on him with cool resolve. Nothing in her face, however, betrayed the lie. Quint had to make a decision as to whether to believe her. She noticed that he'd begun to perspire under his collar. He couldn't risk not believing her, she knew. Wetting his lips, he said, "Well, that's too bad."

Feeling bolder, Kit said, "Why'd you do it?" She fired the question at him like an interrogator, demanding, "Do you hate him that much?"

Quint dropped his pretense and snapped, "Shut up with your damned questions!"

But Kit's anger was mounting sharply, and she wouldn't stop. "You're disgusting!" She spat out the words. "You won't get away with it."

Quint's fists flexed at his sides as he glared at her. On his face was stamped a look of malice and defeat, a deadly combination. "You're right," he said at last. "I do hate him. Wholeheartedly."

"Enough to try to kill him?" she breathed, eyes wide with incredulity.

"If necessary."

She couldn't have known what was to come, or what the ultimate impact of her lie would be. She stood her ground before him, eyes accusing, tone scathing. Again she demanded, *"Why?"*

Quint stormed forward, making Kit flinch with the explosive movement. For a moment it looked as if he were going to swallow her up. *"Why?"* he echoed in a shout. "Because everything comes easy to that arrogant bastard, that's why! Because all he knows is winning. What does he know about losing championships? What does he know about losing anything?"

She couldn't believe what she was hearing. Her face paled with rage. "Hank knows more about losing than most people. He lost a wife seven years ago, in case you've forgotten."

"I haven't forgotten!" Quint shouted at her. "I lost her too, dammit!"

The words hung in the air for several seconds before Quint snorted with disgust and sneered, "That's right. I loved her, too. But she was his wife. Just like everything I ever wanted was his. First Beth. Now the championship. If not for him I would've walked away with that championship."

With the revelation of Quint's jealous secret, Kit began to realize just what she'd unleashed. In a sharp, accusing tone she said, "You cut Hank's cinch so he'd have an accident and you'd be number one? Is that the way you want to win?" She despised the expression on his face, so smug and devious, yet she could not take her eyes from it.

"I'll win whatever way I have to," said Quint. "Just like I did what I had to do to get Beth." He chuckled at his own cunning and reflected, "It took some doing, getting her out there that night. I made up some story about one of the mares being down. She came out to the barn, dressed in her robe. I'll never forget it. She was so close, and I'd wanted her from the first day I'd signed on at the Chaparral. I could see she needed a little persuading, but I figured that once we got into it, she'd enjoy it." His features hardened and his voice dropped to a low rumble of malice. "But she turned me down. Told me she was in love with her husband. I got a little impatient after that. I didn't go through all that trouble to get her there only to let her walk off. All right, so I helped myself to a few kisses, but she shouldn't have slapped me. She never should've done that. When I slapped her back, she went running from the barn. I was so crazy for her, and then so mad when she turned me down, that I never even heard that stallion stealing those mares. Beth must've run right into them and caused the stampede. I heard her screams, but I got there too late."

Kit saw his fists clench as he spoke of the past. He flashed her a look full of hatred and said, "Sure, I wanted her, but if he'd have been there, she wouldn't have been with me that night and she'd still be alive today. He killed her as sure as that stallion did. I swore that night I'd make him pay for Beth's death."

Kit fought down a wave of nausea and said, "Seven years is a long time to wait to get even, isn't it?"

Quint snorted contemptuously. "Who said I waited seven years?"

He was looking pleased with himself for a reason Kit could not imagine. She watched him carefully, not trusting him, wondering whether he was lying. A voice at the back of her mind warned her to be cautious. She swallowed the lump that was growing in her throat and asked, "What do you mean?"

Assuming a stance that was deceptively relaxed, Quint smiled and said, "Poor Hank, chasing after that stallion all these years, when all along it's been me who's been stealing his mares."

It was several stunned seconds before his revelation sank into Kit's brain. She scrambled to fit the pieces together. Then she remembered that Quint had been absent from the

Cody roundup at the same time that Hank's horses had been stolen.

With a look of triumph on his face, Quint said arrogantly, "It was the stallion that made me think of it. A couple of weeks after Beth died, he came back and stole some of Hank's mares. Hank saw him and scared him off. The funny thing is, he never came back again, only Hank never knew it. He always thought it was the stallion after that, and I always let him."

"You made money on Hank's tragedy?" Kit exclaimed. "What a vile man you are!"

"I didn't do it for the money. I never sold any of those horses. I just ran them off. Can you think of a better way to drive a horse breeder out of business than to run off his prime stock?"

Kit's breath was coming in fast flutters. Fear, shock and outrage blinded her to the danger she was in. But right now her thoughts were not for herself; they were for Hank and the terrible wrong that had been done to him by a jealous rival. "You're despicable," she told him.

"Your opinion of me doesn't change a thing."

"You're right; it doesn't. But Hank's opinion of you certainly will change a lot of things when he finds out what you've done."

In a dangerous drawl he asked her, "Who's gonna tell him?"

Kit saw something change in his eyes. Before, they'd been filled with loathing and contempt. Now they simmered with cold determination. She backed away instinctively as the full impact of her lie about the evidence took its final, dangerous form. She spun on her heels to run, but Quint's hand came out swiftly to clamp over her forearm and jerk her back. "Where are you going, Kit?" he taunted her, using his strength to trap her.

"Let go of me!" Kit demanded.

Quint just laughed. "You're hardly in any position to be giving orders."

"I'm warning you," she seethed, glaring up at him, "you'd better let me go. If Hank finds out—"

"To hell with Hank! Let him find out! *After* I take what I want from you!"

She struggled to free herself, shouting, "You're crazy! You don't want me."

"You're right," he agreed. "But he does. He's got it bad for you. I can see it when he looks at you. Well, I'm gonna help myself to something of his."

He put his hands around her and pulled her forcibly into his embrace, her camera bag slipping off her shoulder. Her camera, which hung from a strap around her neck, got in his way. He yanked it off and threw it to the ground. Savagely he kicked it out of the way as his mouth came down on hers so hard that their teeth clashed.

Kit squirmed and struggled to avoid his kisses, but with her waist imprisoned by one of his arms, and his other hand fixed firmly at the back of her head, pinning her mouth to his, she was forced to endure his liberties. He slid his hand from her head to her breast, where his fingers bruised her tender flesh.

It was not an act of desire or lust but one of vengeance and jealousy and the inability to deal with being second-best. Years of frustration and bitterness had led Quint to betray the man who had given him a job and been his employer. But along with Hank and Beth, Quint was also a victim of his emotions. The past and the present collided in his mind until he could not tell one from the other. Suddenly it was seven years earlier, and it was Beth struggling in his arms, calling him cruel names and telling him she would never be his. He felt the terrible anger that had consumed him then. It didn't matter that the woman in his arms at this moment was a different one. This one was spurning him just as the other one had done.

Somehow Kit managed to pull her lips free. She gulped in the air and cried, "Stop! Please!"

Quint looked as if he were coming out of a trance. His arm still wound around her waist with crushing strength, he said to her, "You know, it's really too bad. I actually liked you."

She sensed it was the truth, but it only frightened her more. Breathlessly, she asked, "What are you going to do?" She saw his lips stretch into a cold and empty smile.

"Come with me," he said. "There's something I want to show you over here."

But Kit dug her heels into the ground, refusing to go willingly, sensing that he was up to something and fearing the worst. In answer to her protest, Quint tightened his hold on her, squeezing so tightly that it choked off the breath in her lungs. In a move too quick to deflect, he clamped his hand over her mouth, muffling her scream.

He dragged her, twisting and struggling, along with him, cursing under his breath as she fought him. With her fists she rained blows on him. She scratched deeply into his flesh, and her kicks at his shins made it that much harder for him to drag her along. A twitch grew at the corner of his mouth and spread to his cheek, making it jump violently.

Kit was no longer aware of the sounds of the crowds. As her terror mounted, she heard only the sound of her own scream trapped behind Quint's cruel hand. She struggled and kicked, chest heaving with fury in her desperate attempts to save herself. One deep scratch on the back of his hand forced a brutal curse from Quint. He pulled his hand away to avoid another one, and in that second, Kit twisted her head at an angle to catch it between her teeth. She bit hard into the soft flesh.

Quint let out a howl of pain, releasing her. "You bitch!" It was all the time she needed. Fear forced her legs into action. Terror gave her the energy to dart away just before he reached for her again.

Kit ran, sobbing, blinded by her tears. She gave a frenzied glance over her shoulder, a scream tore from her throat. Quint was coming after her. She could see a crazed look in his eyes. *Faster!* she shrieked to herself. *Keep going! Don't stop! Oh, God, don't stop!* Her heart pumped savagely and the muscles in her legs screamed with pain, but she kept going. She raced zigzag among the horse trailers and vans, not knowing where she was going, just running. She managed to lose him in the maze of vehicles and stopped with her back pressed up against one as she struggled for air. Panting, she crouched down on her knees and looked beneath the trailers. She bit back a terrified sob when she saw Quint's legs moving in on her from one side. She had to do something.

She spotted some stones on the ground. She chose a good-sized one, palmed it and waited. Again she crouched low and peered under the trailers. When she saw his legs reach a certain point, she hurled the stone in that direction. She waited an agonizing second more to make sure his legs were hurrying after the sound of the stone before sprinting off in the other direction.

She ran as fast as she could toward the arena, where she hoped to disappear into the crowd. Quint would never follow her there. But when she looked back again, a wild cry tore from Kit's lips. Quint was coming hard and fast after her. Her trick hadn't worked.

Up ahead she spotted a corral and raced for it. If she cut across it, she'd save precious time. Uttering another cry, Kit reached the corral. She hit the ground at a full run and scrambled beneath the bottom fence post, tearing the knees of her jeans in the process. She felt a muscle rip in her leg and cried out in pain, but it wasn't until she tried to stand again that she realized the severity of her injury. The muscle gave way, her leg crumbled beneath her, and she fell to the ground once more. With trembling arms Kit pushed herself up, gritting her teeth against the sharp pain in her leg. A quick look back over her shoulder, however, and the pain was trivial compared to what awaited at Quint's hands. He was still coming after her. She saw him racing toward the corral. She staggered to her feet and tried to run just as he crouched low to dart under the fence. But when Kit looked back again, what she saw baffled her. Quint had stopped chasing her. He was standing inside the corral, watching her. She stumbled along on her injured leg, turning her head back every few seconds to glance at him. And then she realized that he wasn't looking at her at all; he was looking past her. Kit swallowed hard and turned around. The blood in her veins turned to ice. Facing her across the corral was Old Number Seven.

She realized too late the folly of taking a shortcut through the corral. Her eyes met those of the bull for one brief, fatalistic moment.

Sensing her fear, the bull issued a loud snort from its nostrils and pawed at the dirt. Beyond its lowered head Kit saw the muscles tensing in its thick neck and all along its ominous hump. There was no time to think. With the bull in front of her and Quint behind, Kit turned and made a dash for it. Her body was in motion before the bull charged. Fear made her stronger. Blind panic obliterated the pain in her leg. But the muscle had a mind of its own. Too weak to sustain her, it sent her to the ground yet again. Kit screamed and tried to run, but all she could manage was a slow hobble on her injured leg. With the fence only yards away, Kit fell once more. The bull was in hot pursuit. She could hear the breath shooting out of its nostrils, smell its musky odor, feel the ground reverberating beneath her from the pounding of its hooves. She was unaware of the tears streaming down her cheeks. All she knew was that in a matter of seconds number seven would become number eight. She looked hopelessly at the fence. She wasn't going to make it!

She pulled herself to within feet of the fence, shut her eyes as tight as she could and braced herself for the slashing horns, willing herself to pass out so that she wouldn't feel the pain.

But the pain never came. From somewhere beyond her frenzy, Kit heard her name. It sounded like Hank's voice. Oh, God, she groaned in agony, did her mind have to play tricks on her at a time like this? But in the next instant she felt herself grasped by a pair of strong hands and dragged under the fence to safety.

Number Seven hit the fence hard, shaking the posts that were anchored in the ground. Deprived of its quarry, it whirled around, looking for another. It spotted Quint standing in the corral. With a speed and agility that were surprising for its size, the big bull charged again.

Quint had watched Kit's frantic struggle with a twisted grin on his face. His smile froze when he saw the bull charge in his direction. Triumph turned to sudden panic and panic to raw fear. He turned and ran, but whatever grace he possessed in the saddle eluded him now when the fingers of fear were clutching at him. He tripped over his feet and stumbled as he tried to flee. He moved like a man who'd had too much to drink as he staggered for several feet, lost his balance and fell.

He never had a chance. The bull's horns came down, nearly touching the ground in a wide, sweeping arc that caught Quint under the arm.

From where she watched on the ground outside the corral, Kit screamed and closed her eyes. Did she really see the bull lift Quint into the air on its horns and toss him about like a rag doll? Had she really heard his cries of pain and the snapping of his bones? Or had she dreamed the terrible events of this day? She opened her eyes, hoping to find the awful scene gone, then watched numbly as a quick-thinking rodeo clown, alerted by the screams, sprang into the corral, risking his own life to distract the bull. Several men ran into the corral to carry Quint out. Where his body had lain, the dirt was stained red.

It had happened so fast. One moment she'd been on the verge of disaster, and now she was on the other side of the fence, safe. Kit blinked back the tears and turned away from the horrible scene. Still dazed, she raised her eyes and flared them wide at finding Hank beside her. Then she remembered having heard his voice calling her name, and someone's hands pulling her under the fence to safety. It had been Hank. She opened her mouth to speak, but all that emerged was a strangled sob. She sagged against him and he held her close, his strong arms winding around her for protection.

"Shh," he whispered. "It's all right. You're safe now." He stroked her head to calm her and spoke to her in a soft, soothing voice. He held her like that until her sobs ceased and he felt her trembling subside, all the while trying not to think of what would have happened if he hadn't gotten to her in time. He rose to his feet and drew her along, scooping her up into his arms.

Kit looked into Hank's eyes. In them she saw his fear and her own. Her voice scratched painfully at the back of her throat. "Hank, I—"

"Shh. Not now. Tell me later. Right now I just want to get you out of here."

She laid her head against his shoulder and let him carry her away from that dreadful place. She felt safe in Hank's arms, protected from both Quint's madness and the bull's fury. But her heart ached with the knowledge of what she'd discovered. How, she wondered dully, would she ever tell him?

Later that evening Kit hobbled around the motel room, packing for their departure in the morning. Hank had sent Pete back to the corral at Frontier Park to search for her gear. The camera was broken, but fortunately she had a spare in the trunk of the car. A doctor had confirmed that the muscle in her leg was torn, but probably not as severely as it felt. After packing, Kit took a long, hot shower and got ready for bed.

She hadn't spoken much since they'd gotten back to the motel, and Hank didn't push her. She'd had a terrifying experience, and he respected her right to deal with it in whatever way she needed to. Still, her reticence worried him. It wasn't like Kit to be this quiet and withdrawn. Several times he caught her looking at him with a tense look on her face as if she wanted to say something. A sense of apprehension had settled over him by the time he climbed into bed. He watched her at the dresser as she brushed her hair. She seemed to be stalling. Why? he wondered. If she didn't feel like making love tonight, that was all right with him. He wouldn't press her. He felt himself being shut out the way he had excluded her, and he realized for the first time how lonely that could make a person feel, how she must have felt, and how brave she'd been to persevere with him.

He waited until she'd climbed into bed beside him before saying anything. He drew her into his warm embrace and just held her, making no overtures for anything more than that. And then he asked, "Do you want to tell me about it?"

Kit shivered and pressed her body closer to his. She'd been trying for hours to think of a way to tell him, but she'd been unable to find the words that would soften the blow. Now that he'd asked, she knew she had to say something. Breaking her silence, she gasped, "Oh, Hank, it was so horrible!"

"It must have been terrible for you," he said, strengthening his hold. "Being chased by that bull and then watching Quint." A chill ran over his own flesh when he recalled the grisly scene in the corral. The outcome had been even worse, for Dan Quint had not made it to the hospital alive.

"What were you doing there?" Hank asked. "You shouldn't have been anywhere near that corral." Her close brush with death had scared him witless, and he could not help but show it now, his anger a natural defense against the fear of losing her.

"I know, but—"

Hank's emotions, pent up all afternoon, were getting the better of him. Impatiently, he demanded, "But what?"

"He was chasing me. I ran into the corral because I thought it was a shortcut. I never thought—"

"Who was chasing you? Quint?"

His constant interruptions and the way he fired the questions at her weren't making it any easier for her to tell him. "Yes, Quint."

Hank withdrew his arm and sat up, leaning on an elbow to look at her. "Why was Quint chasing you?"

She hesitated, then blurted it all out. "Because I lied about the pictures. Then he told me what he'd done and... Oh, Hank, he hated you so much."

"What are you talking about?" he asked, confused. "What pictures? And what does his hating me have to do with anything?"

With a shudder Kit told him, "Hank, it was Quint who cut the cinch yesterday."

"You have proof of that?"

"No," she admitted, remembering that Quint hadn't actually confessed to it.

"Then what makes you think he did it?"

She looked into his questioning blue eyes and drew in a breath. "Because there's more," she said. "Much more."

In a faltering voice, pausing now and again to catch her breath for support, Kit told Hank everything she'd learned from Quint. She could feel his anger rising as she spoke, but he stoically remained silent until she'd finished.

Hank was too choked with emotion to speak at first. The story Kit had told him rocked him to the core. He scarcely knew where to begin to sort it all out. Beth. Quint. The stallion. All these years he'd been wrong about all three. So that's what she'd been doing out there that night in her robe. He'd tried so hard to believe her innocent of any wrongdoing, but the possibility of her unfaithfulness had stuck in his belly all these years like a rotten seed, growing on his own uncertainty. Part of him found welcome relief in the knowledge at long last that Beth had not been unfaithful to him. His fury against Quint, however, grew to explosive proportions. Not only was Quint the indirect cause of Beth's death, but he'd made Hank think the worst about her all these years, compounding his own terrible guilt. With the man dead, though, there was nothing for Hank to do with that fury except bear it. He closed his eyes to the agony of the past seven years. Beth was gone. Quint was gone. Only the stallion remained.

He felt Kit's touch on his arm. Softly she asked, "Are you all right?"

He pulled in a deep breath and let it out slowly through pursed lips. "Yeah. I'm fine." But he wasn't fine, not really. Learning the truth about Beth had put a long-held doubt to rest. Discovering the truth about the stolen mares put other things into perspective. Now he knew why he'd never found a trace of the stallion's tracks. Still, nothing could change the fact that what he feared most had almost happened. He'd almost lost Kit. If it hadn't been for him, she'd never have been put in such grave danger and he'd never have risked losing her. He sank back to the pillow, drawing her with him. For a long time they lay there, each content just to be close to the other.

After a while Kit stirred. "Hank?"

In a low voice he answered, "Hmm?"

"How did you know where I was?"

All the anger had washed out of him, leaving him tired in its wake. She could hear it in his voice. "After I finished my ride and went back to where you and Pete were, I found only Pete there. I raced around like crazy, looking for you. I asked people if they'd seen you. Someone said they'd seen a woman eating a candy bar and taking pictures over by the corrals. I figured it had to be you. When I found your things over by the trailers, I knew something was wrong. That's when I heard your screams."

He shuddered, recalling the bolt of fear that had shot through him at the sound. He'd raced as fast as he could in their direction, only to find her in terrible danger. He hadn't even seen Quint at first. All Hank had seen was the bull bearing down on Kit. His heart had nearly exploded in his chest as he'd run to save her. It was only later, when he'd had her safely in his arms, that he'd seen Quint.

Her voice, soft and pleading, broke the ensuing silence. "Hank, make love to me."

He turned away from his thoughts to look at her. She looked so vulnerable and open, so incredibly sexy. His eyes devoured her. "Yes," he breathed huskily. "Yes." His lips sought the comfort of hers, his hands the sanctuary of her body. She was a haven in a storm, and he held her as if he were clinging to life itself. Their bodies united in a mutual understanding of passion and need, a common goal to forget everything else and know only this moment, this heartbeat. The fears of the afternoon vanished, and doubts about tomorrow were nonexistent as they explored and discovered each other all over again.

Chapter 13

Kit sat on the fence, watching as one of the men turned a wild-eyed sorrel horse into the corral where Hank was waiting astride Dakota. The sorrel's body was rigid, and the horse gave several disapproving snorts as Hank threw a loop around its neck. It ran, then planted its feet and struggled against the rope. Hank held the lariat tight, not with a fighting feel, but patiently, until the horse's fears began to subside. When it moved forward, Hank rewarded it by throwing slack in the rope, and did it again and again until the horse got the idea. Then he roped one of its rear hooves. Another fight ensued. When at last the horse leaned away from the rope, allowing that hind leg to hang in the air, Hank let the lariat go loose.

He left the sorrel to think about its predicament for a while and went over to Kit. "So? What do you think?" he asked her.

"I think you're going to put everyone else to shame at Douglas," she announced confidently, referring to the next round of competition, in August, at the Wyoming State Fair. He shook his head in wonder at her unbounding faith in him and jerked a thumb toward the horse in the corral. "I was talking about him."

She looked at the horse thoughtfully for a moment, then said with equal assurance, "I think he'll make a good range pony."

Hank smiled. She was a fast learner. She had a good eye, too. Kit had picked this sorrel out of the bunch Hank had bought with some of his prize money, and she'd urged him to train the sorrel first because there was "something about him."

Hank pulled Dakota's head around with the rein, making the animal's nose touch his knee, and rubbed his mount's forehead in a gesture of affection. "I try to make the right things easy and the wrong things hard," he explained. "A horse has a mind. He gets scared or sure of himself, bold or uncertain. He says to himself 'maybe I will and maybe I won't.' You've got to listen to what he's telling you. Which reminds me. I'd better get back over there before that one starts making plans." He trotted back to the sorrel to resume its training.

In the days that followed, Kit watched each morning as Hank trained the sorrel. She saw that Hank had a rare way with horses. He used discipline without aggression. He taught them how to be caught by making it uncomfortable for them to run from him and easy to approach him, all the while allowing the horse the dignity of escape. "You can't force a horse," he explained. "He'll just fight you if you do."

This time that Kit spent at the Chaparral was calm in the wake of all the previous excitement and the tragedy at Cheyenne. They didn't talk much about Quint and what had happened. What was there to say about it, really? Since

he'd been back at the Chaparral, Hank seemed to have resigned himself to the facts of Quint's treachery and death.
He threw himself into his work and practice sessions, turning in faster times and sharpening the skills he would need
to carry him through to the national finals in Las Vegas in
December.

At night they made love in his bed. Afterward, her
frankness made it easier for him to speak of Beth and of
that night. It was as if the revelation of Quint's secret had
unlocked a door inside Hank. Maybe he'd never be able to
shout it to the rest of the world, but in the quiet of the
night, secure in familiar surroundings as they lay in each
other's arms, he spoke to Kit about his memories. He confided to her the pain and frustration of the past seven years.
She didn't judge or condemn, and she didn't offer advice.
She listened, and she understood.

Hank and Kit had fallen into a comfortable togetherness. Hank had to admit that he'd grown accustomed to
looking up from his work and seeing her there. And the
men liked her. She had gained their respect the day she'd
saved the mustangs from going over the edge of the cliff,
but she had earned their admiration by sticking this thing
out to the end.

Hank felt like a kid of twenty again, trying hard to im-
press her with his skill and prowess. Some things, he
thought with wry amusement, never change. She had a way
of making even the most menial chore seem vitally important by her presence alone. Just knowing that she was
watching made him work harder.

Day after day Kit watched Hank rope and ride, and no
matter how many times she saw it, it never failed to thrill
her. She, too, would have been quick to agree that some
things didn't change, however, for hard as Hank was on
himself in his work and practice sessions, he was equally

severe when it came to blaming himself for the death of his wife.

Kit had tried everything from earnest persuasion to anger to convince Hank that he wasn't to blame. He wanted desperately to believe her, but despite having taken up competition again, he still had to come to terms with his feelings. It would take time and patience, Kit knew. Nor had he told her he loved her, though she was learning daily more and more about him through his own words. She tried to tell herself it didn't matter; she didn't have to hear the words to know it was true. But Kit also sensed that one part of Hank was beyond her reach and that as long as the stallion stood between them, she would never hear from him those words she longed for him to speak.

In spite of the uncertainty, Kit felt a certain comfort here at the Chaparral. She felt at home. The land was suited to her, for it possessed no pretense. The mountains were straightforward in their beauty, candid about their power. Even the heat, about which she'd protested in vain to Sid Burns, was preferable to the stagnant warmth of the city. The air was dry and clean and good to breathe. There was a sense of freedom out here like that she'd known only in her youth in the Adirondacks. And if all that weren't enough, there was the sheer thrill of watching Hank in his element.

She had taken to helping with the chores, starting out with little jobs at first, then tackling some of the more rigorous work. At the end of each day her muscles were sore, but it was a good, solid hurting that made her feel alive. The rubdowns Hank gave her each night worked wonders to loosen stiff muscles and invariably led to a session of passion atop the sheets—after which she slept soundly and peacefully in his arms.

Little by little Kit learned more about Hank, satisfying not only her physical hunger for him but an emotional hunger as well. They'd talk in bed in hushed tones about the ranch and Hank's aspirations for it, about the competition that was coming up, about Kit's work and her family. They spoke of intimate things and the world at large. And for a while it seemed that maybe everything would be all right. But as July came to a close and the August heat lay heavy over the land, Hank's tension began to rise again, centering on the one thing they did not speak of—the stallion.

They'd been back at the Chaparral for over a week when Kit awoke one night just before dawn. She stirred in bed and turned to Hank. He wasn't there. She rose and went to the window. A lopsided moon appeared over a bluff in the distance, looking like a giant tear in the gray cloak of dawn. Life was beginning to stir in the wilds. A coyote pup scampered from its den to frolic in the dew-dampened grass. An imperious great horned owl watched from a treetop perch. A bison calf nursed sleepily as its mother grazed. But all Kit saw when she looked from the window was the empty corral and a ranch still silent as day crept slowly over the horizon.

She went back to bed to wait for Hank, who, she presumed, had gone downstairs. She dozed off and awoke sometime later with a start. Her brow knit with worry to find Hank's place in bed still empty, she went to the window again. A strange feeling nagged at her. She rubbed the back of her neck, trying to figure out her sudden apprehension. Where was Hank? Had he gone downstairs to read and fallen asleep on the couch in the study? She'd noticed that he'd grown restless this past couple of days. Last night she had awakened to find him standing at the window looking out at the night. She'd coaxed him back into bed with fiery kisses, but even as they'd made love she'd felt his tension. Something was bothering him, and even though he wouldn't say it, she knew what it was.

Kit gasped when she realized where Hank must have gone. She turned from the window and ran to get dressed. In minutes she was hurrying out of the house and down the path that led to the stable.

He was there, saddling Dakota, when Kit burst in. He turned a dark gaze upon her. "Your timing stinks, Kit. I have no time to pose for pictures."

Breathless from having run all the way, Kit demanded, "You're going after him, aren't you?"

He replied curtly. "That's right."

"You can't do it!" she cried.

"Oh, can't I?" His movements were quick and to the point as he tightened the cinch.

"You don't understand—" she began.

"No, Kit," Hank cut in sharply, "it's you who don't understand. This is something I *have* to do." He hung one of the stirrups on the pommel of the saddle while he adjusted its length, saying as he did, "I thought you'd figured that out."

Kit took a helpless step forward and said, "I have. At least, I *think* so."

"Then you should know how important this is to me." He went around the horse to adjust the other stirrup.

"And competing?" she asked. "I thought that was important, too."

He looked at her from over the saddle and said, "Sure it is."

"You have a competition coming up in the next few weeks," she reminded him.

Hank shrugged and said, "If I miss the one in Douglas, I can make the next one somewhere else."

"And the championship?"

"There's always next year."

She hesitated, then said, "And me?"

Hank's muscles tightened. Damn her questions! His eyes beseeched hers from the other side of the horse. "Kit, don't. Please. This has nothing to do with you."

At the earnest plea in his voice, Kit wavered. What if he went out there and didn't catch the stallion? Would it always be like this, with him blowing in and out of her life like the wind, chasing after that damned horse? What if Hank *never* caught him? He'd been wrong when he'd said this had nothing to do with her. It had everything to do with her...with them. Didn't he know how hard this made it for her to commit herself to him? And then she remembered—he never had asked her to do that. And so all the arguments she could have given him remained unspoken. She asked simply, "How long will you be gone?"

He took a deep breath and answered, "As long as it takes." He was relieved that she wasn't going to try to talk him out of it, but he was taken totally by surprise when she announced, "I'm going with you."

"Forget it!" He snapped back to work, grumbling, "The mountains are no place for you."

"Give me a break, would you?" she groaned. "Haven't I already proven to you that I can ride well enough?"

"That's only part of it," Hank argued. "Don't forget, there will be no one to cook breakfast for you in the morning."

"So? I'll eat whatever you eat."

He rolled his eyes and emitted a low epithet. What she didn't know was that when he was up in the mountains chasing the stallion, sometimes he didn't eat at all. He tried a different tack. "There are wolves and coyotes up there, and grizzly bears. And it gets damned near freezing at night."

But Kit stood her ground before him, as undaunted now as she'd been that very first day. "If you're trying to frighten me, forget it."

"I'm telling you, Kit, that's wild country up there. We didn't go nearly so far in search of the mustangs when you were along. It could take me days to find his tracks. *Weeks*, maybe."

But stubbornness was one of the things Kit had in common with him. "I came back to Wyoming to take pictures of Hank Reardon. I'm being paid to do this. If you ride out of here, I go with you."

"You're being paid to take pictures of my comeback," he argued. "Which, I might add, there won't be if I don't catch this damned horse!"

"I'm being paid to take pictures of the man," Kit corrected him. "But I can't do that if you chase me away whenever I get too close. You know, Hank, from everything I've seen and heard, you didn't use to be that way."

He gave a short, derisive laugh and said, "Yeah, and I didn't use to be thirty-eight years old either, but things change."

Holding the reins loosely in his hand, he went to pass her, but Kit stepped in front of him, blocking his way out of the stall. "Precisely," she said. "Things *do* change. So why are you still living in the past?"

There was too much truth in the question for Hank to deny it. He himself had been beginning to think he would spend the rest of his life looking behind him. He didn't even try to answer.

For several wordless moments they stared into each other's eyes, trying to read all those nameless emotions that were mirrored from deep within. She sensed something change subtly inside him. The air was suddenly lighter around him, and a smile, almost imperceptible, softened his features just enough for her to see. Gently, she said, "I'll go get my things."

He assessed her in the thin morning light. "You're that sure of me?"

"No. Only of myself."

His eyes lingered on her face a while longer before he nodded reluctantly. "Go and pack your things. And bring something warm to wear. You'll freeze up there dressed like that."

Only then did she realize that in her haste to stop him, she'd forgotten to put on a shirt. The cotton camisole she'd been sleeping in scarcely hid the contours of her breasts and the smoothness of her back. He'd taken it off her on other occasions and was strongly tempted to do the same right now, but Kit was already dashing from the stable, shouting over her shoulder, "Wait for me!"

Hank yelled after her. "If you're not back here in ten minutes, I'm leaving without you." But just as she knew he'd do it, he knew she'd be back.

When she returned ten minutes later, breathless, saddle-bags crammed with food and clothing, Kit found Bayberry waiting for her, already saddled. Once before, she'd asked Hank why he'd bothered to have a horse saddled for her if he hadn't thought she'd be back. She smiled wryly at the memory as she mounted.

Hank responded with a quick warning. "Don't be so sure of yourself, green eyes," he told her as he swung into the saddle. "Remember. I don't get in your way, and you don't get in mine."

She thrust out her hand. "Agreed."

They shook hands to seal the partnership, and rode out into the gray light of dawn.

They followed a creek that chuckled toward the cottonwood banks of the Snake River in the valley bottom. At one point Hank gave a tug on the rein and led the way across the creek, sloshing through the shallows and the waterweeds to the other side. With no foothills to soften the perspective, the mountains' jagged walls rose sharply thousands of feet above wildflower meadows and forests of spruce that were just becoming visible.

Gradually the sky lightened until day was fully upon them and the massive strength of Grand Teton, the tallest spire of the range, filled the view with its gargantuan beauty. The air was fragrant with the scent of white and lavender columbine, wild vetch, lupine and Indian paintbrush. They rode through glades of fir, pine and spruce, crossing several streams in the process, all the while winding slowly higher into the mountains along little-used paths and sometimes no paths at all.

Kit rocked along in the saddle as her surefooted mare stepped delicately over snags and picked her way across rocky creek beds. Kit ducked now and then under low branches and sometimes, on steep downhills, had to lean back so far in the saddle that she was almost standing up in the stirrups. The sky was a crisp blue, like delft china, she mused. The air was warm and strangely alive.

They rode on into the morning, stopping only for brief periods to rest and water the horses and fill their canteens from bright and gurgling streams. The mountains were like a balm, the summer air a salve for any lingering tensions. Even Hank looked relaxed as he rode along at a leisurely pace. It was as if he hadn't a care in the world. Surely a misleading notion, thought Kit as she watched him out of the corner of her eyes. But he was at ease right now, and despite the solemnity of the mission, there was even a smile on his face.

They didn't speak much. Each was quietly appreciating the things around them, and sharing that appreciation with the other in an unspoken way. It felt good to be here together like this. Somehow, it seemed so right. He turned to her, a spark of mischief dancing in his eyes. "Want to see something?"

"Sure," she replied, wondering what he was up to.

"See that boulder over there?"

With her gaze she followed his outstretched arm toward the boulder fifty yards in the distance and said, "Mmm-hmm."

Uncoiling the rope that hung from his saddle, he deftly fashioned a lasso and twirled it over his head as he urged Dakota into a gallop. The rope sailed through the air and landed securely around the boulder, without horse or rider breaking stride. He swept past the boulder, retrieving the rope with a practiced flick of the wrist and repeated the trick several more times to Kit's applause.

"You're pretty good with that," she remarked when he galloped back to her.

"*Pretty* good? I'm *damned* good. There was a time when I was the best." He was feeling pleased with himself as he gathered up the rope and hung it back over the saddle. "I come out here sometimes and practice on the bison calves. Man, do their mothers put up a holler. The Parks Department would have my hide if they knew what I was up to, but what the hell, it doesn't hurt the little guys."

She had wondered how he'd quenched that wild, competitive spirit all those years he was off the circuit. Now she knew. The truth was, he'd never really stopped competing at all; he'd just stopped doing it for the crowds.

Later that afternoon Hank looked up from the stream into which he'd led Dakota for a drink, to find Kit's camera focused on him. As comfortable as he felt with her, he'd never get used to that thing pointed at him. "Do you have to do that?" he groaned.

Kit lowered the camera from her eye and wagged a finger at him. "Remember, you're not supposed to get in my way," she reminded him.

He led Dakota out of the stream and came up to where she was standing. He took a sip of water from his canteen and replaced it over the pommel of the saddle, saying to her, "I'll remember it. Just you remember it, too." He swung his lean, muscular frame into the saddle, which creaked under his weight, and looked down at her as she stood on the ground by the side of his horse. "Someday soon I'm going to remind you not to get in my way. Maybe tomorrow, maybe the day after."

Looking up at him, she said, "I'll remember it."

But the agreement between them was put to the test, and the partnership in danger of ruin, when Hank's horse slipped on the rocks of the creek later that afternoon and horse and rider went into the cold water. In Hank's thrashing around to regain his balance, his bedroll and saddlebags came loose and washed away by the swift current before he could catch them. The fast-moving water carried Hank's belongings over a jumble of rocks, where they fell out of sight.

Hank sloshed his way back to the bank, cursing and muttering. He was soaking wet and had nothing left to change into. But before he could think about his own discomfort, he quickly ran his hands over Dakota's flanks and legs, checking for bruises. Finding none, he walked the horse around and watched its movement for signs of injury. Satisfied that Dakota was fine, Hank climbed back into the saddle, frowning. He tried to stop his teeth from chattering, for despite the fact that it was August, it was cool up this high in the mountains.

His lighter mood of earlier had dissipated, much like the warmth of the sun as it sank beyond the treetops. His clothes gradually dried, but all that wetness next to his body had left him with a permanent chill and in a bad mood. Kit's offer of her blanket to throw over his shoulders was met with a flat rejection and a curt "No thanks."

"Don't you think you're carrying this 'you don't get in my way and I don't get in yours' thing just a little too far?" she said, annoyed by his dark mood.

"What would I do if you weren't here?" he questioned.

"You'd freeze."

"Exactly."

She rolled her eyes in the face of such logic. "But I *am* here," she insisted.

"Not by invitation."

She took a deep breath to calm her growing irritation and said, "All right, Hank, have it your way." If he wanted to play this stupid game, she'd oblige him. After all, he was the one who was cold and would soon be hungry, and the long night was still ahead.

They rode the rest of the way in silence. At last they stopped near a stand of cottonwoods and dismounted, unsaddling the horses without speaking. Kit pulled her saddlebags down and spread her bedroll between some clumps of sage while Hank walked off in search of a log to sit on. He found one about twenty-five yards away. While the horses grazed, Kit went looking for dried twigs with which to make a fire. She returned with an armful, which she snapped across her knee and placed in a pile. With soft breaths she coaxed the flame of a match to ignite the kindling.

Twilight played in soft shadows over the valley in which they were camped. A storm flashed about the mountaintops in a flickering finale to the day. Stars soon glittered like diamonds across the ebony sky. A crescent moon appeared over one of the jagged crests, hovering precariously as though snagged there before rising into the sky. The campfire sent yellow sparks into the night, casting warm shadows over Kit's face as she sat crosslegged on her blanket, eating some of the leftovers from last night's dinner at the Chaparral that she had pulled out of the refrigerator this morning and had warmed up over the fire. When she finished eating, she carried the plate and utensils to the nearby stream to clean them. Back at her blanket, she packed them away and took out her hairbrush. She longed to bathe away the dust and grit of the long day's ride, but she'd have to wait until morning for that. So she sat there before the warm fire, brushing the day's tangles from her hair, her mind wandering but always coming back to the man who sat twenty-five yards away in the cold darkness.

He was doggedly determined to ignore her. He knew he could have accepted her offer of the blanket. He could have shared her supper and the warmth of the fire she'd made, but if he had done that, he might also have given in to her subtle demand that he cease his search for the stallion. Oh, she said she understood about that, and maybe she really did. But the bottom line was that she would have preferred him to saddle up right now, ride back to the ranch and give up the crazy chase. And she'd be right about it. He knew it was crazy, and if he was going to be here at all, then it was even crazier to have her with him. For he knew that if anything or anyone could get him to change his mind, it was her.

He watched her from the shadows. The flames of the fire licked her dark hair, illuminating the natural embers that tinted each silken strand red. He longed to crush her hair in his fingers, to lift it to his face and breathe in its fragrance. The fire's glow played against her face. Something inside him went weak. She suddenly seemed so far away, the twenty-five yards between them like a canyon, and Hank felt alone. The irony of it stunned him. There'd been a time when he'd come often to these mountains to be alone beneath a blanket of twinkling stars. There had been a strange kind of comfort in the solitude, which was like an understanding friend who asked no questions and offered no advice. But that was before Kit had come into his life. The solitude meant different things to him now. It reeked of emptiness, loneliness, of voluntary self-exile to a place he no longer wished to inhabit.

Kit's eyes were closed. The hairbrush lay idle in her lap. She was thinking about Hank and this place and where she fitted in. She didn't hear him come up beside her, but even before he spoke she somehow knew he was there.

In a low voice he said, "I don't expect you to understand why I do it."

She opened her eyes and looked up at him. "Does it matter whether I understand or not?"

Yes, dammit, Hank wanted to shout, it mattered, almost too much. "He and I have a score to settle."

"But why, Hank? Why, when it was Quint who stole the mares?"

He shook his head in protest, saying, "I know that, dammit. But don't you see, Kit? If the stallion hadn't come that night, she'd still be alive and Quint would never have gotten the idea to steal from my herd."

He made it sound so logical, so simple. Yet she knew it was not. "What if you never catch him?" she asked.

It was a question Hank had never dared ask himself, and he didn't like hearing it now. "I'll catch him."

In the wake of the uneasy silence that followed, Hank stood there shifting from foot to foot, not out of nervousness but from the cold. Kit, on the other hand, looked warm inside the sweater she'd pulled on over her shirt. If she offered him a blanket now, he wasn't so sure he'd turn it down. "That sure is a warm fire," he said. "You did a good job."

"Thanks." If he wanted to share the warmth, why, she wondered, didn't he just ask? Damn his stubborn pride.

"I, uh, noticed you were cooking something before. Could it have been the turkey we had last night for dinner?"

"Yes. It was."

"Oh. That's what I thought. I could smell it, you see. From all the way over there."

She leaned over to peer past him at the log, which was just a dark shape in the distance, and muttered, "I see."

"I was thinking that maybe Dakota might like to try a bit of that turkey. Is there any left?"

"Oh, gee, no, I ate it all. Well, that's all right, there's plenty of green grass around for Dakota. I'm certain he's well fed. As a matter of fact, we're all well fed. Except, of course, for you, Hank. Don't tell me you're hungry?"

"Me? No. I'm not hungry."

"Mmm-hmm. Then what are those sounds I hear coming from your stomach? Are you sick or something?"

He was sick of the cold and tired of being hungry and was ready to call a truce, if that was what she meant. But his stubborn streak was in control now. With a breath of disgust, he muttered, "No, I'm not sick or something," and turned to leave.

When he'd stomped a few steps back to the log, Kit called out teasingly behind him, "Oh, Hank. Do you think Dakota might want this?"

He retraced his steps to the fire, but when he saw what was in her hand, he exclaimed with disbelief, "A candy bar? You can't expect a horse to eat *that*!"

Kit feigned an apologetic look. "You're right. I wasn't thinking. It's just that this is all that's left and I don't want it." She patted her belly, adding, "I'm stuffed."

She looked up at him as if something had just occurred to her, prompting Hank to ask, "What?"

"I don't suppose... No, I guess not."

"What, dammit?"

"Well, you wouldn't want this, would you, Hank?"

His eyes glinted ominously at her from out of the darkness. "Woman, if you value your life, you'll hand over that candy bar... now."

Kit laughed at his threat and tossed it up to him, saying, "There. See how easy it is when you just ask?"

He ripped the paper off the candy bar and tore into it. In three bites it was gone. "Feeling better?" Kit asked.

"No," he griped. "Do you have any more of those things?"

"Sorry."

But instead of going, he lingered. "Well, then, thanks. If there's nothing else, I guess I'll be going. Back to my log, that is." He looked longingly at the fire and held his hands over it. "Sure feels good." He eyed her blanket close by and said, "Do you think you'll be warm enough in that?"

"Oh, I'm sure I will." She sighed audibly, adding, "But of course it's not the same."

"As what?" he asked.

"As having someone beside you. You know what they say about body heat."

"Is that an offer?"

"It's a request."

He looked at her with sly understanding. He knew exactly what she was up to. "Well, I can't let you freeze up here, now can I?"

As he dropped to the ground beside her, she opened up the blanket to him. They lay down together beneath it, the space between them rapidly filling up with the heat of their bodies. After a while Hank asked, "Is there anything else I can do for you?"

A flutter caught in Kit's throat, turning her answering voice breathy. "Yes," she whispered. "There is."

She didn't have to say it and he didn't have to ask. Their mouths came together in a kiss of understanding and need and their bodies blended into one harmonious rhythm beneath the light of the stars. All around them the mountains cut the silent darkness, sealing them off from the rest of the world.

When Kit awoke the next morning, the mountains were still there, but they didn't look as ominous as they had under the cover of night. With the sun bouncing off their eastern faces, they reminded her of picture postcards from Switzerland, snows looking like powdered sugar against the deep cerulean sky. She saw that Hank was already up, saddling Dakota. With a yawn and a stretch, Kit got up and trudged over to Bayberry. She bade the mare good-morning and spoke softly to her as she saddled her.

They rode out of the valley before the sun was fully up. Neither mentioned the night before, but each was acutely aware that despite their intimacies under the stars, nothing had changed.

Shortly before noon they came to a rise. Hank dismounted and climbed to the summit to survey the area. Kit trailed after him. At the top of the rise, Kit gasped at the sight that greeted them.

A large herd of horses grazed in the sunlight, swishing tails and snorting occasionally. The herd was calm and content in the midday heat. Hank's gaze flew over them, searching for one whose presence was everywhere but that was nowhere to be seen.

Kit, too, was looking. Just then something from the trees—a movement, perhaps—caught her eye. Squinting against the sunlight, she made out the shapes of two horses nearly obscured by the forest cover. One was snow white. The other, camouflaged by its coloring, was black and white. In an excited whisper, she said, "Hank! Over there!"

He swung his gaze in the direction of the wood and stared, wide-eyed. It was the stallion.

Chapter 14

Hank's heart thumped in his chest. He stood there, unable to move or tear his eyes away.

Kit turned a questioning gaze on him. Why was he just standing there? Had he decided not to go through with it? she wondered, torn between hope and disappointment.

After what seemed an interminable amount of time, Hank turned away and started back down the hill. Kit ran after him. "Hank, what are you doing? You're not giving up, are you?" Even as she said it, she knew that deep down inside, she didn't want him to.

"Are you kidding?" he answered. "I haven't come all this way and waited this long to give up now."

When they reached the horses, Hank mounted and spurred Dakota, not toward the stallion, as Kit had expected, but in the opposite direction. She galloped after him into one valley after another, not understanding his actions and wondering what he was up to. In a small glen ringed by forest, he jumped off Dakota and began to tear at the wild brush and vines.

Kit watched, bewildered, worried that Hank had lost his mind. "What are you doing?" she cried.

He rushed up to her, arms laden with branches and foliage, eyes bright. "I'm going to trap him," he said excitedly. "Right here. It's perfect."

She looked around. The glen was bordered on three sides by dense forest. At the rear was a hill too steep for a horse to scale. It was possible, she supposed, for Hank to chase the stallion into the area, but how would he keep him here? Then she realized what he was up to. Her heart began to pound at the possibility. Without thinking, she dismounted and hurried to help him.

Together they constructed a makeshift corral, using branches and vines and foliage to conceal the boundaries. Their plan was for the stallion to run into the concealed enclosure and not realize its folly until too late. Kit didn't want to think about what would come after that; how the stallion's capture would affect her relationship with Hank, or whether there would even be a relationship. She'd come too far to turn back or to start asking questions.

It was dusk by the time they finished, and Kit went to sit down while Hank put the finishing touches to the corral. Kit surveyed their handiwork and was forced to admit that it just might work.

Later that night they sat before the fire in quiet contemplation. It wasn't hard to guess what Hank was thinking about. She knew that even if she'd wanted to talk him out of it, it was too late. She could feel the tension in him as he sat silently beside her, sharing her blanket.

"When are you going after him?" she asked.

"First thing in the morning," he answered in a voice that left no room for doubt.

"What if they're gone?"

"They can't have gone far. It won't be hard to pick up their tracks."

He sounded so sure of himself, as if he'd gone over everything in his mind and had it worked out to the last detail. Seven years of planning were about to be tested. Hank's own skill and cunning were on the line. It had all come down to this, and nothing would stop him. His voice came low through the darkness. "Do you remember what I told you yesterday?"

She remembered his speech about not getting in his way, and murmured, "Mmm-hmm."

"If we should get separated—and I expect we will—just give Bayberry her head. She'll find her way back home."

"And you?"

Hank took a deep breath before answering. "I'll be back."

"When?"

"That depends on him." He fell silent after that, and she knew he was beyond her reach. She went to sleep, leaning against his shoulder.

Hank was up at the break of dawn. While Kit slept curled up beneath the blanket, he walked the length of the make-shift corral, testing its strength and its ability to fool the stallion. It had to work, he thought. It *had* to. He could feel the nervousness in his stomach. His muscles were straining with anxiety. The tenseness of his mind and body increased as the sun slowly worked its way into the sky.

Kit awoke and found Hank saddling Dakota. She could tell from the way he moved that he was determined to see this thing through. He looked like a soldier preparing for battle, checking his equipment, focusing all his energy on meeting the enemy. But just who was Hank's enemy? Kit wondered as she watched him. Was it the stallion? Or was it Hank himself?

She scrambled out of the blanket, still dressed from the night before, and ran off to saddle Bayberry. She, too, had sworn to see this thing through to the end. If Hank was riding out after the stallion, she was going with him. But when she led her mount by the reins over to Hank, he put a damper on her plans with a taut "Where do you think you're going?"

"With you. Who knows? You might need me out there."

"I told you before, this is between me and him."

"All right," she answered, throwing up her hands at her inability to reason with him. "Let's just say I'm coming along for the ride."

"Do what you want," he said to her as he slid one boot into the stirrup and mounted. "Just don't—"

"I know," Kit groaned, climbing into the saddle. "Don't get in your way. Don't worry, Hank. I wouldn't dream of doing that."

Her bitter sarcasm lay between them as they rode out. It was all forgotten now—the lost bedroll, the hunger-filled night, Quint, Pete, the Chaparral, the last seven years. All that mattered was the finale of the long drama, whose outcome hung in the air as they rode through the morning back to where they'd spotted the horses the day before.

By midmorning they'd reached the place. Quietly they dismounted, tied their horses to a thicket and crept up the hillside. At the top of the rise, Kit felt a surge of blood through her veins and Hank emitted a low growl of triumph when they saw the herd spread out below them. It was a big herd, with over two hundred mustangs, mostly mares, foals and yearlings. Hank recognized some of his own stock among them, their strong, sleek lines standing out against the ranginess of the mustangs. He had never thought he'd see those horses again, but now, as he peered over the top of the rise, he was hardly even aware of them. His eyes swept the herd, looking for one particular horse. Satisfying himself that the stallion wasn't there, Hank turned his head slowly in the direction of the forest.

He spotted the mare first, snow white against the dark woodland. He made out the shape of another horse beside her. Despite the camouflage of the trees and the deception of its coloring, Hank knew which one it was. He grew edgy with excitement. He grabbed Kit by the hand and yanked her back down the hill. At the bottom he spun her around to face him, planting both hands on her shoulders and squeezing them to gain her attention. "All right, look. I want you to wait here. I'm going to head him back in this direction. When you hear us coming, get out of the way. Don't let him see you. I don't want to scare him off when he's almost in the corral." He was speaking rapidly, blue eyes bright with excitement. "It shouldn't take long to flush him out—maybe about an hour. I'll see you then." He released her and ran to his waiting horse. Kit watched, speechless, as Hank spurred Dakota into a full gallop and disappeared over the rise.

That was it? No goodbye. Just a hasty parting of the ways. For several minutes she just stood there, paralyzed with uncertainty. Hank had told her to wait there. But when had she ever followed Hank's orders? She hadn't come all this way and put so much on the line to give up now. She made a dash for her horse and within minutes she was galloping after him. She wouldn't get in his way. She knew this was his battle and he had to fight it alone. Still, she wouldn't be left behind.

At the top of the rise, Kit slowed her mare and led her into concealment among some trees. From there she had a good view of the valley below, of the grazing herd, and of

Hank, who'd circled from the left and was slowly winding his way down the hill toward the forest, where the two horses waited unsuspectingly.

The wind—what there was of it on this still August morning—was on Hank's side. The horses had no idea of the danger that was approaching until it was too late and Hank came bursting upon them at full gallop, lasso twirling over his head.

The piebald stallion and his mare came bounding out of the woods, earth flying from their hooves. A sharp whinny alerted the herd of the danger. Heads popped up and ears pitched forward. All at once there was bedlam as hundreds of mustangs panicked and stampeded in all directions.

The stallion cut right through them, mane flying, neck straining. His white mare galloped after him. Hank, astride Dakota, was in hot pursuit.

Kit watched from the trees, pulse racing, heart hammering, feeling Hank's vengeance as her own, knowing the desperation of his chase and sensing the impending truth of the stallion's capture. But just when things looked so certain for Hank, fate intervened. Instead of running in the direction in which he was being chased, the stallion swerved suddenly, zigzagging through the stampeding herd, and took off in another direction. "No!" Kit cried. "Not that way! This way! Over here!"

Kit was not the only one taken by surprise by the stallion's actions. The white mare became lost in the herd, trapped by the moving bodies of horses all around her. When Kit saw her next, she was galloping off in the opposite direction. Kit glanced anxiously at Hank, who raced doggedly after the stallion, oblivious to everything else around him, and then back at the mare. Kit didn't think; she simply acted. With a kick at Bayberry's sides, she took off after the mare.

* * *

The piebald stallion did its best to shake the pesky man from its tail, but Hank rode through the herd like the wind in an attempt to steer the stallion toward the trap. When the horse turned unexpectedly and headed off in another direction, Hank followed him out into the open valley. Dakota's powerful strides pounded the earth as Hank urged him faster, *faster*.

It was a grueling chase through woods and valleys that continued as morning turned into afternoon. The stallion was a clever creature, fleet-footed and sure of itself, and to Hank's chagrin it managed to maintain a slim lead.

Hank realized he'd underestimated the stallion, but he didn't know how much. A canyon wall appeared before them, and relief surged through Hank. The stallion was trapped! But the beast didn't slacken its pace. Instead, it dodged straight for the wall. For one terrifying moment Hank thought the horse meant to smash itself against the splintered rock in a final, desperate attempt not to be taken. *"No!"* he cried. "Not like that!" He couldn't believe they'd come this far for the story to end like this.

With a pull of the reins, Hank slowed Dakota down. If that piebald wanted his freedom that badly, he could have it. Hank muttered a bitter epithet and was about to turn away when he saw something that changed his mind. He watched, incredulous, as the stallion charged the wall and disappeared into it. Hank blinked hard. He nudged Dakota forward and approached the wall of rock, which rose over a hundred feet above him. The base was covered by thickets of dense shrubs. Hank examined it, suspicious. Cautiously, he urged Dakota forward. Sharp thorns pricked at his chaps as they moved through the tangle of vine and root. Several minutes later he emerged into full sunshine.

He pulled in his breath to see the canyon wall behind him. Ahead stretched a sun-dappled plain.

It wasn't hard to pick up the stallion's tracks in the grass. He followed them into the afternoon and came upon him by accident, never expecting to find the horse around the next bend, grazing in a meadow. He saw the stallion's head come up, and their eyes met in a look that seemed to say, "This is it," before the horse galloped off.

The chase ended abruptly at a precipice that dropped hundreds of feet to an icy river. Hank let out a whoop of triumph. "Now I've got you!" With speed and dexterity he loosed the coil of rope from his saddle and twirled it in the air while slowly urging Dakota forward. The rope sailed up and circled the stallion's neck, and Hank tightened it with a snap of the wrist.

The stallion fought the rope, but Hank held on tight. After a while the animal ceased its struggle. The breath shot out of its nostrils in loud, angry bursts as Hank dismounted and approached. The horse edged away. It glanced over its shoulder at the cliff, then back at the man. With no further hesitation, it lunged for the cliff.

It happened so swiftly and unexpectedly that the rope was yanked out of Hank's hands, ripping the leather of his gloves and burning his flesh. Heedless of the pain, Hank watched in mute horror as the stallion leaped over the edge.

Hank could not believe his eyes. Blind fury overwhelmed him at the thought of his having been cheated out of his victory. Before he could stop himself, his body was in motion and he dived off the cliff after the horse.

He hit the water with a splash and swam through the icy river in long, powerful strokes. His lungs felt as if someone had kicked them in, and he thought his arm muscles would burst as he cut through the current, forcing himself to keep going. He could see the end of the rope just up ahead and propelled himself toward it. By some miracle he reached it. He held onto the rope for dear life, using the first few minutes just to catch his breath. Then he pulled himself along the length of the rope, slowly, torturously, calling upon his spent muscles and exercising the diamond-hard will within him. Somehow he made it to the stallion's neck. Wrapping his arms around it, he grasped a handful of coarse, wet mane and clung for dear life as the horse swam through the icy water.

They emerged on a cottonwood-studded bank, panting heavily, the fight having gone out of both of them. Hank led the horse up the bank and tied him to a tree. Then he walked away and collapsed on the ground.

Hank's mind whirled. Had he really caught the piebald? The object of seven years of pain and frustration was standing several yards away. Yet even as he lay there watching the stallion, Hank knew it wasn't over. He wasn't thinking about Dakota, who would find his own way home, not that the loss of his mount meant walking back to the Chaparral. He was thinking about the real battle that still awaited him.

After a while Hank got up and approached the stallion. "We've come a long way, you and me," he said to the animal. "I've misjudged you, and for that I'm sorry. I'm not asking for your forgiveness or your understanding. I just want you to know that after today it'll be over. But it's not over yet. I think you know that."

The stallion looked at him. Something in its eyes conveyed its own understanding of the situation.

"Okay, pal," said Hank. "Let's get to work."

And he broke this horse the way he would any other. When the time came to mount him, Hank led the stallion back into the river, reasoning that the water would soften his falls. He was right. The stallion put up a good fight, and several times Hank hit the water. With the rope grasped firmly in his hand, he jumped back on again and again until, in the end, he had won.

But later, as Hank sat with his back pressed against the trunk of a tree, the now-tamed stallion tethered close by, he couldn't help but wonder just exactly what he had won. He felt no surge of pride, no rush of vindication, no sense of satisfaction at the long-overdue righting of a wrong. There was just the old pervading emptiness, which had become so much a part of him and now intruded upon his victory.

For Hank it was a hollow triumph. Capturing the stallion only made him realize that it was he who was a prisoner, of his own guilt, his own obsession, his own misguided notions of what was right.

He sat there long into the night, watching the moon rise in the dark sky and stars shooting overhead, disappearing behind the tall peaks. The gentle movement of the water against the bank was constant and reassuring. From the distance a coyote howled and a night owl called. A calmness settled over the earth. Even the stallion was resting comfortably not far away.

As he sat there, unable to sleep, Hank felt a change come over him, subtly at first, then more demandingly. He'd been thinking about Beth, for whose sake he'd embarked on this seven-year quest. Of Pete, who had begged him to give it up. And of Kit, who understood and made no demands. She'd touched something inside of him that went far beyond the physical. He'd always assumed that with the capture of the stallion, the past would be behind him forever. But it wasn't that way at all. Wasn't that what she'd been trying to tell him? She'd seen what he hadn't been able to see—until now, that is. He realized with a start that it wasn't the stallion he'd been chasing all these years; it was himself, trying desperately to return to a time that was free of the heartache and the guilt. In a way the stallion had come to represent Hank himself. He'd been unable to admit that the problem lay inside. It had been so much easier to focus blame on the stallion. He realized that if it hadn't been for Kit, he might never have seen it.

He thought then of the way he'd almost lost her, not only because of Quint but because of his own foolish obsession with something that had never existed. He wouldn't blame her if she never wanted to see him again, and yet a part of him wondered fearfully whether she'd still be at the Chaparral when he got there. There was a good chance she was back there by now. The thing to do was to get back there himself as soon as possible and tell her the things he should have told her long before this.

He eyed the stallion through the darkness. There was his ride home. Wouldn't the boys and Kit be surprised when he rode up on the stallion? He fell asleep smiling, thinking of the looks on their faces and feeling strangely at peace within himself.

He awoke the next morning with a start. His eyes snapped open to bright sunlight. For a moment he thought it had all been a dream, but no, the stallion was still tethered to the tree, and his muscles ached when he tried to move, evidence of the previous day's battle in the water.

The stallion whickered softly when Hank approached, and it did not flinch when he untied the rope and led it into the water for a drink. When they'd both drunk from the crystal-clear river, Hank walked the horse back onto the bank and mounted. The horse's strong shoulders quivered under him and a tremor raced along the broad back, but it made no move to toss him off. Hank leaned forward to pat the sleek, spotted neck. "Come on," he said. "Let's go home."

They rode away from the river. Hank kept the stallion in
check until they reached a wide open plain, and then, unable to help himself, he urged the horse into a gallop. Together they flew over the ground. The stallion was fast and
strong, and Hank couldn't remember when he had felt such
exhilaration. Later they stopped to rest in the shade. Hank
plucked some tender grass and fed it to the piebald. "You'll
like it back at the Chaparral," he said to the horse as he
stroked its fleshy muzzle. "Maybe I'll even see if I can
round up that pretty white mare of yours and bring her
down, too. First, though, there's something I have to do."
He was thinking of the corral he and Kit had erected in the
woods. He couldn't leave it there and take the chance that
some unsuspecting mustang might wander in and not find
its way out. It was best to take it apart and leave the place
the way he'd found it. So he mounted the stallion's bare
back once more and guided him back in the direction from
which he'd come.

They rode into the afternoon. When they came to the
canyon wall that had deceived Hank yesterday, the stallion
did not even flinch when Hank led him through the thickets to the other side. Hank smiled wryly. No wonder he'd
been unable to catch this horse for so long, with hiding
places like that. They galloped across the open plain, in and
out of the same valleys they had dashed through yesterday, up and down familiar hills. They were going along at
a leisurely canter when something in the air caught the
stallion's attention. Hank felt the sudden tension in the
horse and brought him to a halt. Then he heard it, a distant rumbling like that of thunder. Hank dismounted and
laid his ear to the ground. The earth reverberated with the
echo of hooves, hundreds of them. Hank looked back up
at the stallion, understanding.

The horse's attention was focused on something they could neither see nor hear at first, but as they waited, a sound began to grow from the distance. The thunder became louder and the earth shook. Hank leaped onto the stallion's back and galloped him to the nearest rise. From there they had a view of the surrounding countryside. Below them a herd of horses was on the move, raising a great cloud of dust in its wake. The stallion called to them, but they were too far away to hear. He grew agitated and danced around. The tentative friendship he'd built with the man over the past day was just not strong enough to hold him. Hank looked out over the moving herd and then back at the stallion. He understood only too well the call of freedom, the lure of the wild. Yet he'd waited too long, and fought too hard, to let the stallion go. He pulled on the rope and turned the horse's head away. But it wasn't the same after that. The exhilaration was gone. In its place came a realization that Hank could not ignore. Surrender, he realized, did not mean yielding to tyranny but giving in to respect. The stallion had not surrendered to him; it had merely acknowledged its respect. Hank, with his human heart and all-too-human emotions, could only do likewise.

They rode to a spot that was open, where the summer breeze blew up the ends of his hair and the piebald's mane, and billowed Hank's shirt at his back. He dismounted, walked around in front of the stallion and looked him in the eye. A look of mutual respect raced back and forth between man and horse. Hank lifted the rope from around the stallion's neck. "Well," he said, "what are you waiting for?" He brought the palm of his hand down on the stallion's rump and sent the animal back to freedom.

He watched from the hill as the stallion galloped after the herd. He didn't see the white mare, but he knew she must be somewhere among them. With the rope dangling from his hand, Hank heaved a sigh, turned around and started back down the hill on foot. His heart swelled with the pride of having done the right thing, and his heart relaxed as if the weight of the past seven years had just been lifted. Hank let out a laugh. He felt good, dammit. Good for the first time in a long time. First he'd go back to the corral and dismantle it. Then he'd head for home. If Kit wasn't there, he'd fly to New York. He'd find her wherever she was and tell her that he loved her.

Chapter 15

In the soft light of late afternoon the moon hung in a pale sliver above the Tetons. Glacial ice glinted in the fading sunlight. Knife-edged crags shredded wispy pink clouds, and distant thunder rumbled from behind the peaks. The rush of white water was loud and constant at these altitudes, but the boldness of the mountains was tempered by the approach of twilight.

Kit loved this time of day, especially up here. It was a sort of limbo, not quite dark, but no longer really day. The air was thinner and harder to breathe than it was down below, but it was also clearer and crisper and much cooler. She pulled a flannel shirt from her saddlebag and slipped it on over her T-shirt.

She was tired, having spent a sleepless night being foolishly frightened of the dark and feeling alone, so terribly alone, without Hank. She'd awakened to greet the dawn like a returning lover, grateful for its warmth and hopeful that it would bring with it her true lover, whose blue eyes had seared a path clear to her soul. When he'd failed to appear by late morning, her hopes had begun to decline. By afternoon she'd grown anxious, beginning to pace, wearing a path in the grass. Where was Hank? Why wasn't he back by now? Had he chased that horse clear to Colorado? Had he forgotten about her? She was reluctant to stay, yet she dared not go. The thought of spending another night alone in the wilderness without the protection of Hank's presence was not one she wished to dwell on, but the thought of not being here when Hank returned with the stallion was even more disturbing.

She wanted to see his face when he came in, to share his pride and his victory, to tell him how very much she loved him. She was willing to try even harder than before to understand him. With the capture of the stallion, at least now she felt she had a chance to win Hank's love...the love he had never actually admitted. There were no guarantees in life, but he was worth all the risks. Besides, the only thing that could go wrong would be for Hank not to have captured the stallion, and that was a possibility Kit did not want to think about.

She was so engaged in thought that she didn't hear him approach. It was Bayberry's whinny that caught her attention and drew her head up. Her eyes flared wide upon seeing him.

"Hank!" She took a half step forward with an intake of breath but stopped, darting a look past him, searching for the stallion. It wasn't there. Neither was Dakota. Kit's first impulse was to run to him, but something stopped her. Her relief at seeing him was swiftly overshadowed by a deep sadness. How terrible Hank must feel to have failed! Kit's heart went out to him. And with the sadness went a sense of resignation over things never meant to be. She knew that only with the capture of the stallion could they get on with their lives. Now they were right back where they'd started.

He came walking toward her, and in spite of the predictable effect on her senses, she knew it was over between them. Her one hope, the stallion, was gone.

"Hey, green eyes, I thought you would've been back to the Chaparral by now."

He didn't sound angry, she marveled. Nevertheless, she herself found it hard to be polite. "Yes, well, I was just about to leave."

Hank looked over at her horse and the saddle, which lay several feet away on the ground. Her bedroll wasn't even tied up yet, he noticed. "It looks to me like you're getting ready to bed down for the night."

"It will only take me a few minutes to pack up," she said. "I was about to do it when you showed up."

She must be angry because he hadn't returned last night, he figured. He'd told her to go back to the ranch. Wasn't it just like her to do as she pleased? The idea of her alone out here wasn't a pleasant one, but he could not help responding to her defiance with a warning. "Go ahead—ride out if you want to, but remember, there's all kinds of things out there. If you stay close to a fire, it's not likely they'll bother you, but if you go roaming around at night, there's no telling what you might run into."

Kit had backed herself into a corner with her own bluff. She'd be crazy to ride at night. "Well, maybe you're right."

"Good. I'm glad you see it my way. Now, why don't you help me gather some wood for a fire? Then we can bed down for the night."

"Together?"

"Of course together. I don't plan on spending any more time on logs, if that's what you're thinking."

She was thinking that he was crazy if he imagined they could pick up where they'd left off. His failure to catch the stallion had changed everything. She didn't want a part-time lover, a man who came and went with the wind, one who might or might not be there when she awoke in the morning. She understood why he'd chased after the stallion, but she also knew that for her anything less than permanency would never be enough.

Hank looked at her curiously and asked, "What's the matter with you?"

Defensively, she shot back, "What makes you think anything's the matter?"

"Well, for one thing, you just nearly bit my head off. Hey, Kit, look, I'm sorry for leaving you alone last night. Really. But I told you that if we got separated, you were to—"

"I know what you told me," she cut in. "But like you said once, nothing is easy. Walking in and out of someone's life may be easy for you, but to me it comes hard." He watched her grow angrier as the words came, her lovely face flushing with emotion.

"What are you talking about?" he wanted to know.

"I'm talking about us. You and me. I'm talking about your obsession with that horse. I'm talking about how hard it is for you to admit your feelings. Sometimes I feel as if I'm drowning in my love for you and all you can do is throw me a line that's too short. What are you so afraid of, Hank? Of being loved? It's too late for that. I already love you. Of what, then? Of loving? If you'd forget about that stupid horse, you might realize that it's not as scary as it seems."

Hank came forward in several long strides. "You're right. About me, about the stallion. Somehow I got the two of us confused. All this time I thought it was him I hated, when it was really myself. And for what? For something I didn't even do.''

Kit was panting from her own ire and looking at him questioningly. Did he mean what he was saying? And where did that leave her?

"I guess what I'm trying to say, Kit, is that if it weren't for you, I don't think I would ever have realized that. I owe you a debt of gratitude for it.''

"Gratitude?'' Her voice cut shrilly through the twilight. "It's not your gratitude I want, Hank. It's your love. But that's something I'll never have. As long as that horse is still out there, you'll never be able to love me the way I need to be loved. I'm sorry you didn't catch him, Hank, really I am, but if you think you can just take out after him whenever you want for the rest of your life, then you haven't really learned a damned thing about yourself or about the things that really matter.''

"But I did catch him,'' he said.

She gave him a skeptical look.

"I *did*,'' he insisted.

"Right. Then where is he?''

"I let him go.''

"You *what*? You chase a horse for seven years and then when you catch him, you let him go?''

In answer to her disbelief Hank just shrugged and said, "I can't keep what doesn't belong to me.''

She searched his face, looking for a sign that he was telling the truth and not playing a joke on her. Something in his expression spoke of honesty. She knew he was an arrogant man, proud beyond belief and stubborn to a fault, but he was also an honest one. The truth was written plainly in his blue eyes. She shook her head, wondering at the irony of it all. "You mean it's over? It's really over?''

He took in a deep breath and let it out slowly. "It's over."

The revelation, coming so unexpectedly after she had assumed the worst, stunned Kit. Did that mean there was hope for her? And yet she noticed that he still hadn't told her he loved her. Oh, well, she thought with dismay, maybe some things just weren't meant to be. With a sigh she said, "I guess I may as well turn her loose. There's no sense in keeping her here now."

Puzzled, he asked, "Turn who loose?"

She motioned behind him. "Her."

Turning to look over his shoulder, Hank gasped to see the white mare standing in the corral. His head spun back to Kit. "Where did *she* come from?"

"I brought her in."

It was his turn to be stunned. "But how? When?"

"Yesterday. I chased her in. I figured the stallion might like to see her here. There's no sense in your getting angry about it. What's done is done."

But anger wasn't what Hank was feeling at the moment. He was feeling pleasure in her tenacity, pride in her determination, and a love so overwhelming it rocked him. He couldn't take his eyes from her face. She was so beautiful, so necessary to his life. "Kit, I—"

She put a hand up to stop him. "Don't say it," she said. "I understand."

He smiled and asked, "And what is it you think you understand?"

"I understand if you don't love me."

She was so open and honest—and wrong. He opened his mouth to speak, but the words froze on his tongue when the white mare whinnied from the corral. Kit gasped. "Hank, look!"

They both watched, speechless, as the piebald stallion appeared not twenty yards away. For a moment he just stood there. Then he came forward as calmly as could be and walked right into the corral, where he was met by his mate.

Hank looked on in wonder and astonishment. The stallion, it seemed, was willing to give up its freedom to be with its mate. For Hank it was a lesson well learned.

Kit, too, was watching. A tear formed in her eye and fell onto her cheek. She turned and walked away.

"Hey, where are you going?" Hank called.

"What does it matter?" she answered over her shoulder without breaking stride. "You have everything you want now."

"Come back here!" he yelled.

"No! I won't. You don't understand."

"Dammit, woman, I said come back here!"

She didn't hear it coming. Without warning the rope sailed into the air and landed around her. With one swift pull it was fastened tightly around her, pinning her arms to her sides. Kit began to struggle against it, but her strength was no match for his, and she found herself being pulled toward him. When she was within arm's reach, he grabbed her, drawing her easily into his embrace.

"Quit that squirming and listen to me!" he demanded, but he was smiling. His breath was warm against her cheek, his hands strong at her back. "There's something I want you to know. It wasn't because of you that I caught the piebald, but it was because of you that I was able to let him go, and in doing that, I let go of the past. None of that matters anymore. It's gone, Kit, gone for good. All that matters is you and me. I love you, Kit. I love you and I want to share my life with you. I can't promise you neon lights and fancy parties. I work hard and I ride hard, but

I'm faithful to the woman I love, and that woman is you. What do you say, green eyes? Why don't you stick around?''

Kit remained perfectly still in Hank's arms, hearing his words of love and feeling stunned with joy. The rope slackened, enabling her to wind her arms around his neck. She drew his head to hers and kissed him. Here in the Teton wilderness, and in this man's arms, her heart had found its home.

*   *   *   *   *

*. . . and now an exciting short story
from Silhouette Books.*

*

HEATHER GRAHAM POZZESSERE
Shadows on the Nile

CHAPTER ONE

Alex could tell that the woman was very nervous. Her fingers were wound tightly about the arm rests, and she had been staring straight ahead since the flight began. Who was she? Why was she flying alone? Why to Egypt? She was a small woman, fine-boned, with classical features and porcelain skin. Her hair was golden blond, and she had blue-gray eyes that were slightly tilted at the corners, giving her a sensual and exotic appeal.

And she smelled divine. He had been sitting there, glancing through the flight magazine, and her scent had reached him, filling him like something rushing through his bloodstream, and before he had looked at her he had known that she would be beautiful.

John was frowning at him. His gaze clearly said that this was not the time for Alex to become interested in a woman. Alex lowered his head, grinning. Nuts to John. He was the one who had made the reservations so late that there was already another passenger between them in their row. Alex couldn't have remained silent anyway; he was certain that he could ease the flight for her. Besides, he had to know her name, had to see if her eyes would turn silver when she smiled. Even though he should, he couldn't ignore her.

"Alex," John said warningly.

Maybe John was wrong, Alex thought. Maybe this was precisely the right time for him to get involved. A woman would be the perfect shield, in case anyone was interested in his business in Cairo.

The two men should have been sitting next to each other, Jillian decided. She didn't know why she had wound up sandwiched between the two of them, but she couldn't do a thing about it. Frankly, she was far too nervous to do much of anything.

"It's really not so bad," a voice said sympathetically. It came from her right. It was the younger of the two men, the one next to the window. "How about a drink? That might help."

Jillian took a deep, steadying breath, then managed to answer. "Yes . . . please. Thank you."

His fingers curled over hers. Long, very strong fingers, nicely tanned. She had noticed him when she had taken her seat—he was difficult not to notice. There was an arresting quality about him. He had a certain look: high-powered, confident, self-reliant. He was medium tall and medium built, with shoulders that nicely filled out his suit jacket, dark brown eyes, and sandy hair that seemed to defy any effort at combing it. And he had a wonderful voice, deep and compelling. It broke through her fear and actually soothed her. Or perhaps it was the warmth of his hand over hers that did it.

"Your first trip to Egypt?" he asked. She managed a brief nod, but was saved from having to comment when the stewardess came by. Her companion ordered her a white wine, then began to converse with her quite normally, as if unaware that her fear of flying had nearly rendered her speechless. He asked her what she did for a living, and she heard herself tell him that she was a music teacher at a junior college. He responded easily to everything she said, his voice warm and concerned each time he asked another question. She didn't think; she simply answered him, because flying had become easier the moment he touched her. She even told him that she was a widow, that her husband had been killed in a car accident four years ago, and that she was here now to fulfill a long-held dream, because she had always longed to see the pyramids, the Nile and all the ancient wonders Egypt held.

She had loved her husband, Alex thought, watching as pain briefly darkened her eyes. Her voice held a thread of sadness when she mentioned her husband's name. Out of nowhere, he wondered how it would feel to be loved by such a woman.

Alex noticed that even John was listening, commenting on things now and then. How interesting, Alex thought, looking across at his friend and associate.

The stewardess came with the wine. Alex took it for her, chatting casually with the woman as he paid. Charmer, Jillian thought ruefully. She flushed, realizing that it was his charm that had led her to tell him so much about her life.

Her fingers trembled when she took the wineglass. "I'm sorry," she murmured. "I don't really like to fly."

Alex—he had introduced himself as Alex, but without telling her his last name—laughed and said that was the understatement of the year. He pointed out the window to the clear blue sky—an omen of good things to come, he said—then assured her that the airline had an excellent safety record. His friend, the older man with the haggard, world-weary face, eventually introduced himself as John. He joked and tried to reassure her, too, and eventually their efforts paid off. Once she felt a little calmer, she offered to move, so they could converse without her in the way.

Alex tightened his fingers around hers, and she felt the startling warmth in his eyes. His gaze was appreciative and sensual, without being insulting. She felt a rush of sweet heat swirl within her, and she realized with surprise that it was excitement, that she was enjoying his company the way a woman enjoyed the company of a man who attracted her. She had thought she would never feel that way again.

"I wouldn't move for all the gold in ancient Egypt," he said with a grin, "and I doubt that John would, either." He touched her cheek. "I might lose track of you, and I don't even know your name."

"Jillian," she said, meeting his eyes. "Jillian Jacoby."

He repeated her name softly, as if to commit it to memory, then went on to talk about Cairo, the pyramids at Giza, the Valley of the Kings, and the beauty of the nights when the sun set over the desert in a riot of blazing red.

And then the plane was landing. To her amazement, the flight had ended. Once she was on solid ground again, Jillian realized that Alex knew all sorts of things about her, while she didn't know a thing about him or John—not even their full names.

They went through customs together. Jillian was immediately fascinated, in love with the colorful atmosphere of Cairo, and not at all dismayed by the waiting and the bureaucracy. When they finally reached the street she fell head over heels in love with the exotic land. The heat shimmered in the air, and taxi drivers in long burnooses lined up for fares. She could hear the soft singsong of their language, and she was thrilled to realize that the dream she had harbored for so long was finally coming true.

She didn't realize that two men had followed them from the airport to the street. Alex, however, did. He saw the men behind him, and his jaw tightened as he nodded to John to stay put and hurried after Jillian.

"Where are you staying?" he asked her.

"The Hilton," she told him, pleased at his interest. Maybe her dream was going to turn out to have some unexpected aspects.

He whistled for a taxi. Then, as the driver opened the door, Jillian looked up to find Alex staring at her. She felt . . . something. A fleeting magic raced along her spine, as if she knew what he was about to do. Knew, and should have protested, but couldn't.

Alex slipped his arm around her. One hand fell to her waist, the other cupped her nape, and he kissed her. His mouth was hot, his touch firm, persuasive. She was filled with heat; she trembled . . . and then she broke away at last, staring at him, the look in her eyes more eloquent than any words. Confused, she turned away and stepped into the taxi. As soon as she was seated she turned to stare after him, but he was already gone, a part of the crowd.

She touched her lips as the taxi sped toward the heart of the city. She shouldn't have allowed the kiss; she barely knew him. But she couldn't forget him.

She was still thinking about him when she reached the Hilton. She checked in quickly, but she was too late to acquire a guide for the day. The manager suggested that she stop by the Kahil bazaar, not far from the hotel. She dropped her bags in her room, then took another taxi to the bazaar. Once again she was enchanted. She loved everything: the noise, the people, the donkey carts that blocked the narrow streets, the shops with their beaded entryways and beautiful wares in silver and stone, copper and brass. Old men smoking water pipes sat on mats drinking tea, while younger men shouted out their wares from stalls and doorways. Jillian began walking slowly, trying to take it all in. She was occasionally jostled, but she kept her hand on her purse and sidestepped quickly. She was just congratulating herself on her competence when she was suddenly dragged into an alley by two Arabs swaddled in burnooses.

"What—" she gasped, but then her voice suddenly fled. The alley was empty and shadowed, and night was coming. One man had a scar on his cheek, and held a long, curved knife; the other carried a switchblade.

"Where is it?" the first demanded.

"Where is what?" she asked frantically.

The one with the scar compressed his lips grimly. He set his knife against her cheek, then stroked the flat side down to her throat. She could feel the deadly coolness of the steel blade.

"Where is it? Tell me now!"

Her knees were trembling, and she tried to find the breath to speak. Suddenly she noticed a shadow emerging from the darkness behind her attackers. She gasped, stunned, as the man drew nearer. It was Alex.

Alex . . . silent, stealthy, his features taut and grim. Her heart seemed to stop. Had he come to her rescue? Or was he allied with her attackers, there to threaten, even destroy, her?

*   *   *   *   *

Watch for Chapter Two of SHADOWS ON THE NILE coming next month—only in Silhouette Intimate Moments.

Starting in October...

SHADOWS ON THE NILE

by

Heather Graham Pozzessere

A romantic short story in six installments from best-selling author Heather Graham Pozzessere.

The first chapter of this intriguing romance will appear in all Silhouette titles published in October. The remaining five chapters will appear, one per month, in Silhouette Intimate Moments' titles for November through March '88.

Don't miss *"Shadows on the Nile"* —a special treat, coming to you in October. Only from Silhouette Books.

Be There!

IMSS-1

In response
to last year's outstanding success,
Silhouette Brings You:

Silhouette Christmas Stories 1987

Specially chosen for you in a delightful volume celebrating the holiday season, four original romantic stories written by four of your favorite Silhouette authors.

Dixie Browning—*Henry the Ninth*
Ginna Gray—*Season of Miracles*
Linda Howard—*Bluebird Winter*
Diana Palmer—*The Humbug Man*

Each of these bestselling authors will enchant you with their unforgettable stories, exuding the magic of Christmas and the wonder of falling in love.

A heartwarming Christmas gift during the holiday season...indulge yourself and give this book to a special friend!

Available November 1987

XM87-1